H. E. COOPER

THE VESTIGE AGENT

AWARD WINNING

DESTINY'S TIME SERIES

Dedicated to the LJCs in my life.
    This book wouldn't be here without either of you.

For the Reader[1]

---

1. Three Societies shape the world you're about to enter. Need a quick reference? Flip to the Extras at the end—I've tucked a summary there just for you. Fair warning: those Extras include some spoilers, so proceed with caution.

This book also uses some non-English speaking words. Where they are more complex, I've added a footnote like this to clarify the meaning. I hope it helps. Enjoy!

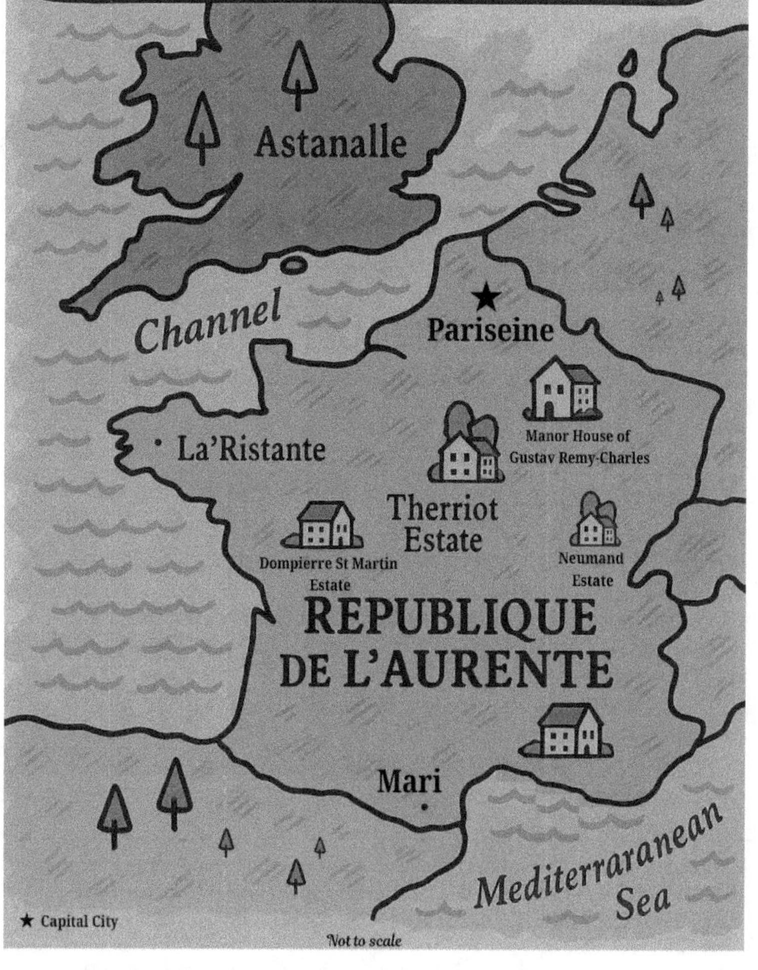

RÉPUBLIQUE DE L'AURENTE AND ASTANALLE IN THE 17TH CENTURY
Astanalle
Channel
Pariseine
La'Ristante
Manor House of Gustav Remy-Charles
Therriot Estate
Dompierre St Martin Estate
Neumand Estate
REPUBLIQUE DE L'AURENTE
Mari
Mediterraranean Sea
Capital City
Not to scale

Chapter One

1613 A.D. Astanalle, ARK1 dimension

> **Mission purpose:** *Find a missing prophecy*
> **Code name:** *Amelie*

MY BREATH COMES OUT in ragged gasps as I cling to the rough, weathered stones. A biting wind cuts through my clothes, leaving a chill that fails to dry the sweat trailing down my face. The salty droplets threaten to sting my eyes, blurring my vision and masking the perilous drop below.

My feet are balanced precariously on the uneven protrusions of the ancient castle wall. I push up to the next handhold, my fingers curling around the cold, unforgiving stone. My left foot flails about until it finds a solid anchor. I inhale deeply. "You've got this," I mutter.

Summoning every ounce of strength left in me, I claw my way up the final few feet, my fingers reaching for the opening above like a lifeline.

A closed stained-glass window blocks my path.

"Oh, come on!" My fist hits the stone ledge in frustration, and my balance fumbles for a moment. A dim glow illuminates the image of a face on the glass. It seems to be mocking me. Teetering on the edge of disaster, I slam my hand on it in defeat, loathing the thought of climbing even higher.

The window swings open without resisting.

"Oh." I peer in. "Typical," I mutter, feeling stupid but relieved.

Grasping the stone ledge with sweaty hands and trembling arms, I pull myself through the narrow opening. The effort all but takes it out of me, but once I'm almost fully through, I let gravity do the rest and slide down unceremoniously, landing with a thud. Sprawled out on the wooden floor, breathless and shaking, I spit out a section of hair from my long ponytail and thank whatever deity helped me this time. That was an uphill battle.

Lesson number … I've lost count. My latest lesson learned: Scaling castle walls in the seventeenth century is not the same as rock climbing in the twenty-first century. Even my armpits are crying.

My breathing slows and I listen for any disturbance caused by my entry. All I hear are sounds of the festivities below, a birthday celebration for the young master that has gone late into the night.

Time to move.

I sit up and groan. My arms throb with pain and feel like overcooked noodles as I push into a standing crouch, rubbing my aching side through the slick, black outfit under my jacket. The discomfort makes me feel older than my seventeen years. My hands feel raw and I touch them. I wince and drag in a sharp breath through my teeth.

"Oh, wait." Frantic, I feel for the one nail I've managed to grow long. The edge is jagged. I release my breath on a sigh and slump in defeat. Of course it's broken. Should have worn gloves. Didn't think of that—this was a last-minute plan after all, and the only way to slip in unnoticed.

"It is what it is," I tell myself, whisper-quiet. Gritting my teeth and looking ahead, my eyes adjust to the darkness, and I find my bearings. The moonlight illuminates a door on the far side of the room. Silent as a cat, I move toward it and step into a corridor, my senses alert to every sound and movement.

Everything's in semi-darkness, apart from a flickering oil lamp casting shadows on the wall at the end, and I'm glad my hair blends in with my outfit to keep me hidden. I visualize the blueprint of the castle in my mind, tracing the corridors and chambers until I pinpoint my location—just a few rooms away from my target.

Moving swiftly down the dimly lit corridor, I stop at the thick wooden door of the master suite, its surface adorned with ornate carvings. Leaning closer, I press my ear against it and listen for sounds of anyone inside. Just in case.

The silence envelops me like a shroud.

My hand settles on the carved metal handle and I nudge the door open a sliver, peering into darkness. No movement, only the vague silhouette of a canopied bed and the edge of a wardrobe looming in the gloom. Satisfied, I widen the gap just enough to slide through. The air inside smells faintly of old lavender and cold hearth ash.

I wait until my breathing steadies, then pull a small flashlight from my waistband and flick it on. The beam slices through shadows and glints off the gilt edges of furniture as my eyes sweep the room, searching. The light barely skims the top of a polished writing desk when it lands on a low chest of drawers, old but sturdy, its brass handles gleaming dully.

With a fluttering of excitement, I walk over and study the carvings on the front. A work of art. I snap a picture with my fitted company-issued 2.0 Vestige Lumé bracelet, then crouch down and dry my sweat-slicked hands before running them over the second drawer on the left. I almost lost my life for this, so it had better be here.

Easing the drawer open, it creaks in protest and gets annoyingly stuck on one side. I jiggle it a bit and it gives a piercing squeak. I freeze, glancing at the door. In this room, the party sounds quiet in comparison.

One last tug and the drawer obeys, my muscles unclenching in response.

Shining light on the contents—heart pounding in anticipation—I glance through the papers on top and move them aside. An insignia stares up at me. I grin. Lying nestled beneath is a thin glass case, hopefully holding the document I've been sent to retrieve.

I pull on some nitrile gloves, anchor the flashlight between my teeth, then lift the glass case out with care, revealing a thin copper wire running beneath it. My heart stutters. A pressure plate. I trace the wire with my eyes to where it disappears into a small hole in the drawer's back panel—likely connected to some medieval alarm system, probably bells in the servants' quarters. With steady fingers, I slide a hairpin from my ponytail and wedge it under the pressure plate, holding it in position as I disable the trap. The case comes away freely, and the knot in my chest unravels.

A fine web of dust dances up in the beam of my flashlight, marking the spot where the case has lain undisturbed for ages. The glass itself is cool to the touch and heavier than it looks. I can feel the weight of history in it, or maybe that's just the sweat from my palms. Steadying my breath, I place it on the floor and locate the wax seal, which I break with a satisfying crack. Then I run a gloved finger along the seam of the case until the lid gives. It slides free, and for a second nothing happens. There's just me, bent over some ancient box, sweating and out of time, a fugitive in a world that technically doesn't exist.

Then the smell hits, stale and parched, with a ghost of ink long since faded and old paper gone acid sharp. Prying the flashlight from my mouth before I start drooling, I lean in and, with the reverence of a believer, reach for the single sheet folded inside. It's smaller than I thought, weightless, colorless, just a slip of pale yellowed parchment, but it's the most beautiful thing I've ever seen.

With trembling fingers, I unfold it gently under the flashlight's beam and scan for the mark I was told to find. And there it is, in the lower right corner, the "mirror signature"—backwards, impossible to read unless you know the trick. The last known prophecy of Leonardo da Vinci, tangible and pulsing under my hands. I'm so giddy I almost forget to breathe, but somewhere in my head a voice is screaming, "Go! Now!"

If they catch me with this, it's over.

Which is when I hear it: the unmistakable scrape of a boot in the corridor. I nearly drop the parchment in panic, scrabble to replace it in the case, and then think better of it. With hurried movements, I refold the parchment and whip out a synthetic rubber bag to protect it. Except it isn't the right bag. I was so focused on how to enter the castle that I forgot to pack it.

What I see instead is a large Ziploc bag holding a handful of Skittles I haven't yet eaten.

I consider my options and sigh. Time to improvise.

I tip the Skittles into my mouth and tuck the historic document inside the now-empty bag. It just fits. Once sealed, the bag slips easily inside my jacket.

Footsteps sound outside the room. Moving fast, I return the case and push the drawer closed. It squeaks louder this time.

I switch off my flashlight, tuck it back into my waistband and slink over to the wall next to the door. My mouth feels like it'll burst, it's too full to chew. But it sure tastes better than cold metal.

The footsteps come closer.

Walk past. Please walk past.

The footsteps move past the door and I slump in relief.

The footsteps stop. They move back, toward me. I freeze, eyes wide, as the door swings inward with a sudden burst of force. I slide to the right. The door slams against the wall, missing me by a hair's breadth.

The shadow of a man leaks into the room, the light from his lantern giving him a stretched appearance.

I try to blend into the darkness.

The man steps into the room. It's the young master, William.

What's he doing up here, instead of enjoying his own party?

He glances at the chest of drawers. Then he turns around.

I shrink backward, pulling my ponytail over my nose to hide my face as my mind chants, *I am the shadows. I am invisible.*

It doesn't work.

William makes a surprised sound in his throat. Placing his lantern on the floor, he takes on an aggressive stance.

"Who are you? Come out lest I kill you!"

My mouth is still full of Skittles. At his shout, one pops out.

We both watch as it bounces on the floor between us, made visible by the pale moon. It rolls into the brighter light of his lantern then stops, center stage.

William stares at the red Skittle then bends down as if to pick it up. Uh oh. Well, it can't be helped. I doubt history will remember one tiny red Skittle.

Let's get this over with. I step into the light.

William's head jerks up and he stands, appearing tense. He looks me over once, then twice, confusion sweeping his brow. "Amelie?" he says to me. "What are you doing here—and dressed like that?"

I'm surprised he doesn't mention my puffy cheeks, or maybe he finds it attractive when a girl has her mouth full.

A lecherous smile crosses his face and he takes a step toward me. "Haven't had enough of me, eh? Maybe I should cease teasing you and show you what love means."

Eww. Snort-laughing, I gag, and a Skittle gets caught in my windpipe. I choke and a bunch of Skittles fly out of my mouth. Stupid. Stupid. Stupid. Gasping for breath, I throw a hand over my mouth and cough a few times then munch the remaining Skittles and swallow.

William frowns at the colorful candy but shakes his head. "You don't believe me? Aye, that may be. I will have to show you."

He launches himself forward and tries to grab me, but I'm not half-drunk like him and I'm much faster.

I shift to the side. He loses his balance and face-plants on the floor.

As I move to leave, he somehow manages to get up and grab the hem of my jacket, pulling me back toward him, hard. I roll with it, using his own force against him, and he loses his balance again. We hit the floor—or rather, he does. I fall on top of him, narrowly missing his lantern.

Recovering, I turn and push myself up from his stomach. He grunts. Slipping out of his grip and shaking myself off, I head toward the door—but hesitate on hearing a sound coming from the corridor.

It's all the time William needs.

Surging up from the floor, he grasps my ponytail. With a brutal yank, he wrenches me backward, ripping a cry of pain from me. William hauls me roughly against him, my back slamming into his chest.

"Enough!" I stomp down hard on his foot at the same time as rearing my head back. His nose crunches with the force. William yells and lets go. I swing around and knee him in the groin.

He goes down wailing. Crouching before him, I hit a few of his pressure points to overstimulate his brain and knock him out.

The silence is beautiful.

Standing, nostrils flaring in annoyance, I turn toward the door, massaging the back of my head.

A beautiful blond boy is standing in the doorway, holding a lantern and staring at me, wide-eyed.

I freeze. He seems young, maybe around seven. Perhaps I can convince him I'm a damsel in distress.

I wince. "Ow," I moan as I hold the back of my head and take a step forward. I try to squeeze out a tear for good measure. "Please sir, can you help me? This gentleman tried to force himself on me and I've managed to get free. I want to leave, but I'm so ashamed of what happened. Can you help me get away from this place without being seen?"

After a moment, he nods.

I smile in relief and walk toward him.

He's staring at me and I wonder if he's never seen a woman in trousers before. Though this catsuit is less like men's trousers and more like a second skin.

"You must think me strange to wear this outfit," I say.

His smile is shy and he looks down. I bend forward and detect a faint odor of paint.

I lift his chin with the crook of my finger and grin. He grins back.

"I do beseech you to rescue me," I say.

"I will help you, my lady. Follow me," he replies. I'm surprised by his accent. He mustn't have been born in Astanalle.

I'm not given time to ponder as he leads me further into the castle, then down winding stairs that seem to have no end. After what feels like forever, we exit into the cool night air through a side door.

Catching my hand, the boy pulls me along a cobblestoned courtyard and past a slumbering guard at the gate, who smells drunk. We continue along a dirt path and around a lake to a nearby forest.

"You can escape through there," he says, pointing to the forest. A narrow path between two trees winds into the darkness.

I crouch before him, smiling in gratitude. "Thank you for helping me. I am saved. What would you like in return?"

The boy looks down again.

Feeling compelled, I unclasp my necklace. The pendant is a silver fleur-de-lis representing my real name, Lily. It's made to look like an antique and was a gift from my parents on my thirteenth birthday.

Reaching out to grab his hand, I pause when he whispers, "A kiss."

A kiss? Then again, he believes he's rescued a damsel in distress.

With a soft laugh, I take his hand, dropping my necklace in his palm and closing his fingers over it. Looking at him again by the light of the bright moon, I touch his cheek. He stares intently at me and I smile back.

"My knight in shining armor."

Reaching up, I kiss his cheek.

The boy has a soft smile on his face as I pull away, and he examines me as if committing my face to memory.

"What is your name?" he asks in a quiet voice.

I don't know why, but I give him my real name. "Lily."

He smiles. "Will I see you again, Miss Lily?"

"Maybe one day." Guilt throbs in my gut at the lie.

He opens his mouth to say something, but we hear a shout from the castle. Concerned it might be because of me, I tell him, "I must leave now."

He looks over his shoulder toward the castle. Turning back to me, expression serious, he nods.

I stand. "Farewell, my friend."

"Farewell, Miss Lily."

We smile as I start walking backwards. Then I turn and run into the safety of the dark forest, leaving him behind.

Chapter Two

Present Day, United States of America, Earth dimension

My mind spins as wildly as I do in the vortex of time and space. Did that sweet kid get into trouble because of me? I never even asked his name.

A blinding light zaps me back to the present, and I crash-land onto the cushy pad at Vestige Headquarters. I'm back on Earth, with my employer.

A hand reaches out to help me up, and then I'm face to face with my colleague, Sam. She has a collection of non-prescription glasses. Likes to wear them as a fashion statement. Today she's wearing bright red ones and I'm close enough to see the purple underside.

"Nice specs, Sam. New?"

She grins. "Yep. Got these little beauties on sale. They're getting lots of praise. Might wear 'em all week."

"You should."

"Thanks. And welcome back to the twenty-first century. How was Astanalle? Did your mission go well?"

I hide a grimace. "Well enough. Where's Peron? I should probably check in with him."

"He's in his office. Said to tell you to take twenty and freshen up before you head in."

"That sounds like a great idea." I need a hot shower.

Sam waves me off as I shuffle to the "de-virusing" zone—where mystery vapor sprays us down like we're contestants on a game show. Two minutes later, I'm squeaky clean and off to my quarters, ready to unwind.

The heat of the shower eases out my tense muscles. Like a river of warmth, it soothes my back and I find myself staring at a plaque on the wall. It's the logo for my employer, Vestige, a secret organization that was founded by Alex Vestige in the Middle Ages after he discovered time travel. Alex came to be known as the Vestige Protector, a title that has continued down the line until today, although we don't have a reigning Protector right now. Our later Protectors uncovered portals into other worlds and the rest is history.

When I first joined Vestige, I was told I'd have constant training to prepare me for my work. When I discovered it was like school, I almost backed out. But then I found out multi-dimensional time travel was more than just theory and Vestige was the only known company with the technology.

That sparked my interest, but I thought they were pulling my leg. I kept chuckling—until I walked into HQ and realized no one else was.

Then I saw someone disappear into thin air as they were embarking on a mission. My beliefs were upended in an instant, my entire world view altered. I blinked. It stayed. So I guess it's real.

But I often wonder if I'm cut out for this. A teenage girl stumbling through time portals, fumbling with gadgets my father mastered decades ago. His faith in me feels like a weight. Everyone else sees what I am: an imposter with a famous last name.

I just hope I haven't botched my chances to prove myself with this last mission.

Chapter Three

At twenty minutes on the dot, I head to Peron's office.

When I get there, his secretary isn't around. Peron must have seen me arrive though, as he calls out from his office, "Come in, Lily."

He sounds displeased. I hesitate, struck with a sense of foreboding.

Peron clears his throat. Even in that, I hear irritation.

I walk into his office and stand to attention.

Peron Davies is my boss. He oversees my missions. Right now, he's making me wait as he studies a document. My mind shoots in a billion directions, wondering what would make him upset.

After an eternity, he straightens with an exhale and stares at me, as if trying to see all my secrets.

I stare back and plaster a smile over my tension.

"At ease," he says after a long moment.

I deflate and relax my stance.

"Lily, it's come to my attention that a certain sugary obsession of yours may have landed in the past—in another dimension, I might add."

A wave of heat shoots from my face down to my toes and I tremble, fearing the worst. They're going to get rid of me. They'll wipe my memory and fire me. I'll never have the chance to prove I'm as good as Dad—

"Lily." Peron interrupts my manic fears.

I look up. The dread must be stamped in bright pink all over my face.

Peron's eyes soften. "How could you take something like Skittles to the seventeenth century? Only Vestige-approved items are permitted through the time vortex."

"I'm sorry. I really am. It wouldn't have been a problem except—" I sigh and bow my head. "It was an accident."

Then a thought occurs to me and I jerk my head up. "But hang on—how do you even know?"

"Funny you should ask," he says. I detect a note of sarcasm in his voice. "A painting appeared, stemming from that region and dated the year of your visit. A painting that doesn't seem to have existed before. And guess what it shows?"

He reaches down and picks up his tablet, pulls up a picture and hands it to me.

I enlarge the screen and my eyes widen. A handful of Skittles are laid out in an assortment of colors, all with a definitive white "S" on their surface. A red one takes center stage, as if mocking me.

Good grief. What have I done?

I look for the artist's signature and see a squiggle on the bottom corner that looks like an "M." Whoever M. was, he painted well ... it's realistic. Too realistic. I grind my teeth at my obvious lack of luck. Where did it come from? My dad never mentioned anything like this in his spy days. Why do I always mess up?

Peron clears his throat, drawing my attention away from the accusing picture.

"Skittles aside, did you complete your mission?"

I nod, grateful to have something good to share. His eyes light up and he pulls on nitrile gloves with barely concealed excitement.

I pull the prophecy from the jacket I'd shrugged back on in my haste to get here, realizing too late that the document is in the Ziploc bag. The one I emptied of Skittles.

A weight hits my gut. Have the rainbow colors transferred from the plastic to the document?

I look up at Peron and cringe as my struggling sense of achievement flees.

He frowns and indicates that I pass it over.

A horrible feeling starts in my abdomen, like tiny, sharp feet are crawling up my torso toward my neck. Hands shaking, knowing I can't avoid the wave of disapproval that's about to hit me like a tsunami, I hand over my impending doom.

I'm not disappointed.

"What—what is this, Lily? Is this a *Ziploc* bag? Where is the approved synthetic rubber bag we gave you?"

I look down, hands trembling. He doesn't wait for me to respond. He opens the bag, pulls out the prophecy, and gasps.

"And what is this? These colors on the parchment? Are these from your candy? This is disastrous. You've ruined the prophecy!"

I wish I could shrink into the floor and become invisible. I may have retrieved the document, but one stupid mistake has turned my mission into a failure.

Peron huffs in annoyance. "Lily, this lack of professionalism leaves me questioning if you are the right person for this line of work. You knowingly violated our policy on artefact preservation. I want you to go and reflect on this, while I try to salvage the prophecy and determine whether I should give you any more assignments."

I salute him then march out with my back straight, tears held in check, until I reach the safety of my room. There, I surrender to the waves.

Chapter Four

Over the next few weeks, I keep my head down and study hard in my Vestige classes. From Espionage to Language to History, Politics and Customs, and even Mixed Martial Arts, I apply myself more than I've ever done, in the hope that this won't be my last chance.

It isn't made easier by the fact that Alyse Georges, the teacher's pet in most classes, continues to make me look bad in front of the professors, in particular Professor Crabb. They've both taken issue with me since the day I arrived. I think it's because I was the youngest spy to join Vestige in fifty years, and I unintentionally offended Crabb when we first met.

But then, I once heard one of Alyse's minions saying I got this job through my dad, who'd been a spy at Vestige before me. And really, they were kind of right. Peron recruited me because he knew Dad. I guess he thought I'd gotten his cool genes. He's no doubt regretting that decision now.

A sheet of paper being slapped on my desk brings me back to reality. I jump a little and look up to see Alyse's sneer. She moves away to hand out test scores to the rest of the class and I look down. There in bold red ink like a victory flag, an "A-" stares up at me. I blink, then smile.

Alyse sits down at her desk near the front of class. "Professor, I hate to bring this up now, but ..." She waits expectantly.

Crabb smiles at her. "What is it, Alyse?"

She glances back at me and a bad feeling pools in my gut. "Well, you see, I had thought being the better person would mean letting it go, but now I realize I'm not helping anybody by keeping this a secret."

"What secret?"

"Oh dear … well, I mean, I hate to say this in front of everybody." Crabb opens his mouth to speak.

"I saw Lily cheating on our latest test," Alyse says in a rush.

Crabb looks at me, frowning. He glances between us and seems to come to a decision.

"Lily, see me after class."

"What? I didn't cheat."

"Lily, it's best you deal with this terrible practice now, before it becomes a habit. You'll thank me someday," Alyse says.

I curl my fingers, wanting to claw at her smile.

Everyone is staring at me. Some are nodding like they believe Alyse. I hear a few snickers.

I huff and then clench my jaw. "Where's your proof, Alyse? For all we know, it was you who cheated."

She bats her lashes at Crabb, lips quivering. Game over. He pivots, finger jabbing the air between us, and proceeds to champion Alyse's integrity while assassinating mine.

A hot burst of anger fires through me, but I stifle it and remember I'm already walking on thin ice. Staring down at my desk, I take the rubbish Crabb dishes out with gritted teeth. No doubt as usual, Alyse got an A+, though I'm not sure if it was for her efforts or because of her relationship with the Professor. She's his niece, after all.

I block out the unjust treatment by imagining myself in another place, like I always do. Today, I'm a wealthy shopper in a colorful bazaar, someone who can take her pick of the merchandise. As my thoughts float away from the classroom, I feel a calm settle over me. I'm deliberating between a rare marble statue and a fine yellow diamond necklace when I realize class has ended.

Looking up, I catch Alyse's evil smile as she swings out the door, her entourage in tow.

I wait as the class empties, packing my bag slowly. After the last student exits, Crabb closes the door and turns to me.

"Lily, you are going to clean this entire room and think about what cheating means."

The door opens and a janitor brings in a bucket of water then exits. With a sinking feeling, I walk over and look down at the murky contents. Didn't they at least have the decency to give me fresh water?

With an internal sigh, I crouch down and try to see if there's anything creepy in there, lest I get my hand bitten like has happened in the past.

Crabb clears his throat and I look up. "This is what you will clean with today," he says.

In his hand is a small cloth.

After two hours I still haven't finished, and my hands are stinging from my recent ascent up a castle wall.

My teeth unclench when Crabb tells me to stop. I get off my stiff knees and try to stand, hiding a groan. Now I know how Cinderella must have felt. I inspect my short fingernails. When did dirty water ever make anything cleaner?

"Lily, I expect you back here after class tomorrow to clean the rest of the room. If I didn't have to be somewhere else, you would be cleaning this entire room today, your other classes be damned," Crabb says. "As it is, I'm still deciding whether to fail you on the test. Cheating will not be tolerated."

I bite down a retort and nod. He eyes me suspiciously, then hands me a pass to explain my absence to the next Professor. My stomach protests that I'm already an hour late and missed lunch, but I take the proffered pass, grab my stuff and move to leave.

"I'm warning you, Lily," Crabb says. "I will not tolerate your behavior much longer."

Anger fills me again and I stalk out without a backward glance. Alyse must be filling his head with stories. If I were any more well-behaved, I'd be a statue. Guess breathing counts as rebellion now.

I roll my eyes. *Noted.*

I fake a gasp. Oh no. I blinked too loudly. Crabby might alert the authorities.

I huff. This is ridiculous.

Dad and George Crabb were colleagues back in the day. Dad was one of the best Vestige spies before he retired. From what I've heard, Crabb was pretty awful to him. I bet he was jealous. And even if Dad jokes about it now, it must have left a mark. Of course, why would Crabb treat Dad's daughter any differently?

Throwing off my irritation, I turn a corner and head to my locker for the next class, reading Crabb's note. It's accusatory in nature and blames me for being late. How is that a pass?

Shaking my head, I reach the locker and turn the dial. It's slimy. I can picture some guy's filthy hands grabbing the wrong dial after lunch or fitness training. Gross.

Pulling a tissue out of my pocket, I wipe my hands then the dial, before turning it to a certain point and using a fingerprint scanner to complete the process. My locker pops open. It's empty, except for a small pink note.

A warning bell knocks against my brain. *Alyse.*

The note has one word on it: Toilet.

Dread crawls up my spine and slides back down into my gut like a cockroach on a water-slide.

Giving my locker a quick sweep and relieved to find it clean, I drop in my books from last class and close the locker, taking a moment to change the code and hoping I'll remember it.

How did Alyse access my locker? Though Code Breaking 101 is one of our first classes, these lockers have fancier security. I bet one of her peeps did it for her. She does have some ... let's say "talented" friends.

Tucking the "pass" into my pocket, I head to the nearest ladies' room and push open the door.

An unpleasant odor wafts in my face. I keep my mouth closed. The place is empty, so I shove into each stall and glance into the bowls. Yuck.

Disgusted at what the cleaner has to face every day, I get to the last stall and almost backtrack. The smell makes me want to gag.

Nudging the door open, I hold my forearm over my nose as I shuffle into the cubicle. Peering down, I recognize my Old English language textbook, half submerged. And someone has taken a dump on it. Craptastic.

I flush the toilet, but the book is a goner, with bits of human filth still sticking to it. There is no way I'm sticking my hands in that muck.

I back out of the stall.

Goodbye, book. Hope I won't need you again.

Turning, I rush to the sink and scrub my hands, trying to clean the image from my mind. Thank goodness I just had one item in that locker this morning. I wouldn't even use the locker if it hadn't proven so convenient.

Hands scrubbed raw, my vision blurs. Frustration robs me of breath. I close my eyes and count to ten, taking shallow breaths inside my elbow as I strive to get control over my emotions.

I can't let Alyse see me crumble. She'll think she's won.

When my heart slows its frantic beating, I straighten and stare at the girl in the mirror. "You can do this. You're worth more," I tell her.

Leaving the bathroom, I head to Reception instead of class, where I file a complaint. I don't want to be blamed for flushing my textbook down the toilet and I definitely don't want to be forced to retrieve it.

I look at my watch. Class is about to end.

Instead of making a late entrance, I head in the other direction and jump in the elevator. I'll give Professor Nobby the pass tomorrow. At least she's a little more understanding.

I grab a snack from the canteen on the way to the dorm. On arriving, my emotions threaten to swell again, but I shut the door behind me before I break down.

Leaning against the door, I slide to the floor and tremble. "Why are people like this?" I ask myself. All the repressed anger and hurt and annoyance and frustration jostle for room in my mind. I grab my plush toy dog from the floor next to me and scream into its side.

Slumping back against the door frame, I use the back of my hand to wipe away tears, but they keep coming. Soon my nose is blocked, so I breathe deep through my mouth and try to calm down.

I can't lose control now. I can't give in to them. I have to stay here and prove to Peron that I can be trusted. I can be as good as my dad on my own. I didn't get in because of him. I didn't. At least, I hope I didn't.

Bleakness rolls in like a thundercloud, threatening to sink me under the weight of depression, but something in me refuses to give in. I have endured bullying and threats of failure and removal since I started at Vestige, and I've survived. I'm a survivor.

Determination wars with despair and I choke the bitterness down. I will not be fired unjustly. I will not have my memory wiped clean. I will not be a sleepwalker in a world of hidden wonders.

I want adventure. I want to keep the good memories I've made at Vestige. I want to explore other worlds and see other cultures and learn and grow and live.

My fingers curl into a fist, locking onto a new resolve.

Giving up isn't an option. Letting them win? Not a chance.

I won't back down. Not now.

Not ever.

CHAPTER FIVE

THE NEXT MORNING, PERON sends me a meeting invite for nine sharp. I eat breakfast in my room, smuggled from the cafeteria again, and do some stretches and push-ups to get my blood flowing. Then, I head to his office.

I pass a few students and turn a corner, almost bumping into Jason. I'm quick to step aside, but he stops and smiles at me. "Hey, Lily," he says.

I stare at him for a moment, lost as to why he would be talking to me. He was the star quarterback of his school before he joined Vestige. Alyse has been after him for ages, but they're still "just friends."

I don't know how anyone could be friends with a girl like her.

It dawns on me that I haven't responded, and I probably look like a dork staring back at him. I open my mouth to say hey back, but Alyse calls his name.

We both turn and she shoots me a glare as she nears, before smiling at Jason. "Are you coming to class, Jase? We're waiting for you!"

"I'm coming." He glances at me again, hesitating. "See you, Lily." He smiles and leaves.

I'm dumbstruck. When has Jason ever given me a second of attention?

Alyse cuts into my thoughts like the viper she is.

"What? Jason's talking to you now? He's feeling sorry for you, after your little accident in the ladies' room yesterday." She laughs and walks away.

My face grows warm, but I remind myself it wasn't "my" accident. Shaking my head in disgust, I summon my resolve and continue to Peron's office.

The meeting with Peron leaves me reeling.

He's decided to give me another chance. A mission in Pariseine, in the ARK1 dimension. For six whole months.

Struggling to hide my glee, I race back to my room, not giving a hoot about who sees me.

I'm getting fitted for some outfits later today, then leaving for a quick visit home tomorrow and then I'm off to the seventeenth century.

I throw open my suitcase, piling in necessities while mulling over Peron's words.

"I've watched you, Lily, and can see you have applied yourself. I'm willing to trust you again. This is an opportunity for you to prove you are suited to this line of work. I personally think you have what it takes, if you just apply yourself like you've done with your studies."

Like I've done with my studies? Given the grades Crabb gave me, I was surprised Peron saw my efforts. Perhaps Professor Nobby put in a good word.

Then Peron hinted that every classroom and corridor has concealed cameras.

I should have known.

Peron apologized for Crabb's behavior, saying he would revise my grade and give me an A for Crabb's test. I guess the videos satisfied him I hadn't cheated. I chuckle at the memory, feeling vindicated, until I recall him saying it was character building and would toughen me up for missions.

Gee, thanks, Peron.

But I suppose he has a point. Maybe.

I finish packing and lock the door on my way out to the fitting. Then I have to go back inside to change my top, realizing I spilled breakfast down the front.

Why didn't Peron say anything? Was I always this messy? I search my mind but draw a blank.

There must be a lot on my mind. I need a break before starting this mission. A quick trip home and then I'll be ready to run into the fray of multi-dimensional time travel, guns blazing ... at least metaphorically. Or not.

And this time, I'll prove Crabb wrong.

Chapter Six

My stomach growls. I wish we had room service.

I get off my bed and start pacing back and forth, trying to psych myself up for a trip to the cafeteria.

I check the time. The clock reads 8.20am. My stomach growls again.

I'm going. Feel the fear and do it anyway. With any luck, Alyse and her cohorts will be busy elsewhere.

Taking a deep breath, I pull my door open and peer out. The hall is empty.

I lock my room and walk steadily, if a little nervously, to the elevator and down to level minus nineteen. When the doors slide open, a few students mill about but no one aligned with Alyse. Relieved, I head for the cafeteria.

"Lily," someone calls as I'm about to enter the cafeteria. I freeze, heart pounding, and swallow hard. Of course she'd find me.

"Well, if it isn't the redeemed wannabe-spy!"

I turn as Alyse walks toward me, her sneering entourage in tow.

Dread takes me prisoner, until I remember: I'm Lily Destin, daughter of the famous Michel Destin, and I'm about to embark on a mission Alyse would salivate over. Taking a deep breath, I let resolve wash over me and raise my chin.

"Alyse."

"My uncle tells me you have a mission." She laughs as if that's a ludicrous idea, and her friends laugh with her. "I'm surprised

Peron is willing to trust you again. I was sure you were on the way out. Pity."

I start to turn but the venom in her voice halts me.

"You won't succeed, Lily Destin. You were born to fail. You don't have what it takes to be a spy. Soon even Peron will have to admit to that." She comes right up in my face and glares.

Unprepared, I take a step back and she laughs.

"It's just a matter of time. Lily, Lily, how very silly. She'll try her best but end up dead," she says in a sing-song voice. Her friends laugh again and a few stare at me menacingly.

Blood rushes to my face and I turn my back on them, clenching my fists. Someone pushes me from behind and I fall, sprawling, landing half inside the cafeteria. I knock my elbow hard and bite back a yelp. Heads turn but no one makes a move to help when Alyse strides in and places a foot on my back.

"I'd watch my back if I were you, Lily Destin."

I see a red bucket in the corner of my vision and hear it sloshing. They're going to dump it on me in front of everyone. Trying to push myself up, Alyse's heel digs painfully into my spine. Where are the cafeteria staff? I look around desperately, seeing the concerned but fearful faces of the new intake, even though they're about my age. Where are the security cameras? Can Peron see this? I wish he'd see and discipline Alyse.

The sloshing gets nearer and I squeeze my eyes and mouth shut, tensing for the onslaught.

It never comes.

Alyse gasps and her foot leaves my back. I open my eyes and see the red bucket moving away.

Has Peron come to save me?

"Stop, Alyse!" That's Jason's voice. I'm stunned. "This is stupid and immature. I thought you were better than this. I didn't leave one school to enter another. We're adults. Act like one!"

He sounds angry and I twist my head up. I've never seen Jason look angry before—and at Alyse, no less. And I never thought he'd be this decent and come to my rescue. I guess I misjudged him.

Alyse's expression screams pain, but she's the first to look away from his glare. She glances at me heatedly then storms off. "Come on, guys. We have better things to do than waste our time on her."

I watch them leave, my mouth hanging open unattractively. Jason shakes his head then glances down at me. My mouth slams shut.

Squatting down by my side, he appears concerned. "Are you all right, Lily?"

Embarrassed, I push myself up to a sitting position and cradle my throbbing elbow.

I look up at him to find his face inches from mine. I freeze. He studies me as if seeing me for the first time and his Adam's apple bobs. Glancing down, he sees me guarding my elbow and reaches for it. I hold my breath as his warm fingers trace and examine it. He gently closes his hand around it, as if to take away the pain.

Releasing my breath, I say, "Thank you. For what you did back there. You're the first person to—"

"I'm sorry, Lily."

I glance up, startled.

"I'm sorry they bullied you. I didn't realize until yesterday, when I overheard Alyse laughing about your book. I got so mad. I can't excuse Alyse's behavior, but I hope I can make it up to you."

My jaw goes slack again, but I manage to find my wits.

"Thank you. That means a lot, Jason."

He stares at me and my face warms. A prickling on my left side tells me we have an audience. I look and catch a few dreamy-eyed girls with soft smiles. Actually, everyone seems to be smiling.

"Lily, I like you—a lot."

That draws my attention back and I stare at Jason, shocked. It looks like he wants to confess, but then it's like he becomes aware of our audience and checks himself. He clears his throat.

"Can we be friends?"

This could be another one of Alyse's games, but he seems so genuine. I want to believe him.

"That would be really nice," I say.

He smiles and I smile back, heart feeling light.

Jason stands and leans down to help me up. I'm a bit wobbly at first and he pulls me against him for a moment to steady me. His muscles are the real deal. Another boy's embrace flashes in my memory. I pull back and Jason releases me. It feels awkward for a moment, but Jason recovers and offers to take me to the sick bay.

I shake my head. "Thank you, but I'll be fine. Right now, I'm famished."

"Really? Me too. Want to grab a table? I'll get us breakfast."

"Sure." Have I entered an alternate reality? I spy an empty table away from the others and walk over to it, hoping to avoid the attention we've garnered.

As I sit, Jason dings a bell and a cafeteria lady comes out. They talk, then she goes back into the kitchen. She comes out a few minutes later with a tray and two steaming bowls of food.

Jason thanks her and turns, tray in hand, to search the room. Spotting me, he smiles and heads over.

He places the tray on our table and takes the seat opposite me.

My mind is buzzing. This is Jason, Mr. Populaire, and he's sitting with me. He went against Alyse for me. And everyone here saw it.

Jason gives me a bowl and takes his, and we start to eat in silence. The salmon steak is cooked in a lemon butter sauce and is delicious. I take a mouthful of greens, remembering my mother's wisdom about food: fat unlocks the nutrients in greens, protein metabolizes the fat. This meal would be perfect in her eyes and I'm sure she'd appreciate, as I do, how Vestige supply a full range of meals around the clock. Some agents have to work nights so this would be dinner for them, but who says you can't enjoy a full meal at breakfast?

Jason finishes before me, but waits as I eat, studying me with a mysterious smile on his face. After a few moments, the nerves in my belly have dissolved my appetite. I put my fork down.

"What?" I ask.

He hesitates. "I never thought it would be this easy. To sit with you, here, like this." He waves a hand around.

I'm waiting for the punchline and look at him quizzically.

He clears his throat again. "I've wanted to do this for a while, but you always seemed so closed off that I ..." He shakes his head. "I was a coward, believing you'd shut me down. I should have taken the risk."

If he's saying what I think he's saying … my toes curl in anticipation.

"What are you saying?" I ask.

He licks his lips. "It's probably too soon, I know. I was wondering if … maybe if you'd want to go out with me … sometime."

What. The. What?

Did Jason just ask me out? I must be in that alternate dimension after all. Or maybe Alyse knocked me out and I'm dreaming.

"Lily?" Jason sounds unsure.

I look at him, really look at him, wishing I could have something special with a guy like him, but fearing a repeat of the past. What on earth do I say?

"This isn't one of Alyse's schemes, is it?"

"What? No!" He says, sounding a bit offended.

"Sorry. I had to ask, given all she's done in the past. She is capable of this."

Jason nods. "I guess."

I study him for a moment, afraid to hope. "Jason, thank you. I mean it. But … I'm about to head off on a long-term mission. And … I don't want you to cop any trouble from Alyse because of me."

He looks disappointed.

"I don't mean to friend-zone you, but I would love it if we could be friends—for now. When I'm back, if we both feel the same way, maybe then …" If I can trust him.

He smiles slightly. "I should have taken the shot months ago."

"I wish you had," I say.

His smile carries a hollowness I feel, and I want to kick irony in the shins.

I finish my meal as we talk about my upcoming mission—as much as I'm allowed to say, anyway. Jason walks me back to my room and surprises me with a goodbye hug. Hesitantly, I hug him back. It feels awkward, but warm and comforting too.

Jason leaves with slumped shoulders and my regret lingers. I tell myself I've made the right choice.

Back in my room, Alyse seems like a long-forgotten threat, thanks to Jason. But it gets me thinking that if I were in charge of Vestige, I'd push for changes. Like an anti-bullying culture, for starters. And room service—or at least vending machines with decent food on every level. And perhaps a team of psychologists. Sometimes I think I need one.

I laugh at the direction of my thoughts and focus on the task at hand. I'm about to get a reprieve from Alyse and her drones. And Jason—the guy she's been after for ages—asked me out! Eat that, Alyse.

With a grin tugging at my lips, I think of Jason—how sweet he was. The memory lingers as I step into the shower, warmth spreading through me. Maybe, just maybe, things are finally falling into place.

Chapter Seven

Present Day, Australia, Earth dimension

TODAY IS THE DAY my life will change. It's the day I become a new person. The day I can walk away from the bullies and be free. Free to prove the naysayers are wrong about me.

I'm packing in my room after enjoying a week at home, telling myself to be strong as I prepare for my return to Vestige. There's a chance I may face Alyse or Crabb again, but then it will be over. I will be liberated for an entire six months, unimpeded by my tormentors.

My heart feels light at the prospect.

I'm traveling to the République de L'Aurente, which is located in ARK1, the first world our Protectors uncovered a portal into. The same world I just came back from, for my mission in Astanalle.

Amazingly, this dimension is similar to our own world, with the same genealogies, but history has taken a different turn, like a Choose Your Own Adventure novel. Things are altered here and there, so our cultures aren't quite the same. The differences pave the way for interesting trips whenever I have the joy of a mission there.

One thing I'd love to do is investigate my doppelgänger, if she exists. It would be interesting to see what she's doing, what her life is like. But it's not allowed. Too risky.

I shake my head.

I shouldn't try to compare. I am grateful for my life and it's pretty good, considering. I've seen ARK1. I've seen some of the other dimensions. Some parallel worlds are bizarre, making my wildest imaginations seem dull in comparison. To be honest, I'm a little relieved to be going back to the ARK1 realm—I can understand it, and trips there can feel like a holiday.

I stare out the window for a moment. A kid on a skateboard whizzes past, oblivious to the vast conglomeration of worlds out there.

Having access to so many dimensions means that Vestige have a huge responsibility. Before the first Protector died, they showed Vestige's body of leaders how to search for portals. Now, a new dimension is found every eighty years or so, like our own endless expanding universe. Pretty mind-blowing stuff.

I mean, seriously, multi-dimensional time travel? Can someone cue the Dr Who theme tune?

A light knock on my door breaks me out of my reverie. Mom stands in the doorway, watching me. She's beautiful in her caramel-colored satin dressing gown, her glossy brown hair clipped back. People say I get my looks from her, but I fail to see how I could be as gorgeous or sophisticated.

"Lily, darling, I know how eager you are to go on this second-ment in France, but please promise me you'll be safe? That you'll keep in touch? I want to know how you're going."

"I will, Mom. Don't worry about me. I'll be fine."

I will, I tell myself. Though I won't be in France. I hate lying to Mom, but it's for her protection. Mom doesn't know about my real job. She thinks I'm in research.

She sighs. "All right, honey. I'm just glad it's not your father who's doing this. At least you're single and don't have a family to support." She shakes her head. "Trust me, you'd better enjoy it while you can. Just be careful, all right?"

"You know I will." I smile at her with my brave face on and she moves in to hug me. She's soft and warm and safe.

Dad chooses that moment to come in. He grabs us in a group hug and we squeal.

"Ah, my two favorite girls in the world." He smacks a kiss on each of our cheeks and grins, distracting me from my fears. Mom and I grin back like idiots.

I love my parents. They're the best thing I have in this world.

The moment ends and Dad repeats some of what Mom said, the staying safe and keeping in touch part.

"Keep your head in the game, Lily. It's all right to enjoy your surroundings, but you don't have time for romantic attachments. You're there to work, remember."

"Dad," I whine and try to hide my blush. "Really?" I roll my eyes. As if that would happen.

"Michel, Lily is seventeen—a young woman. What's the harm in a little flirting? It's Paris. The city of love!"

"It's the city of light, Mandy. The city of light. You do realize France has over two million more women than men, right? That's not a dating pool—that's a dating ocean with sharks. Paris is a city with aging demographics and caffeine dependency. And those Parisian men? They don't chase women, they collect them like limited edition espresso cups."

"And your point is, darling?" Mum wears an amused smile.

"Mandy, I've seen the documentaries. The Eiffel Tower is a beacon for heartbreak—a giant metal arrow pointing to France's national reserve of beret-wearing Casanovas. *Aging* Casanovas, might I remind you. I won't have my daughter become another notch on some Parisian's baguette. If she wants to date—one day when she's much older—then I'd like to be able to recommend the man myself."

"What?! Eww, no! Dad, I don't need you to be my matchmaker." And if he has his way, I'll be an old maid.

To my relief, Mom says, "Michel, Lily needs to make her own decision about these things."

Dad looks like he wants to argue, but I can almost see the cogs turning in his mind. He clears his throat.

"Well, don't get involved with anyone over there. You're too young for that, Lily. I want you to be my little girl as long as possible, all right?" His look is hopeful.

"Dad, I can't believe we're having this conversation right now. It's unnecessary. I've only had one boyfriend, and that was a disaster!"

I don't want to think about that particular memory or give them another reason to ask me why we didn't work out. The less they know, the better.

Dad seems pleased at this news, which is insulting, so I give him a mock punch in the gut. It works as a distraction.

He responds, quick on the offence, and we tackle each other right there, complete with grunts and shouts of victory, to my mother's dismay. She bolts out of the way.

I'm glad I have a big enough bedroom to allow for these minor scuffles. I had to rearrange my room after the first time we did it, when some of my favorite things got smashed.

We're still straining against each other when my kid brother Patrick—Trick, as I like to call him—rushes through the door to see what the fuss is all about. "Yeah Dad! Get her!" he cheers.

He turns to Mom. "Hey, you want to bet on who will win? I'm betting on Dad!"

Mom shakes her head and walks out the door with an indignant huff, a small smile playing on her lips.

Dad wins the fight with a skilled takedown, and I'm left panting on the floor. Trick cheers again and beats his chest like a gorilla. Dad lets go and helps me up while grinning. I brush myself off with a begrudging smile.

"All right, fine. You win. Now out, both of you, so I can finish getting ready."

I stand with my arms crossed as they jostle each other out of my bedroom and shake my head at their antics.

Trick pushes for a fight with Dad in the corridor while I massage my sore shoulder with a grimace. The last thing I hear before I shut my door is bodies hitting the wall as they grapple with each other.

An hour later, I'm standing outside and watching my breath turn to smoke in the cool air when a car pulls up. An old man named

Alfred climbs out and gives me a wave. He's been sent by Vestige to take me to Bankstown airport in western Sydney.

I have to catch a private plane to get to my employer's head-quarters. It must be crazy expensive, but I guess they can afford it, so why not?

"Good morning, Miss Destin," Alfred says as he comes around and opens the door for me, forever the gentleman. I smile in appreciation.

"Good morning, Alfred. Thank you."

I get settled in while Dad helps him load my luggage into the boot, then Alfred comes around to get into the driver's seat. I notice his hands are shaky and concern grips me, but he starts the car with little effort.

I turn and wave a final goodbye to my family through the back window, watching as they disappear over the hill. Then I swivel back around and sink down into the seat.

As suburbia crawls past, I remember what I'm about to face. Anxiety hums in my gut, scuttling up my ribcage to my heart.

I breathe out slowly, wanting this day to be over.

Chapter Eight

ALFRED DROPS ME OFF at the airport and hands me a missive which he says is from Peron. I take it and tow my luggage to a reserved section to catch the private plane.

I have a while to wait, so I read the missive and a weight falls off my shoulders. I'm going to the Australian Vestige headquarters, not the USA. That means no Alyse. I smile and breathe easy for the first time in what feels like forever.

I glance at my phone to check emails, then sink into my seat. People zip past, engrossed in their screens yet never stumbling. Swept up in the current of their own busy lives.

I've been there. I wonder how many amazing encounters we miss in our preoccupation with our gadgets.

My phone buzzes, as though mocking me.

I check the screen. Dad.

"Hey, Dad."

"Lily." His voice booms through the handset. "Have you made it yet?"

"Yes, Dad. I'm here, safe and sound. No need to worry. I'm waiting for the plane."

"Well. Good. Just wanted to check up on you."

"Okay …" I stifle a chuckle.

"Yes, well … Tell Peron I said hi and that we're still on for a chess game when I see him next."

"Okay, I will."

"Thanks, Lily. Remember what I told you—keep your guard up against the men over there. Trust no one."

"Dad." I sigh.

"I mean it, Lily. No one."

We say our final goodbyes and he puts Mom on the phone. She sounds a bit teary. You'd think this was my first time flying or that I was never coming back, with the way she sounds, but I reassure her and we end the call on a positive note.

I put my phone away with a smile and shake of the head and make a mental note to pass on Dad's "message."

Dad and Peron go way back. I first met Peron just after I started high school, and he spent most of his later visits watching me—he is quite eccentric. He invited himself over when I was fifteen and nearing the end of my school year. He and Dad were sequestered in Dad's study for over an hour. I could tell Dad wasn't happy when they came out, but he called me over and let Peron offer me employment with his "research company." With the promise that they would let me finish the end of my school year to meet compulsory schooling requirements. I'd commence training in his company straight after.

I was open to the idea, so they took me into the study. After signing the job acceptance letter and a confidential agreement, I found out what the company really was: a secret organization with connections to Governments around the world. I was hurt that Dad knew and never told me, but that hurt paled in comparison to the awe I felt when I discovered my father was a Vestige spy and had a stellar reputation to boot. My respect for him soared to new heights and warred with the sting I felt at him keeping this amazing secret from me.

The conversation went a bit like this:

Me: "How could you keep something like this from me? I'm never going to speak to you again!"

Dad: "C'mon, Lily, can't you understand? You've signed the contract. You're aware of our terms now. We're sworn to secrecy in this Agency—need to know only. The one man who broke this covenant put his fiancé in danger and they both came to an unbelievably bad end. His story is a reminder that we cannot break our pledge."

Me: A sullen silence.

Dad sighs: "Lily, this is how I'm protecting our family. Please understand."

Me: ...

Dad: "I'm sorry, honey. Forgive me, please?"

Me: Sniff

A few days of silent treatment later ...

Dad: "Lily, are we still doing this?" Sigh. "All right. How can I make it up to you?"

After a while my respect won out and our relationship was restored. Coincidentally, that was the same week we drove out of the second-hand car dealers with a shiny blue Toyota. An early birthday present from Dad.

To everyone else, I had become a research historian like my father, and we worked for the same employer. In reality, I joined the elite ranks of time travelers making history and keeping the balance between dimensions in the multiverse.

Dad and I grew closer and he supported me during my first few missions. Though they were small and though I had years of martial arts training behind me thanks to Dad, I still struggled and faced resistance from my peers. However, with Dad's mentoring I improved fast and became a passable spy. He was so proud of me.

I also grew up a little and learned to appreciate his position in all this. I wasn't giving back the car though. She was a little old, but I loved her all the same. I named her Macey.

Chapter Nine

My plane arrives on time. I settle in and the plane soon lifts off. The flight goes smoothly and I end up chatting with a colleague who is also headed back to headquarters. The slight turbulence is making him sweaty, and his glasses keep sliding down his nose. He seems unaware of how many times he has pushed them back in place as he drones on and on about the dangers of flying, the risk of propellers, and the worries of an unbalanced wingspan ratio.

After a while, I make an excuse to use the ladies. On my way out I run into the cabin crew. They're chatting about a recent holiday one of them took and they smile as I approach.

"Any chance of an upgrade?" I ask.

They all laugh and one of them hands me a drink and a snack.

"This is the best you're gonna get, honey," she says.

I take the offering with a smirk and find a seat near the front, hoping for some peace and quiet.

Sipping my orange juice, I remember my assignment. My excitement grows.

One of my favorite places to travel to is present-day Pari-seine, in the République de L'Aurente. It reminds me of Paris, France.

Because ARK1 is similar to our world, Vestige set up as many bases there as they have in our own dimension. It's become like a companion world to ours.

I often stay at Vestige's training unit in the République de L'Aurente and I can't wait to go back.

A glance out the window shows we're almost there. The Australian desert spans the horizon, hot and dry and wild and ... well, deserted.

My thoughts turn to reports of the latest attack on Vestige headquarters. A young man was abducted, tortured, and left broken and bloodied on the sidewalk in present-day Tokyo. The police had thought it might be the Yakuza, but we knew better.

Vestige has enemies, but there has been an unspoken, unbroken truce since World War II. Until last year. Since then, there've been countless kidnappings all over the globe.

Two parties fall under suspicion: the greedy Relic Hunters—their name speaks for itself—or the Sentinels, a religious sect.

The Sentinels believe that Vestige employees are under some sort of demonic influence and have proven to be a dangerous enemy with their warped religious fervor. They employ despicable methods to achieve their ends and the thought of encountering one of them terrifies me. Given the Sentinels wouldn't have left the Vestige agent alive at all, I'm going to bet it was the Relic Hunters who did the kidnapping this time.

I hope the abducted agent isn't someone I know. I'm sure Peron would tell me if it were. I spent four months at the Japanese HQ last year and made so many friends that I was considering a transfer there, but Peron talked me out of it. I've regretted that decision.

Well, if he won't let me go to Japan, maybe I should lobby for South Korea. I had a wonderful time there on my last holiday with the family.

"Oh my gosh!" A high-pitched shriek jars me back to the present.

Looking behind me, I expect to see my nervous colleague having a breakdown. Instead, I spy Vanessa, one of the girls in Alyse's outer circle of friends, staring at her phone. Registering her presence like a dark rain cloud over my happy thoughts, I swivel back around and try to look interested in the view outside. Why are they in Australia and not the USA? I grind my teeth. It's probably related to a mission.

"What?" her companion asks.

"I just got The Retisense booked for my party on Saturday! They're like my favorite band!" She gives a fake scream and they laugh.

"OMG, I can't wait! It's gonna be awesome."

"It's going to be ah-may-zing!"

They laugh again, but Vanessa stops.

"Keep it a secret, okay? I don't want Alyse to know."

My ears prick up, straining to hear every word now. What's this? Keeping something from Alyse, are we?

"You got it, Ness. There's no way I'm spilling this. More for us, I say. Why should she get all the attention?"

"Mm-hmm." They fall into a fit of giggles and I smile slowly, relieved that not all her friends are blind followers.

I take a sip of juice and end up getting cookie crumbs all over my mouth. Realizing I raised the wrong hand, I brush my face off and raise the other, my mouth connecting sloppily with the cup.

A voice comes over the speaker and I jump. The juice sloshes over the side of my cup and splatters on my clothes. Great.

"Cabin crew, prepare for landing."

I swallow, brushing drops of moisture from my lap. A glance out the window shows the Australian Vestige headquarters coming into view. The cabin crew materialize and check luggage compartments, trays, and seatbelts.

"Sir, please put that under the seat in front of you."

I turn to see my nervous colleague holding a black contraption, trying to measure the air pressure. He fumbles as he tucks it away. I smother a snort.

A thought floats in like black smoke, bringing a sense of foreboding with it. What if a certain spiteful girl tries to thwart or pull me off my assignment? I take a breath and let it out fast, breathing in again to calm my nerves.

I'm about to embark on the mission of a lifetime, ready to be sent through the multi-dimensional time vortex.

The sooner I leave, the better.

CHAPTER TEN

Vestige Headquarters, Australia

THE PLANE TAXIES DOWN the runway and comes to a stop inside a warehouse that acts as a hangar for the aircraft.

As soon as I'm allowed off, I grab my luggage and walk the short distance to the building next door, which acts as the outback office for Vestige researchers.

After ten minutes, I clear the appropriate security checks and walk through a secret door to a huge elevator. When it arrives, the doors open and I enter, rolling my suitcase behind me. The doors swish closed and I watch the lighted numbers change as the elevator takes me underground.

We moved to Australia when I was young, after Dad "retired" from active service to Vestige and became a consultant for them. I'd thought this would be my "home base" for work, so I was surprised when Peron asked that I work directly under him at the USA headquarters. I bet he's keeping an eye on me for Dad's sake.

Still, I'm glad he didn't make me fly all the way back to the USA this time. I have less than two days before I head to ARK1.

The elevator hums and stops on level minus twenty. Metal doors slide open and I step out into the reception area. Janet, the receptionist, assigns me a bunker and hands me a note saying Peron has flown in and wants to see me in his office once I've settled in.

I take the elevator to level minus fourteen and wheel my suitcase through several security doors to reach my quarters. After freshening up, I head back down to Peron's office, not surprised when I'm let in straight away. He must have been waiting for me.

I stand at attention. Today, Peron's thin frame holds up a diamond patterned vest in mustard and green, with a dark yellow shirt underneath. If that's not bad enough, he's topped it off with a plum-colored tie and plum pants. It looks like his clothes vomited on him. Ugh. Everyone knows Peron can afford a stylist, and his wardrobe is literally begging for it.

He considers me now. "At ease, Lily."

I relax and wait, staring at the shiny bald spot on his head.

"Lily, in a few days, you will begin to infiltrate high-society Pariseine. Your mission will be to pass on relevant information to our Vestige contact there and help us track down Jasper Dompierre-St-Martin. What do you know about the case?" Peron starts pacing.

"Sir, Jasper disappeared when he was five. The family suspect the nanny kidnapped him, as neither have been seen since. And didn't you say Jasper has inherited the family land and titles?"

"Correct. What I haven't told you is that Jasper was in possession of a priceless heirloom that had been passed down through the family line to each first-born son on their fifth birthday."

An heirloom? I'll bet my entire bank account the Relic Hunters were involved.

Peron continues, oblivious to my private contemplations.

"The heirloom was a gold necklace, which Jasper was instructed never to remove until he had a son he could pass it on to."

He pauses and contemplates me, twisting his thin moustache absentmindedly.

"Lily, what I am about to tell you must not leave this room. Do you understand?"

I gulp and nod. "Yes sir."

Satisfied, he continues.

"Unknown to most, the necklace, though valuable, only served as a protective counterpart for something priceless. A pendant, which is a mythical vessel said to trigger the onset of power from the next reigning Vestige Protector. In the past, those chosen by Vestige would visit the family to see if they were the next ruler."

My curiosity overwhelms me.

"Why did this family need to keep it? Why couldn't it be stored at Vestige headquarters somewhere, safe and sound?"

Peron smiles.

"The pendant is highly sought after. It brings good fortune to those who wear it, for one thing. However, its real purpose is to select the next Protector, unlock their supernatural abilities and enhance the Protector's power as they wear it. These supernatural abilities manifest uniquely in each person chosen by the vessel and whoever receives this power cannot be defeated. They could rule the world if they so desired. It's fortunate the vessel has always chosen people with character." He looks at me, as if to check I'm paying attention.

I nod and motion for him to continue. He still hasn't answered my question.

"This is why Vestige has lasted so long, and another reason why Relic Hunters and other enemies search for the pendant and the future Protector. We cannot risk them attacking or infiltrating our headquarters and gaining access to the pendant. Nor can we risk those at Vestige becoming power hungry and going rogue."

Peron walks over to his desk and rifles through a file.

"Many centuries ago, it was discovered that the Dompierre-St-Martin family have a gift. This gift allows them to obscure the item's whereabouts when in close contact with it. The younger they are, the more powerful their ability. When wearing the pendant or in close proximity to it, they render the piece, including the protective gold necklace which holds it, invisible to all but themselves, their family, and the Protector."

"How is that possible?"

"Something in their blood or genes seems to interfere with the pendant's power. We are still researching it, but the mystery has so far eluded us. It's an enigma. Some say it's magic." He smiles again.

I scoff at that.

Peron ignores me and continues.

"The Dompierre-St-Martin family were honored to protect the pendant on behalf of Vestige's leaders, and they have kept our secret from the time it was entrusted to them. It served them well. They became one of the most powerful ruling families, an obvious bonus to being Keepers of the pendant.

"In fact, the pendant has always been handed back to the Keepers on the death of each Protector and is passed down from father to son until the pendant calls a new Protector."

My boss appears thoughtful as he pulls a page from the file and paces the room with the paper in hand. After a moment, he stops and regards me.

"Lily, Jasper was wearing the pendant when he disappeared. We need to find him—and the pendant."

I'm a little in awe of this story, of a secret pendant that is central to Vestige—if, in fact, it does have powers. But I'm puzzled.

"Why me? Why do you trust me to find the clues that will help us locate Jasper?"

"I believe you are more capable than you know, Lily. I'm hoping you will take this as an opportunity to prove it to everyone who has doubted you. Unfortunately, you may have to reconsider your career choice if you fail—the Board is unhappy with you. So please, do all you can to succeed."

"Yes, sir," I gulp.

"Good. Now, if you happen to find the pendant itself—should it no longer be in Jasper's possession—you will be able to see it." His tone is light, almost off-hand. "It looks like this." He lifts the paper in his hand and waves it under my nose. It's a picture of a beautiful pendant: a tree with bronze, silver and gold branches intertwined around a crystal at its center.

"Pretty. Does it have a name?"

"It's called the *Arbre de vie*, the Tree of Life. It's so precious that it's kept in a protective case when not in use—the gold necklace the Keeper wears. We updated the necklace about a hundred years ago. The previous one was more like an interlocking piece that fit together with the pendant, and the Board were concerned the *Arbre de vie* was too exposed."

Peron scratches his cheek. "Lily, I want you to be on the lookout for anything related to the *Arbre de vie*. A small jewelry box has been developed for the pendant under each Protector's rule, but some have gone missing over the years. It would be a boon if you can locate those too."

A knock at the door interrupts Peron. On the other side of the glass wall, his secretary is holding a phone and giving him a meaningful look.

Peron seems to know what she's trying to say. He turns to me.

"It looks like something urgent needs my attention. We have you scheduled to leave tomorrow afternoon at two. Come back in the morning and we'll finish the briefing."

"Yes, sir." I exit the room and head to the elevator.

Chapter Eleven

I RETURN TO MY room and log into the library server on my laptop, using the extra security clearance Peron's secretary sent me via encrypted mail. A quick search reveals the Dompierre-St-Martin family aren't wealthy at present, which makes sense given Jasper disappeared back in the seventeenth century. It must be due to having lost the "blessing" of the magic pendant.

The article says the younger brother, Étienne, took over the family business. He developed a terrible gambling habit in his older years and the family fell into financial ruin.

Well, I hope I can go back in time, find clues to the missing son Jasper and correct that piece of history. And save my job in the process.

I'm not sure why Peron thinks I have a chance of success, when I'm sure the Vestige leaders would have sent others to look for the boy and the pendant in the past.

There must be something every other agent missed. There must be a reason Peron gave me the assignment—does he believe I have something they didn't? Or does he think there's no way I'll succeed? Is he regretting his effort to bring me in and now looking for an excuse to get rid of me?

I clench my jaw. I bet Alyse would love to be chosen instead. What would she do if given this opportunity? I shudder, imagining those who might get hurt on the road to her success. No. I won't be like her. This is my chance to show them I deserve to be at Vestige.

My hands tremble.

Operation Jasper needs to be a success. My career—my life—is hanging on it.

Operation Jasper. We don't even know if Jasper is still alive. But if he was dead, the pendant wouldn't stay hidden, right? Or would it? Maybe it's buried underground somewhere with his decaying body. Maybe an archaeological dig will find it one day in the future, once his body has disintegrated and has no power over the pendant anymore. Wouldn't that be ironic?

Now I know the stakes, it dawns on me that I am about to embark on what may be a fruitless endeavor.

I stand and walk to the bathroom, considering myself in the mirror. What do they see when they look at me? A naïve young woman, ready to take the fall for their failure?

No. I will not be that person.

I look closer at my reflection. Why didn't anyone tell me I have cookie crumbs on my chin? I hurry to brush them off.

With renewed seriousness, I question myself again. Do they think I'm an easy target?

What would Dad say?

I smirk. He'd agree with Peron and point out what a wonderful opportunity this is to prove everyone wrong.

And he'd be right.

I pull on every grit of resolve within me, gathering the pieces together into a solid wall of self-protection.

I'll do it. I'll pose as a sixteen-year-old, a cover that will give me the edge I need to stay undetected. And I'll pull it off. An innocent girl being a spy? Who would believe it?

I will find this Jasper if it's the last thing I do.

Chapter Twelve

The next morning, I finish packing what I need for the mission. The new outfits I was fitted for earlier take up most of the room in my suitcase. I add my diary and then head to Peron's office.

His secretary shows me in right away and I stand to attention again.

"At ease, Lily." he says.

I relax my stance.

"Let's continue where we left off, shall we? I'm going to tell you about the history of the *Arbre de vie*." Peron looks at me carefully, as if to make sure I'm listening. I stand a little straighter. He launches right in.

"Alex Vestige discovered the pendant in the twelfth century, then founded the Vestige Order. Now, the pendant had passed from family to family prior to that, we think originating in Jerusalem, but its magical properties were largely unknown except for the prosperity it brought those who wore it. Legend has it that this once belonged to Queen Esther."

I glance up at that. "The Jewish queen, wife of the Persian king Xerxes?"

"Yes."

I raise my eyebrows, impressed.

"Anyway, when Alex discovered the pendant, it 'came alive' according to our writings, and endowed Alex with a power as yet unknown to man—perhaps except for when it is said the Creator walked the earth in human form."

The Creator? God? I'm not sure he exists, but I'll keep that to myself. Peron hasn't finished.

"Alex founded what was then the Vestige Order, to help humanity, and the pendant was a significant help. Our records tell us that when the pendant exhibited a noticeable reaction for certain other individuals who later came into contact with it over the centuries, they would be elected as the next Protector."

"What kind of reaction, Sir?"

"Well, it varied. But it was always quite supernatural. For example, the Protector Nic was said to have glowing eyes. Some even say Nic's eyes shot out beams of light. Interestingly, Nic later exhibited the powers of prophetic dreams and would get sudden insight and knowledge about things. It's said Nic could even see into the spirit realm at times."

Whoa.

"Now, each Protector had a different power, but that power was always what was required at the time to preserve the Order and ensure we could assist humanity."

He stops to scratch a tuft of graying blond hair.

"There's more to this story, Lily. Are you interested?" he asks, as if testing me.

"Of course. Besides, I need as much intel as I can get if I'm to pull this off."

"Good. Now where was I ... ah, yes. During the sixteenth century, the Vestige Protector Henri Bergenoir, moved the *Arbre de vie* from Paris to the most comparable alternate world known at that time—ARK1. The Dompierre-St-Martin family were also willing to move and maintain their role as Keepers. We used our connections to give them lands and title in the République de L'Aurente and they brought much of their existing wealth with them."

He takes a breath.

"But why move it to another world?" I ask.

"There were complications with keeping it in our dimension at the time."

"Let me guess. One of our enemies?"

"You're right. You know Leonardo da Vinci was a key figure in our Order. Before he died in 1519, he prophesied that there would be a great war with the Sentinels if we left the pendant in this world. He said many would die and the pendant would be stolen, which could have devastating consequences. It was enough to convince the Order to take drastic measures, and they decided it would be safest to move the *Arbre de vie* to our companion world."

"I think I'm beginning to understand why there's so much secrecy around the *Arbre de vie*," I say. "It's risky business."

"Risky indeed," Peron replies. "It's unfortunate that a few Sentinels managed to infiltrate Vestige and gain entry to the parallel world before we could increase our security."

Peron runs a hand down his face.

"Thankfully, they haven't been strong enough to pose a threat until now. But back to my point—the Order had been searching for the next Vestige Protector since the last one, Terry, died in Pariseine in 1584. Unfortunately, we still hadn't succeeded in identifying a new Protector before Jasper disappeared in 1594."

So that's why we don't have a Protector right now.

"Prior to the pendant going missing, no one chosen by Vestige displayed any powers. We were at a loss as to where the Protector was and why none of our candidates were selected. However, we have a few people in mind for the Protector now. Once you locate Jasper and recover the pendant, we will arrange for them to visit the family in the seventeenth century."

My eyelid starts twitching. This mission is more critical than I expected. I don't want to think about the possibility of failure.

"We have created a time-slip and will be sending you back to 1629, which is thirty-five years after the kidnapping," says Peron.

"What? Why thirty-five years? That's almost half a century! Jasper would be like, forty years old. Why am I not going to the time when he was kidnapped? Or before, so I can prevent it?"

"I thought you'd ask that, Lily. When Jasper was lost to us, we sent agents to that time but for some reason every mission failed. Quite bizarre." He shakes his head. "One of our gifted leaders prophesied the pendant would be hidden for thirty-five years and then the Protector would appear. We stopped the missions and waited for a new generation of potentials to be born and grow of age."

"What happened with the other missions to 1629?"

"There haven't been any. There was a hold order put on this mission and it got buried under other priorities. They studied the failed missions to identify what went wrong, but there were too many inexplicable situations. The hold order was finally lifted last month and we are ready to try again."

So that's why I've been given this mission. They don't expect success, so they give it to someone they want to performance manage out of the business. Great.

I slump a little then remember Dad's encouragement that every stumbling block sent to take me down is a stepping stone that can take me up. I've got to believe that. But something nags at me.

"Sir, we are time travelers. Surely someone knows who the future Protectors are. I figure it would be in some top-secret file to protect their identity. Given the current crisis, why can't we refer to that?"

Peron pinches the bridge of his nose, where his skin is worn smooth by years of practiced restraint. "Lily, contrary to what you believe, the identities of the Vestige Protectors are kept secret until they are chosen. Those select few Vestige operators who live in or travel to the future are under oath on pain of death to not reveal the identity of the Protectors."

I blink. Peron must see something in my blank expression. He releases a breath.

"This is to prevent the knowledge being leaked to our enemies who would either assassinate the chosen one or try to change their allegiance before they are selected. We study and protect history, along with humanity, and correct the smaller wrongs humanity has caused. No heavy tampering."

"Okay," I reply, stumped, although I do wonder when our vision shifted from helping humanity to being a parental figure, all to "protect history."

Peron finishes the download on Operation Jasper, as he's calling it. After passing on Dad's message (which puts a gleam in his eyes), I salute Peron and he sends me out with a look I can only decipher as hopeful.

Deep in thought, I open the door and walk straight into a well-dressed gentleman.

"Oomph! Sorry."

"Stefan, there you are," Peron calls from his office behind me. "Lily, this is Stefan Georges. He's Alyse's father and a member of Vestige's board of directors. Stefan, Lily Destin, one of our operatives."

Stefan looks back at me with a disinterested smile, but I hold my hand out in introduction. He grips my hand briefly then lets go as if I'm not worth his notice.

"Agent Destin is about to embark on Operation Jasper."

I guess Mr. Georges is in the know, but he gives me a sharp glance. What, doesn't he think I'm good enough either?

On edge, I squeeze out the door and move around him, rolling my eyes when I get to the elevator. The doors open and I walk in. Turning, I see Peron talking to Stefan, who is still watching me. A shiver tiptoes down my spine, settling in my gut. Did Alyse send him to stop my mission? I return his stare until both doors close.

Back in my room, I ignore the butterflies in my stomach as I freshen up and climb into one of the dresses sent from the Wardrobe department. It's unlikely they'll cancel my mission at this late stage. "You're gonna be all right, Lily," I whisper. I check my reflection in the mirror. "This is really happening," I breathe.

I'm relieved I learned the Olde-French language last year and that our teacher makes us speak every dialect but our own in Language class. Keeps us fresh, she likes to say, and I agree. It's going to make things easier when I arrive in a few hours. All I need is to adjust to the more relaxed style of the République de L'Aurente.

My thoughts turn back to the pendant and its elaborate history. I didn't think that type of thing could exist, but then again, most people don't think time travel exists. It does, so why not a magic pendant?

Honestly, why do we even need a Vestige Protector? We've gotten on pretty well with Vestige's current governing body since the last Protector passed away over four hundred years ago. Although, there has been a recent increase in the number of incidents involving our enemies.

Before long the time has come for me to head toward the Vortex Center, where I'll be leaving this world to enter ARK1 and traveling back through time. I grab my suitcase and lock the door on my way out.

Chapter Thirteen

1629 A.D. République de L'Aurente, ARK1 dimension

Mission purpose: *Find Jasper Dompierre-St-Martin*
Code name: *Lily Therriot*

"Lily! Come quickly!"

I glance up at Cherie's excited whisper and put down the leather-bound book I'm reading with a smile.

It's been a week since I arrived in ARK1 and I'm still surprised at how fast I've become friends with Cherie and Charlotte, my "long-lost" fifteen-year-old cousins. Although twins, it's a relief they're not identical. They are the daughters of Raimond Therriot, a celebrated member of Vestige and my contact with Peron.

Gathering the skirt of my pretty yet cumbersome light blue satin dress, I join Cherie at the bay window overlooking their beautiful, sculpted grounds. Curious as to what has caught her attention, I spot a shiny black carriage coming down the path toward the mansion.

The carriage draws to a halt, silencing the clip-clopping of the horses. We watch as the carriage door opens, our faces pressed against the glass. Out steps a well-dressed young man, his golden hair peeking out of a fancy dark green hat. I can't see him clearly, but I already know who he is.

The twins haven't stopped talking about him since I arrived.

His name is Monsieur Coupier, a tutor sought after by the daughters of all the wealthy families. Why? Well, not only is he famous for being one of the most talented and knowledgeable tutors around (a great feat at twenty-two years of age), but rumors say he is also the most handsome.

I follow Cherie across to the music room to grab Charlotte and trail behind them, admiring their sweet, amber curls as they prance down to the drawing room. Their sense of anticipation is catching, but I can't stop the nerves playing hopscotch in my stomach.

Why am I nervous? I'm on assignment. This is absurd.

It has nothing—absolutely nothing—to do with the fact that the moment we step into the drawing room, my gaze locks onto the most breathtaking man I've ever seen.

For a second, I forget to breathe. This is monsieur Coupier?

There's something undeniably masculine about him—it's intense. His tailored clothes emphasize the strength beneath. Thick golden hair, neatly gathered at the nape of his neck, contrasts with his vibrant, untamed green eyes. They pull me in, like the heart of a wild forest in spring, but I'm torn between wanting to lose myself in them and resisting their allure. Goodness. He's dangerously irresistible.

Charlotte nudges me and I realize I'm staring at monsieur Coupier, biting my lip like an idiot. And he's staring back. My cheeks warm and I shift uncomfortably, averting my eyes. At last, I remember to breathe.

Raimond Therriot clears his throat and introduces our new tutor. "Good, you are all here. Monsieur Coupier has been engaged to instruct you girls in music and art."

Cherrie giggles. The pride in "Uncle" Raimond's voice is understandable. According to Charlotte, he's secured us the tutor everyone wants but few can get.

How can monsieur Coupier be so successful at such a young age? Must be his looks. Thankfully, this dimension doesn't believe in garish cosmetics. Anything less than perfection would be a crime against that chiseled face.

Guilt tugs at me for the unkind thought. Maybe he worked hard for it. I owe him the benefit of the doubt. And respect, too, given that he'll be teaching us.

Composing myself, I look back up with a smile.

He's still staring at me, as if he's never seen a girl before.

My smile falters and I glance away. Why is he staring at me? Am I that unusual? Is it obvious I don't belong here?

I struggle to pull myself together and manage to look up at my uncle, not ready yet to glance at monsieur Coupier again. Swallowing, I almost choke on the dryness scraping like flint against my throat. I wish I'd had a sip of tea before coming down.

Uncle Raimond continues with the introductions, gesturing to Cherie to move forward, which she does.

"My eldest daughter, Mademoiselle Cherie Therriot."

In the corner of my eye, I see monsieur Coupier has already moved toward me (me!) and is reaching his hand out to grasp mine in the traditional gentleman's kiss. I look back at him, surprised. I might be the oldest, but courtesy dictates he greet the twins first.

Cherie is too busy gawking at monsieur Coupier's divine face to notice his hand. Her hand reaches out with enthusiasm and whacks his off course.

Monsieur Coupier looks down at his hand then glances at Cherie. It seems he may not have heard Uncle's introduction.

Everything moves in slow motion.

Cherie, intent on having her hand kissed, is caught, propelled forward by her own eagerness. She ducks as if to curtsy and takes another step ... onto the hem of her skirt.

She face-plants straight into monsieur Coupier's chest. He twists and catches her, eyes wide and mouth agape. Cherie jerks back, mortified. A rosy glow spreads up her neck and reaches her cheeks.

I don't know whether to gasp or laugh. Charlotte snorts beside me, her reaction obvious. Uncle just frowns, like he's not sure what's going on.

Monsieur Coupier proves himself a gentleman, helping Cherie to find her feet with a quiet throat-clearing. She stares at the floor. The silence is awkward.

I can't take it. A giggle escapes—too late to rein it in. All eyes snap to me, and I freeze, pulling what Mom calls the stunned mullet face.[1]

Great. Way to go with the etiquette, Lily.

A snicker from my right. Cherie's glare shifts to Charlotte, who tries to look innocent. She fails, her mouth twitching. Mine does too, at the funny expression Char is pulling.

Then Cherie cracks, laughter spilling free.

Relief floods me. I close my eyes for a moment and join in, caught in the wave of giggles.

When I open them, a slow smile is growing on monsieur Coupier's passionate mouth. The merriment in his eyes makes my heart light. Until they turn on me again.

A delayed shockwave hits my gut and catapults up to my heart.

Th-thump—thump—thump.

"My deepest apologies Monsieur," Cherie says. "It wasn't my intention to—to ..."

Monsieur Coupier tears his gaze away to assure her. "No need to apologize Mademoiselle. All is well. I am pleased to make your acquaintance."

Cherie's face clears and she sighs with a smile. Uncle looks on, amused.

Monsieur Coupier kisses her hand and walks over to Charlotte to do the same, his movements smooth and controlled. Like power restrained.

"Ah, this is my younger daughter, Mademoiselle Charlotte Therriot," Uncle says.

"A pleasure," monsieur Coupier says. After a few more words and smiles between Charlotte and monsieur Coupier, their introductions are finished.

Then the man turns with purpose and steps my way. His eyes arrest me and I'm unable to move. Why is he affecting me like this?

---

1. The expression "stunned mullet" is a phrase occasionally used in Australia to describe someone who looks shocked, bewildered, or dazed, much like a mullet fish that has just been caught or stunned. Imagine a fish out of water with its wide-eyed, blank stare, and open mouth.

I watch as he holds his fist against his mouth for a moment, his expression suggesting he's recalling something funny.

Then he's before me and Uncle says, "And this is my niece, Mademoiselle Lily Therriot."

Interest sparks in his eyes. "Mademoiselle, I am enchanted. It is an honor to meet you. I am Monsieur Marc Coupier." The resonance of his voice affects me.

"Monsieur." I have to clear my throat. "Monsieur, it is a pleasure to meet you."

With a smile that looks like triumph, he takes my proffered hand and kisses it gently. His mouth is soft and warm against my skin. I melt inside and want to bite my lip again.

He lifts his head and catches my gaze. "Oh, but the pleasure is all mine." There's that look again, like he's found something humorous and won a trophy all at once.

He's still holding my hand and his stare is becoming intense. Is he a player? I experience a flash of regret.

Either way, I can't maintain eye contact, not with him looking into my soul.

I glance away to catch my breath, all too aware of his skin against mine.

Red alert! Red alert!

I slip my hand from his grasp and step back with a frozen smile. A look of something that could be disappointment flickers across his face.

Shields up! Up, up!

I will keep my head on straight and not get distracted ... or fooled.

Four days later...

Monsieur Coupier, or Marc, as I secretly call him, has visited a total of three times since our introduction.

Each tutoring session, I've kept my distance, trying to ignore his stares and trying not to stare back when he's not looking. He's the most beautiful man I've ever seen. I admire his long lashes and straight nose, his full lips and strong jaw. There's something almost magnetic about the way he moves, the kind of presence that demands attention without asking for it.

I look over at him now. His blond hair catches the light like threads of sunshine, his eyes clear as he paints—a vivid green. A white shirt complements his lightly tanned skin. It's like he doesn't care that pale skin is in vogue, and he doesn't have to. He's gorgeous.

Yesterday, he moved the grand piano to make room for us to watch him play. He'd rolled up his sleeves, and the veins and muscles stood out on his forearms as he pushed the piano.

I swallow hard at the memory.

And I'm staring at him again. I feel a tiny shift in the air that tells me he's about to glance my way. My stomach flips, and I drop my gaze, pretending to focus on anything else.

Ugh. Idiot.

Marc has this quiet intensity that makes him seem untouchable, but he also has this calm, collected vibe that feels ... real. No cheesy pickup lines, no smug smirks—just a quiet confidence.

Still, I'm not falling for it. Gorgeous guys like him always have a catch. They use their looks like a secret weapon, charming their way into the lives of girls too naïve to see the truth.

I clench my jaw, pushing back the memories that try to claw their way in. Not now. Not him.

But then I glance at Marc again, and for a moment, my doubts waver. He's fully tuned into us when he teaches. His passion for his subject practically glows in his eyes. He's patient, kind even, like he cares that we get it. And for one second, I wonder ... maybe this time it's different.

So then ... why does he keep staring at me?

Chapter Fourteen

A week later, Uncle Raimond pulls me into his study and hands me a case file. Turns out the last Vestige spy who investigated Jasper's disappearance thirty-five years ago, discovered something. Jasper's nanny had been sighted in the south, close to a village named La'Ristante.

Even though that was some time ago, Uncle and Peron plan a field trip to the area.

Uncle tells the girls he is letting me visit an old friend of my mother's family. They want to join me, but he insists their lessons are important and refuses to let them shirk their learning. Amused, I say goodbye to two pouting girls. If only they knew.

The carriage ride is long and bumpy. By the end of the first day, I'm bored with staring out at the same scenery. My chaperone, an older woman named Félicité, has slept the entire way. By the third morning, my bones ache and I'm sure I look as rumpled, dusty, and tired as I feel. Félicité doesn't seem to be faring any better. Although we'd stayed at a small inn last night, exhaustion lulls me to join her in sleep—albeit a light, fitful one.

"Mademoiselle ... Mademoiselle Therriot, please wake up. We're here."

I come to and open my eyes slowly, blinking the grit away until my surroundings are clear. A fellow Vestige agent, who Uncle introduced to me earlier as Louis, has opened the carriage door. He'd been sitting with the coachman for a while up top.

Once he's satisfied I'm awake, Louis moves on to help the coachman unload our bags from the back of the carriage. I stretch my aching form and wince. Turning to Félicité, I shake her gently. "Madame Félicité, wake up. We're here."

She wakes with a groan and I feel terrible that Uncle suggested someone of her age accompany me. She must be almost fifty but looks eighty. At least the average life expectancy in ARK1, at seventy, is twice that of Earth in this century. The introduction of personal hygiene in the last few decades has made a vast difference.

Louis comes back around and offers me a hand. I stand quickly and whack my head on the carriage roof. Pain shoots through my scalp from where my hair pins have been pushed in from the blow.

"Ow. Crap!" I rub my head gingerly then accept Louis' hand and climb down, ignoring the shock in his face at my unladylike language.

I straighten to find myself facing our lodgings in La'Ristante.

Louis helps Félicité down and takes our bags in with the help of our driver. I follow him in, supporting Félicité and sensing the curious eyes of other patrons in the adjoining parlor. I try to ignore the attention while I wait for Louis to arrange my room, as well as rooms for Félicité, himself and the driver. He and the coachman are both bodyguards and part of Vestige, entrusted with my protection during this trip. Not that I can't handle myself in a fight.

The matron of the inn smiles at me while she provides Louis with the keys to our rooms. She leads us up a flight of rickety steps to the second floor and I take on more of Félicité's weight to help her up.

We find ourselves on a small landing, looking down a hallway with several doors on either side. Although corridors didn't become common until the late seventeenth century on Earth, in ARK1 they became popular in the fourteenth century.

The matron shows us to my room first. Louis leaves my bags on the carpeted floor, then supports Félicité in my place.

The room is quite spacious with all the necessary essentials, and is richly decorated, though a little vulgar for my taste.

The matron turns to me. "Mademoiselle, your guest is in the next room. There is an adjoining door here should you require it."

"Thank you," I respond. She smiles and bows her head in deference to me. Then she closes the door to show the others to their rooms

I turn back to my room and start checking my surroundings for spy holes. Call me paranoid, but this is the seventeenth century and it's safer to take precautions. Anyway, I need to stay in practice. As a final security check, I walk up to the nearest painting and challenge it to a stare-off, watching for wandering eyes.

Satisfied all is secure, I move to the basin and wash my hands and face. Dabbing myself dry, I use the mirror on the wall to adjust my appearance and look at the adjoining door where my guest resides. In actual fact, the guest is my partner on this small expedition.

I move toward the door and consider this week's code of introduction, as advised by Uncle Raimond. No, not a sophisticated knock. It's the call of a pigeon. I'd had to practice for half an hour before he was satisfied I had it right. I can only assume that whoever chose this week's code was either sleep-deprived, overly hopeful, or conducting a social experiment on human compliance. I wonder at the confidence it must have taken to call this a good idea. And yet ... it seems they'll get the last laugh.

Taking a deep breath, I produce the required sound and wait. After a moment I hear a pecking response. Well, I guess that proves it's my partner.

The door opens and I behold an attractive older woman with black hair pulled back in a gentle bun. The lines on her face suggest her age to be around forty years, but who knows in these times. She could be younger.

We smile and she backs away to let me in, closing the door behind me.

We turn and face each other.

"*Ma chère*,[1] you must be Mademoiselle Lily Therriot."

---

1. Ma chère is an affectionate term meaning "my dear." It's less intimate than ma chérie.

"I am. And you are Mademoiselle Victoire Rohan."

She smiles and nods. "*Bonjour.* It is lovely to meet you in person. I expect we shall have some fun together, yes?"

I grin back.

We spend the rest of the afternoon discussing our plans to seek out clues to the whereabouts of Jasper and his nanny—if they're even alive—and to work out what happened to them.

After a hot dinner downstairs, we retire for the evening. I lie awake for a while listening to the sounds of other guests in the inn. Eventually, tiredness overwhelms me and I slip into a blissful sleep.

Chapter Fifteen

The morning light spills through gaps in the curtains as I wake up. It takes twenty seconds for me to remember where I am and what I'm doing here. Then I'm jumping out of bed to get ready for the day.

After dressing and throwing open the curtains, I walk to the adjoining door and hear Victoire moving about, so I knock.

"*Un minute!*" she calls.

I wait as I hear murmuring and some shuffling. Then I'm certain I hear a window close and movement outside. As in outside on the second level, not out in the corridor. Maybe she has a balcony adjoining her room. What was she doing, having a secret party? With a secret friend? I grimace. I don't want to know.

I hear light footsteps headed my way and school my features. When she opens the door, Victoire appears a little flushed and is fixing her appearance. Yep, she has a secret lover. I smirk when her back is turned. Though what she does behind closed doors is not my business.

When she's ready, we head down to breakfast. Louis and our driver are waiting in the hallway, so Louis sends the driver out to ready the horses while he joins us.

"We've already eaten," he says.

I nod. "Was madame Félicité settled in to her satisfaction?"

"Oh yes. Be at ease—she will be well looked after these next few days, until you're ready to return home."

"Thank you."

Victoire and I eat as Louis talks.

"I've made some enquiries and have a few places we can check out, including a few houses where Jasper and the nanny may have been living. I don't hold much hope, but it's worth investigating."

I nod and soon we're finished, freshened up and ready to depart. The carriage is waiting out the front and Victoire and I climb in with Louis' assistance.

"Watch your head, Mademoiselle," he says to me with a smirk. I ignore him.

The carriage jerks forward, heading out to the first location. We will commence on the outskirts, near the sea, where it's probable they may be situated.

The first place we check returns nothing, so we move on.

We travel from village to village, disembarking to stretch our legs and ask questions. After some time, one seasoned farmer recalls a young woman who lived with her boy in a white cottage near the sea, about thirty years ago. He used to trade his produce for fish and other goods in the village and would often see them in front of their cottage on the hill.

Excited by this news, we thank the man and follow his directions to the seaside village.

The air smells briny when we arrive at the outskirts. We stop and the driver agrees to take the carriage "into town" while the rest of us move forward on foot.

As we walk closer to the docks, a sour, fishy odor permeates the air. We pass several fishermen working with their catch and seagulls squawk as they fight over dead fish heads. I look away and hitch my skirts higher as I sidestep a pool of blood, fighting to swallow my bile.

We pass by the wharf and I glance over at the dilapidated houses facing us. They run parallel to the main street of the town. What things have they seen over the years? Could they attest to the truth about Jasper?

We soon clear the area and come upon a small beach. A fresh wind blows off the sea. I pause for a moment to enjoy the clean air and the peace that comes with the sound of waves lapping against the shore.

It's quaint here, not a bad place to grow up if you're willing to work hard for a living. Except for the reeking fish heads.

Victoire points out a white cottage beyond a small cliff overlooking the beach. Hope flutters in my chest. This could be it. The house matches the farmer's description, but we wouldn't have noticed it without his directions.

It doesn't take long to hike up to the cottage. When we arrive, Louis checks the perimeter while Victoire and I head to the front door. Victoire knocks several times.

We hear footsteps and then the door opens halfway. An old woman peers out, her gray hair peeking out of a shawl. She scowls.

"What do you want?"

Victoire cringes for a moment, but recovers her smile and introduces us, before explaining that we are here to visit old friends but are not sure if they still live here.

"Have you lived here long?" she asks kindly.

The woman eyes her a moment, then squints at me.

"I have lived here twelve years. Six with my beloved husband, Alfred, and six since he passed away."

"I am sorry to hear about your husband, may the Creator bless his soul."

The woman crosses her heart. "May he bless his soul."

I study the woman closely. She doesn't fit the description of the nanny—her eyes are the wrong color.

"Thank you for telling us," Victoire says. "Our friends must have moved." She looks perplexed, so I jump in.

"Madame ... *pardonnez-moi*,[1] what may we call you?"

She glares at me before answering. "Jeanne Turenne".

I smile in thanks.

"Madame Turenne, how lovely to make your acquaintance. I am Mademoiselle Therriot and this is Mademoiselle Rohan. We are sorry to hold you up at your front door like this. Only perhaps our friend lived here before you. Do you remember the name of the man who sold you this house, by any chance?"

Jeanne pauses and furrows her brow.

"I seem to recall his name was monsieur Bernard. Oui, Bernard."

---

1. "Pardonnez-moi" means "Pardon me"

"Bernard." I sound the name out, but it doesn't ring any bells. Disappointment fills me. "Thank you, Madame Turenne. You don't know where he moved to, do you?"

She shakes her head. "I am sorry. I cannot help."

"You have been most helpful. Thank you." We say our good-byes and retreat. Once the madame has closed the door, Louis approaches and we start our trek back down the hill.

"There wasn't much behind the house. Looks like the woman is living on her own," Louis says. "No evidence of a male living there now."

"So, this monsieur Bernard … do you think he bought the place off the nanny or Jasper?" I ask. "Or could he have been Jasper under an assumed name? Or is this even the cottage he and the nanny lived in? What if they lived somewhere else entirely?"

"That is what we'll have to find out, Mademoiselle." Victoire sighs.

We agree to head to the main street—the rue principale—to stop for lunch. After enjoying a light meal, we decide to wander around and see if we can find some villagers who remember the nanny and Jasper.

Victoire heads out on foot with the driver, while I set out with Louis.

After a scenic walk and a chat with a couple of villagers, we head back to the rue principale. Dust from the horses and the road clings to my gray dress, coating it in a fine, gritty layer. I sigh, grateful I don't get this back home. Imagine the washing I'd have to do. I shudder. I don't envy the maid who'll have to clean it in this century.

Well, at least the color of my dress blends in.

I look up and see a few men loitering around a run-down tavern. They give us odd looks. One of them seems familiar, like a face from a half-remembered dream. I can't quite place him. I look at him again, surprised to see he's staring at me in a way that makes me either want to squirm or blush profusely. I glance away.

"Monsieur Louis," I say, trying to act casual. "Might you look at me as if we're in conversation?"

"We are," he responds with the hint of a smile.

"Those men outside the pub ... don't look, but I'm sure I've seen one of them before. They look suspicious."

Louis considers me and then nods slightly. We turn and keep walking, while Louis casually glances in their direction. I sense him stiffen and he walks faster. Then it hits me.

"Louis, it's our driver." I stop, pleased with my observation skills.

Louis grabs my arm, urging me to keep walking. We hear footsteps behind us and his pace quickens in response. I increase my pace to catch up.

"Mademoiselle," he says, "you might want to loosen your corset."

I look at him in surprise but do as he suggests. I'm wearing a twenty-first century version of a seventeenth century out-fit that matches the current fashion of this dimension. This "Vestige" outfit, created by Branson Co., is modified for ease of use—and is handy in a fight. I adjust the cinch at my waist and both dress and corset expand. It's oh-so breathable, just like the Branson Co. tagline.

As we turn the corner of a building and move into a new street, Louis pulls me forward into a run.

Eyes wide, I hike up my skirts and race with him down the street, my hair escaping from the tidy bun I'd put it in this morning. Within seconds, heavy footsteps slap the ground behind us. It sounds like they're gaining on us. My senses come alive and my focus sharpens.

Heart thudding. Panting. The crunching of feet as we hit a section of loose stones. My throat burns. What would make Louis, a bodyguard, run?

It doesn't take long to find out. Louis pulls me into a semi-hidden alleyway next to a small brasserie and surveys the area for a vantage point. The smell of rotting fish assaults my nose as we rush pass what looks like days-old vomit. I grimace.

"Mademoiselle, those men are Relic Hunters," Louis tells me between heavy breaths. "I know of one of them. He's extremely dangerous, so I will take him on."

"Our driver is a Relic Hunter?"

"Apparently—and a mole. I'll deal with him later. Are you ready for a fight?"

"Yes."

We're halfway down the lane when it widens into a residential courtyard. It's a dead end. We turn. The three men from the tavern stand in the entryway and are blocking our exit to the alley. They look at each other and grin, then advance.

A Relic Hunter with a vicious appearance says something in creole, staring at me. His eyes rake me up and down and he leers.

"*Ou chen!*"[2] Louis responds in creole, his tone dark and angry.

The ugly dude runs toward us, along with the Relic Hunter who was next to him. Louis moves in front of me to face them off. I step back.

With a swift roundhouse kick, Louis connects with the ugly man's head and knocks him out cold—just in time to face an attack from the other man. He looks menacing and I notice a tattoo on one of his arms. It's a symbol of a sword intersecting a crown diagonally from above. The mark of a Relic Hunter.

The scary man pulls out a knife and swipes at Louis, who ducks out of the way just in time. I scurry further back to safer ground as Louis ducks again, evades then manages to disarm the guy. The fight turns into a punching and wrestling match.

The last Relic Hunter has hung back all this time and I look over at him now, surprised he hasn't rushed to attack me. He just stares at me.

It's our driver. At least I think it is. No, I'm sure. Yes. It is the driver.

He has short dark hair, olive skin, and he appears to be in his mid-twenties. A light shade of stubble runs along his jaw. I have to admit that he's well-built and attractive. I would say he's hot, but it'd be in a creepy sort of way because of how he keeps staring at me.

I raise my chin in defiance and stare back, daring him to fight me. I see the flicker of a smile and he moves toward me. He slips past Louis with agile prowess and corners me into the back of

---

2. In Creole, "ou chen" means "you dogs!"

the alley. But he doesn't attack. He just keeps staring, which sets my teeth on edge.

I stop and position myself for a fight, pulling out an extendable baton with "Justice" engraved on it.

"Say hello to Justice."

He stops and lifts his eyebrows, so I run at him and whack him with it. Somehow, he manages to grab it and pull it off me.

"Justice."

I move backward, positioning myself into a praying mantis pose. Kung fu. Not yoga.

"You're not going to try and fight me are you, *ma bichette?*" His voice is low and enticing.

His little doe? I shake my head. I'll ignore that insult. Must be some macho testosterone thing.

"Why don't you come and find out?"

Now he smiles. One minute he's standing there smiling at me, the next, he's rushing at me. Gosh, he's fast.

I engage him with a strike that would make my father proud.

He recovers too fast and the fight begins in earnest. We struggle to overcome each other for a couple of minutes. Rather, I'm attacking and he moves on the defensive.

My hair has come out of my bun now and is getting in the way. I flick it back and the man stares at it. His eyes trail over me a few times before I identify it: desire. His expression holds a renewed keenness that makes my belly do a little flip. Part of me enjoys his interest, even as it repulses me.

Disgusted with myself, I charge at him again. I sense he's holding back, until suddenly he's in my face, flashing me a grin that could melt wax. It flusters me and before I'm aware of what he's doing, the guy has maneuvered somehow and grabbed me from behind. No!

I struggle, furious at myself for letting him catch me off guard, and he grunts in protest.

"Just stop, Lily. Why are you even trying to fight in this getup? It's unnecessary and must be bothersome for you. Although—" he grunts again as I buck him. "It isn't for me." He chuckles.

I freeze, gasping for air. How does he know my name? And what gives him the right to speak to me so informally?

"That's better," he says. "Now we can have an intelligent conversation."

We're both panting and he has me in a vice grip. Why isn't he knocking me out? Well. I'll have to make the most of the opportunity he's given me.

"What were you following us for? Aren't you our driver? Why have you attacked us?"

"What do you think? You're members of Vestige, aren't you?"

"Wait. What's a Vestige? What are you talking about?" I act innocent and struggle against him with renewed vigor. And then recall he too was supposed to be Vestige—until this betrayal.

"Oh, don't give me that, Lily Destin. I've been watching you since you came to town."

I still. How on earth ... "Who are you?"

"An interested party."

I wait for more. Nothing.

"That's it? No name?"

"Nope."

I huff in protest. "That's rich, considering you're holding me quite informally right now."

"Well, one could say I know you more ... intimately."

Creep. I huff in protest. "How do you know me?"

"It's my job to know you. Every person suspected of being a Vestige spy is followed. I volunteered to be your shadow the instant I saw your picture."

Should I be flattered? "My shadow?"

"Mm-hmm," he murmurs and rubs his stubbled cheek against mine.

I lean away and he chuckles softly.

"Unhand me!"

"Oh, I don't think so, *mon chaton.*"

So, it's *my kitten* now, is it? "Then you're not my shadow," I say, acid in my tone. I think fast. "You're ... you're *mon puce.*"

My flea. And it sounds putrid.

He chuckles again and pulls me even closer. He whispers in my ear, a faint scent of mint wafting toward me. "So you admit I'm yours?"

A shiver runs down my spine and I try to repress it. This is wrong, Lily. Get yourself back in the game!

I change the subject before he gets any ideas. "I'm surprised you've given the game up. You know, being a double agent and all."

"I have my reasons."

Realizing he's not going to elaborate, I ask, "What are you doing here?"

"Following you."

"Why?"

"Why are you here?"

"That's none of your business." What's the bet he already knows?

Louis and the other Relic Hunter are still fighting behind us. How are they holding out so long? I hope Louis is okay.

"Any business of yours is my business, Lily."

Can you believe this guy?

I should be stomping on his foot and executing some other moves to get him off me. But I hesitate. He might prove useful if he's this talkative.

"You said you wanted to talk. So talk."

He breathes in my hair. "Hmm, you smell good. You should consider joining me as a Hunter. We could be good together."

"Never."

He makes a disapproving noise. "Do you know how the Relic Hunters were formed, Lily? You might be surprised."

"So tell me."

"Oh, I will," he drawls in my ear. "When you meet me tonight."

"That will never happen."

"Won't it? I think you'll be interested in what I have to say. And what your society has lied to you about."

That does pique my interest. My loyalty for Vestige wars with my curiosity. Stupid curiosity.

He takes my hesitation as consent. One arm unwinds from around me and a moment later a piece of parchment is being waved in my face.

"This will give you the details of our meeting point. I look forward to our rendezvous."

"Hearing you say it makes it sound dirty."

His soft laugh sends puffs of air on my neck. "If you want, it can be."

That's it. I stomp and shift enough to get my arms free, then grab the parchment and elbow him in the ribs. I break out of his hold, pull a knife from his belt and whirl around to face him. I go on the defense, flipping the knife around at the ready. I can tell he's surprised but he hides it in an instant.

He steps back with casual grace and raises his hands in surrender. He almost looks like he's enjoying himself.

"Mademoiselle," he says.

I ignore his sarcasm and pocket the paper.

I hear fighting outside the alleyway, on the main street. More men pour into the alley. I tense in readiness for what I expect will be some serious fighting.

"Brought your friends with you, did you?" I ask.

"I didn't, but my colleague may have," Mon Puce responds with displeasure in his voice. He turns around and moves into a protective position in front of me.

What the heck?

"What? Are we friends now?"

"I'd like to be," he says, shaking his head at some men rushing at us. They stop midway and divert their course to Louis, who has just taken out the scary dude.

Who is this guy? I move around Mon Puce to help Louis, but he grabs me from behind. I struggle. "Let me go. I have to help him."

Mon Puce holds fast.

Louis fights three men at once, with more on their way toward him. I want to scream. I fight Mon Puce in earnest. More men rush in yelling. They start fighting the men who entered before them and Louis ends up only having to ward off two Relic Hunters. I relax, relieved.

Mon Puce spins around with me in his grip so I'm facing the wall again and I yelp in surprise. I struggle and he grunts in protest. "Stop resisting, Lily!"

Oh, that's it. I didn't want to do it, but I rear my head back, cringing at the broken nose I foresee in his future.

I don't hear a crack though. Instead, my skull connects with the softness of muscle.

Oh.

I misjudged his height and hit his chest. I can imagine him raising an eyebrow right now.

"Just give up." I hear humor in his voice.

I slump.

"You really should think about switching sides," Mon Puce says in my ear. "At any rate, it's more fun with me."

"Impressed by my superior fighting skills, are you?" I ask, face heating at my failure.

"She will do no such thing," Louis says from behind and the flea gives a slight grunt.

"Now release her," Louis says.

The guy releases me and I spin around to look up at him. What is it about this guy that disarms me? Aside from the muscles. And the deep voice. And his overall attractiveness. Oh, shut up!

He stares back at me, not moving as Louis presses something into his back. A knife would be my guess.

I smile at him with sarcasm. "Nice meeting you."

He smiles back. "Oh, it was my pleasure."

He gazes at my lips as if considering taking more pleasure than is his right. I'm surprised when this doesn't sicken me, shocked when I'm tempted. Disconcerted, my smile falters. He looks into my eyes again and I see a flicker of something there.

"Lily," Louis says.

I blink fast. "Let's go."

I move around the cute flea, his eyes following me.

"Until we meet again, Mon Puce." I don't know why I say it, but I do.

He smiles. Louis knocks him out with Justice and he crumples to the ground. I wince.

Louis hands me my baton.

"Justice!" I cradle him lovingly.

I look at the flea again. Is it bad that I'm anticipating our next meeting? What is going on with me? I've just met this guy and he's a Relic Hunter. There will be no next meeting.

It's then that I look up at Louis and notice his split lip. I suck in air through my teeth as I study the rest of his face and neck. "Those men gave you a run for your money, didn't they?"

"They got as good as they gave." He stretches his jaw with a wince. I grimace in sympathy. Seems I fared a lot better than Louis this time around. Hopefully, there won't be a next time.

That reminds me. I look around and see a few men still standing, watching us. The rest are lying all over the place, knocked out or dead. I hope not dead.

"Reinforcements?" I ask Louis.

"So it seems," he says, sounding bemused.

We walk over to the group and a tingle shoots down my spine. I shake it off. Weird.

I nod at them and they return the gesture. "Thank you for your help," I say.

"No trouble," one of the men says. His hair is tied back and sprinkled with grey and he appears quite fit. I'd guess he was in his forties or fifties. What strikes me most are his silver eyes. How unique.

"May I ask who you are and why you assisted us?"

The silver-eyed man seems a little perturbed, but drawls, "You can call me Alain. My men and I enforce the law in these parts. Prevent the exploitation of innocents and so on." He gestures to me at the word "innocents" and I almost feel offended. I don't need rescuing. I know how to fight. Usually.

After today's encounter, I will be training extra hard in Uncle Raimond's secret den.

Louis indicates that we need to get out of the alley before the men come to. I nod at the group again and glance at Alain with a grateful smile. As I pass them, something prickles in my belly. I frown but continue to pick my way across the prostrate bodies as I head toward the alley's exit.

Oh. Wait.

I turn and run back in.

"Lily, what?" Louis asks and follows me.

I wait until he reaches my side. "We have to get pictures of these guys, for our records," I say under my breath.

I snap pictures of the first two guys with my new upgraded 3.0 Vestige Lumé bracelet and press the button to send them to Vestige so we have their identities and evidence of our run-in on record. I take a general sweep of the rest of the bodies, unsure who are with the Relic Hunters and who are part of the "local police."

The men standing are gawping at me like I'm crazy. Finally, the silver-eyed man shakes his head and turns, gesturing for the rest of the men to follow. They pick up a few men from the ground and carry them out, leaving Louis and I with the rest.

Well, that works. I take an updated photo of the bodies, then run over to Mon Puce and snap away. He's lying sprawled on the ground but looks like a model posing for my pictures. I have the sense to look back and make sure Louis is walking out of the alley, before I reach down and touch his arm, irresistibly drawn to this well-built man.

What are you doing, Lily?

I withdraw my hand and stand up, guilt twisting my gut. Mon Puce is not what I'd call him right now. Perhaps it was the way he moved to protect me, but for some reason, I don't want to share his picture with Vestige.

I'll do it later, I tell myself and I hit "save" on my bracelet instead of "send." I'm sure Louis will bring it up anyway, now that we know he's a double agent. I find myself hoping Mon Puce will get away before our cleanup crew arrive though. I nudge him with my toe. No response.

I back away then turn and run toward the street. I can tell Louis is getting impatient.

"Sorry," I say sheepishly. "Company procedure and all."

He accepts this but shakes his head. "I've alerted our men in the nearest town. They'll come soon to collect these perpetrators for questioning—especially the mole." His lips twist as he tucks a Vestige device into his pocket. "Come on, let's get back to the others, before these scoundrels wake up."

I couldn't agree more.

Chapter Sixteen

Later that night, unable to resist my curiosity, I head out to the rendezvous point. I know, I said I wouldn't. And he was probably taken by the Vestige clean up team anyway. But I can't shake the feeling that Mon Puce was being genuine when he said there were secrets I should know. So on the off chance he got away …

I arrive at the destination after the sun has set. It's an isolated part of the wharf. The air is cleaner here. A cool wind blows off the sea and the moon sends her pale light across the water. As I stand waiting, I admire the glassed-in candles lit along the walkway. They cast a charming soft orange glow.

After a few minutes, I wonder if I shouldn't have bothered coming. Maybe he was captured after all.

Then I hear movement and turn.

Mon Puce stands peering at me, quite cat-like. I feel like the proverbial canary.

Taking a step back, I swallow. "You said you'd spill the beans on my organization. So spill."

He stalks toward me and I hold my ground. I'm not afraid of him.

"The first Relic Hunter was a young man named Valentino." He stops two feet away from me. His eyes roam my face and I wonder if he's got a headache from being knocked out.

"He was born in 1606 on what you call ARK1, but soon became an orphan. He was taken in by a man who worked for Vestige. It wasn't long before he proved himself worthy. His adoptive father, who was one of the best Vestige had, inducted Valentino into the secret society when he was twelve. Valentino moved up the ranks at a rapid pace under his father's tutelage and was highly decorated for someone so young. In fact, he was rumored to be the best Vestige spy in a century."

He pauses for a moment and I wait impatiently.

"When he was eighteen, the Vestige Order sent Valentino back five centuries into the past to help a family and "right the wrongs of history" as your society claims to do. While there, he fell in love with a beautiful woman, Adele. He couldn't keep the secret from her for long and soon after she found out, the Vestige leaders heard about it. Angered at the danger Valentino had placed on the mission, they took a vote and the woman was assassinated."

I gasp. Mon Puce gives me a long look and continues.

"When Valentino went to visit Adele and found her dead, he was distraught. He knew the Vestige leaders had played a part and demanded they let him go back earlier in time to save her, promising he wouldn't tell her this time. They refused, claiming it would create a split in the time stream."

"That would be playing with history."

"Regardless of the fact that they had tampered with history themselves, the Vestige leaders said this was justice and it would send a strong message to all Vestige spies ... what Vestige does—even their existence—is a secret they should take with them to their graves, unless given suitable clearance." He says those last words as if they taste bitter.

"That can't be true. Why would they do that? It's not like she told anyone, did she?"

"No, *mon chaton*. She would have kept his secret."

That reminds me of what Dad told me, about the Vestige man who blabbed and set the example for all Vestige spies on what not to do.

"After that betrayal of trust, should it surprise you that Valentino went rogue and established the Relic Hunters in secret?" He pauses. "It is unfortunate he wasn't privy to how time travel technology works, but that didn't stop him trying to find out. Annoyingly, the Vestige Order discovered his plans, stripped him of his title and access, then sent a man to kill him when he returned from another mission ... a mission that took place in your Earth dimension, if I recall correctly."

I frown. How does he know what dimension I'm from? And it's the Vestige Society now, or just "Vestige." The Board made that change in 1979.

Mon Puce continues, unaware of my thoughts. "Luckily, that was after he'd already had the opportunity to establish the Relic Hunter Society in two dimensions, including five hundred years in the past—right after Adele had been murdered."

So that's how it originated.

"When the Vestige assassin confirmed Valentino's death, all records of Valentino were destroyed. The Vestige leaders sought to wipe out everything but the lesson his memory invokes."

I hear the disgust in his voice and can't help but feel compassion for Valentino—if this story is true. I don't want to believe it, but I suspect there is some truth to it given what Dad told me earlier. Am I doing the right thing, being part of Vestige? I hope he's lying.

"That's a tragic tale," I say. "But it's just that—a tale told by a stranger who was fighting me before, not ... not whatever it is you're trying to do now." Recruit me?

"I'm trying to enlighten you. Trying to keep you from being deceived by those who destroyed Valentino."

He holds out an object and I snatch it off him. By the dim light of the candles lighting our path, I see it's a miniature painting.

"This picture is in our record books, something we are shown when we become Relic Hunters."

I look at him for a moment, untrusting, as I pull out my flashlight and turn it on. My eyes dip to follow the light. It blazes across the portrait of a man's chest.

Right. Sure. Not weird at all.

Then I notice a tattoo on the man's collarbone. It isn't a Relic Hunter tattoo, but something else entirely. A symbol.

"What is it?"

"This is a partial picture of Valentino before he was killed. See that tattoo? It meant a lot to him."

"Valentino?"

"Yes, Lily. I think you would be interested to know what the tattoo means. I am giving you the chance to find out something for yourself, something Vestige won't tell you."

Hesitantly, but with a sense of curiosity, I pocket it. His eyes track my flashlight as I flick it off and clip it onto my belt. I wonder if he's seen one before. Guess I'm breaking all the rules now. "How can I trust you? How do I know if this really is a picture of Valentino?"

"It is up to you whether you believe me or not," Mon Puce says softly, his eyes pleading in the candlelight. "I hope you give me a chance to show you something you have a right to know. Something they have hidden from you."

Me? I have right to know some supposed dark secret that the Vestige leaders are keeping. Why me? And if that's even true, why does this man care? What does he want from me?

I'm still wondering that when I get back to the inn. I copy the pictures of my Flea stalker from my bracelet to a tiny chip in my necklace via magnetic transmission, an innovative technology Vestige has developed to compensate for lack of internet in the seventeenth century.

Then, with shaking fingers I erase all evidence on my bracelet. Every single photo of him. I guess I'm not ready to share Mon Puce. There's something about him which intrigues me. Despite his cocky magnetism, he seems sincere at times. I believe there are good and bad people on both sides of our war.

Alyse's face pops up in my mind and I squish it like a bug.

I look at the flea's face from the hologram my necklace throws up. I've undoubtedly seen him in different disguises when he's followed me in the past. I should have been more alert.

I chew on a fingernail. The Relic Hunters know I'm with Vestige, but I can't be that important to them. I won't worry about it.

But what did Mon Puce want and why didn't he knock me out? Maybe he'll tell me next time ... if there is a next time. As dangerous as the others appear, he feels safe somehow. Like he doesn't plan to hurt me. Like he wants me for something else. But what?

I pull out the picture he gave me and stare at the tattoo, trying to ignore the well-muscled chest and arms. It occurs to me that this could be the crest of Valentino's family house.

I'm determined to find out more when I get back to Vestige headquarters.

As I'm falling asleep, I remember the assistance we received in the alleyway today. It's nice to know there's some good people out there helping those in need.

I'm dreaming. In my dream, I'm a warrior. I look down and see a sword in my right hand and a shield in my left. I'm wearing some type of battle gear and my hair is tied back.

I hear shouts. They're coming from behind me. I turn my head and see a horde of men, waiting for my signal, calling out taunts to the unseen army in front of me. They're carrying various forms of weapons and shields and look ready to kill.

Silver eyes.

My eyes flick back. A man stands near, dressed as a captain or some type of leader. He has a crest with a sapling on his shield and he's watching me as if waiting for something, his silver eyes waiting ...

Alain.

With a gasp I wake up. I lie there, shaken. It felt so real.

I don't fall back to sleep.

Chapter Seventeen

It doesn't take long for Louis to question where the photos of the third Relic Hunter have gone.

I'm in the den with him and my uncle two days later at the Therriot residence, as we submit our report to HQ. I feel the sting of failure, woven with the weight of exhaustion from the long journey home and two sleepless nights.

Still, I act bewildered when Louis confirms HQ didn't get pictures of all the Relic Hunters. He looks pointedly at me and I know he's thinking of Mon Puce.

What am I doing? This lie could cost me the opportunity to continue with the mission. Is he worth it?

I don't know why, but I tell them the bracelet must have malfunctioned. Keep a straight face when they ask me to give it to them for testing. I hide the tremble in my hands and hand it over when Uncle promises me a replacement by the next day.

Louis considers me and I tense, holding my breath. I'm relieved when he doesn't say anything. He shakes his head and leaves the room, muttering about getting some breakfast. My shoulders relax and I release my breath.

Uncle Raimond reminds me we're leaving in one hour for our regular visit to the local parish—the Church of the Creator. Guilt resurges and threatens to swallow me whole.

A week later I'm on another assignment, determined to prove myself. I look out for Mon Puce but have no luck identifying him among the faces I come across, not even in the servants. Is it wrong to feel disappointed?

What I do come across however, is intelligence about the nanny. She disappeared a few years after kidnapping Jasper. He would have been about nine or ten when she abandoned him, poor thing. After that, he would've had to find work just to survive.

Louis and I believe the Relic Hunters were behind the kidnapping of Jasper. She could have been offered a nice sum of money to deliver the boy into their hands. If so, did she renege on the deal and use the money to buy a place for them to hide and live semi-comfortable for a few years?

Why would she do that? Why did she seek to escape the Relic Hunters when she'd already put her life and career on the line in stealing the boy? It baffles me.

I just hope that the Relic Hunters didn't find the boy.

Chapter Eighteen

I AM PAINTING A week later, in what we've designated the school room. It's a spacious room with large windows that overlook the gardens. I feel as serene as the warm afternoon sun that casts a golden glow around the room.

Monsieur Marc Coupier has created engaging lessons this week, all while maintaining a measured distance. I'm certain he's sensed the barrier I keep firmly in place, and the realization stirs a tangle of emotions within me. Though I've kept him at arm's length, my defenses unyielding, there's something about him that draws me. But like with Jason, even if I'm attracted, it's not enough—I can only trust my feelings if I know his character is truly good.

Awareness taps me on the shoulder. Marc is standing right behind me. Startled, I stop painting. I look back at him to find him staring at me with a strange look on his face.

"Well, this is awkward ..."

He looks at me quizzically.

Uh-oh. "Did I just say that?"

I watch the smile growing on his face. I guess that's a yes. I cringe.

"I just said that ..."

I turn away and squeeze my eyes shut, desperate to stop the heat diffusing my cheeks, but that seems to make them hotter. I feel like an idiot. I bet I look like a ripe tomato right now.

He clears his throat. I open my eyes ready to face the inevitable mocking, but he surprises me.

"You're doing well, Mademoiselle Therriot. Might I suggest you add some pale yellow here … and here … as a reflection of light?"

He motions with his finger. I am so aware of him I have no idea what he is saying. He could be telling me about the latest movie he hasn't seen (duh, seventeenth century) and I wouldn't even know it.

He gestures to my brush when I don't respond.

"May I?"

Flustered, I manage to nod. With gentle fingers, he takes the brush from my hand, wipes it clean and dips it in white and yellow paint, mixing it to the right hue on my palette. Leaning over me he adds some brush strokes to my canvas. He is so close, his warm breath lifts the tiny hairs on my ear and my blush deepens.

Great. I've progressed from tomato to beetroot. Perhaps I should retire from this lesson and go and live in the garden.

The scent of fresh pine mixed with paint wafts over me. I breathe it in desperately.

I stare at Marc's strong hands and notice a slight tremor as he gives the brush back, but mine are more unsteady and I almost drop it. "Th-thank you."

I wince. I look up at the girls to find them staring back at us. Cherie is open-mouthed and Charlotte has a knowing smile on her face. Ugh. Fantastic.

With some effort, I turn back to my work, determined to block everyone out and regain my composure. It's a struggle and I almost knock my picture off the easel in the process.

The lesson finally ends and we pack up. Marc needs to go to a neighboring family to give their daughter a piano lesson. Pianos were invented in 1540 in this dimension, not like on Earth.

Marc says his farewell, but before leaving the room he looks at me with a mysterious expression. Then he smiles a secret sort of smile and glances away.

My blush comes back in full force.

Frustrated with myself, I sweep from the room, the girls trailing behind me. They are quiet until I reach my bedroom. Then the giggling starts. I turn around to confront them but Cherie beats me to it.

"You have a paint moustache, Lily!" She bursts into laughter.

What? I run to my dressing mirror and almost die. I stare at my hand accusingly. Yep, a swab of blue paint stains the skin. I must have swiped my upper lip without realizing. Raising my eyes to the face that stares back at me like a clown, I wince.

That must be why Marc was eyeballing me so intently. Great. I bet he's laughing all the way to his next appointment.

Charlotte is grinning. "But how could you keep this from us, Lily? You like him—and he clearly likes you!"

"What? That's ridiculous." As if he'd be interested in me romantically. Besides ... "Mesdames, I am not interested in men who use their physical attributes to take advantage of women."

"Are you saying monsieur Coupier does that?" Charlotte asks in a skeptical tone.

"So you do think he's handsome." Cherie giggles.

Ignoring Cherie's comment, I respond with a question of my own.

"How do we know he is a genuine and honorable gentleman?"

"Because Madeleine told me so." Cherie stands with a hand on her hip. "She and her sister Élisabeth have been trying to flirt with him for the past two years. Not once has he flirted back. She says he has acted like a stiff gentleman the entire time." She giggles. "They are so frustrated at not getting him to crack and now, after a few weeks, you have made him melt like butter!"

"See?" Char says. "He is good. I have never heard one bad thing about monsieur Coupier's conduct. He is a true gentleman and a serious tutor, someone parents trust with their daughters. No matter how much that pains them, considering all the marriage offers he must get." She laughs. "With the exception of you, that is!"

I ignore that last comment too.

So Marc is not the player I thought he was. Maybe. Perhaps I misjudged him. Unless he's good at hiding it. Maybe he hasn't been motivated to take from anyone before ... but what can I offer him?

A concerning thought pushes its way in. What if ... no. It couldn't be.

I bite my thumb nail.

What if he's a Relic Hunter? Is there another mole at Vestige? Have they leaked my mission? Is that how Mon Puce knows about me? Have they both been sent to watch me?

I grip my bedframe for a moment before common sense smacks me on the head and I can breathe easier. Right now, there is no evidence to suggest this. It's too early to tell. Besides, I need to focus on my mission.

"But I'll be watching you, Monsieur Coupier. You won't see me fall for anything," I whisper.

My determination is trampled on before it has a chance to solidify.

I'm forced to listen, more anxious by the minute, as the scheming twins' plans unfold. I beg them not to follow through, but they believe they are doing the best thing for me.

I groan as they skip from my room to their own beds.

"Oh, how I miss my Skittles." They have always been my go-to when I needed to stress-eat. It comes as no surprise when I don't get much sleep that night.

The next day, the twins approach their father for permission to engage Marc's services for more lessons. Of course he permits it—he can't refuse them anything. I gather it's to make up for the fact that their mother died giving birth to them. Well, I can't begrudge them that.

When Marc arrives for his next lesson, my uncle has a private meeting with him. A maid confirms she heard him offer Marc more money if he comes over more often. Marc agreed.

I thought he was booked out. How will his other pupils react to him canceling their lessons? There are a few tutors around, so

I guess Marc is giving them more work. Still, I'm surprised he'd stop teaching his regular clientele. It can't be good for business.

I guess that wouldn't matter if he was in the RH club though.

It remains to be seen.

Anxious, I chew on my thumbnail and head for the kitchens to find a replacement for Skittles.

The weeks fly past in a whirlwind of assignments, each leading me to fascinating places. A few close calls keep me on edge, but I push through, crafting believable excuses whenever the twins grumble about my absence. Uncle backs my stories, which makes it easier—but I still hate lying.

On the upside, Marc's lessons have become more frequent, and I feel more at ease around him. We're finally getting along like normal. Thank goodness.

And I've found a substitute for Skittles—mixed berries. Something that actually tastes like the comfort I need. I have Marc to thank for that. He showed up one day with candied berries for us to try, as if he somehow knew exactly what I was missing.

Anyway, I've got another mission and this one promises more than just intel.

Chapter Nineteen

Uncle Raimond briefs me with what he knows about my next mission: the Duke and Duchess of Neumand are holding a hunting party tomorrow and we are all invited. He's already accepted the invitation and is under orders to make sure I go. Uncle hands me a sealed missive and I can't wait to tear it open.

I thank him and take the missive to my room. Once there, I do tear it open and absorb the details of my mission, excited. Once I'm certain of everything, I drop the paper into the fireplace before the fire dies down completely. I mentally prepare myself as it burns to ash.

The next morning, I join the girls and Uncle Raimond as we leave the house. The girls are animated, telling me about the family who own the estate we are visiting as we climb aboard the carriage.

It starts with a jerk then settles into a bumpy ride.

The sun is out and it's already quite warm, so we leave the carriage windows open, hoping the breeze will keep any sweat at bay. I tug at the collar on my dress, wishing I didn't have to wear so many layers underneath. Thankfully, the girl's chatter keeps me occupied during the long uncomfortable ride. Then we arrive, along with about twenty other carriages.

The twins and I are handed out of our carriage and we shake out our rumpled skirts, glancing around with curious anticipation at the other guests.

I admire the stately gardens and the palace as we walk up the stairs and are welcomed by our hosts. The Duchess ushers us into a lemon and white colored drawing room for refreshments, where friends meet each other with boisterous conversation.

I lead the girls to a free spot in one corner where we help ourselves to iced tea and take a seat, admiring the tasteful decor.

Before long, we are joined by some of Cherie's friends. They gush over some cute gentry who've arrived and are eyeing us from the other side of the room. I tune them out, sipping my drink and wondering how long it will be before I can begin my mission.

After a few minutes I sense eyes on me, but when I look about the room, no one is staring at me and I don't see anyone of particular interest. I look back down at my glass, half listening to Cherie and Char doing what teenage girls do when they get together: gossip.

I rub the back of my neck at the return of a prickling sensation. I look behind me and see a tall broad-shouldered man with dark hair turn away and leave the room. I don't quite catch his face but something about him is familiar. I sigh. Operation Jasper has me on edge.

Finally, everyone has arrived. The men head out for the hunt while the women call out their goodbyes. We women then head into another room for more hors d'oeuvres and gossip.

I watch and wait for an opportunity to slip away, forcing a smile which I hope doesn't look like a grimace. Time passes slowly. I'm gritting my teeth with impatience when a woman shrieks and falls into a swoon.

Certain it's faked, but glad of the distraction, I jump up with the others but walk in the opposite direction—backward, toward the door—while every other woman crowds around her. Unnoticed, I exit the room and creep up a winding staircase with stealth.

There is no one about.

The stairs exit onto a shallow landing with enormous windows overlooking the front drive. I turn right and speed-walk along a blue and white hallway. Light falls softly from several tall windows as I glance into each room I pass, my heart beating with rapid awareness.

After about the ninth doorway, at the end of the hall, I locate what must be the Duke's bedroom.

The room is deserted.

I slip inside, grateful that most staff are required downstairs. Closing the door behind me with care, I take in my surrounds.

The décor is too gaudy for my taste, what with all the gold filigree against a mash-up of greens, yellows, pinks and reds. Sunlight pours in through tall windows on the side, lighting up the entire room and imprisoning the shadows in tiny corners.

Glad for the brightness—though it's perhaps a little too bright against the gold—I set to work, searching for a small, rose gold jewelry box said to hold a replica of the *Arbre de vie*.

I will need to take snapshots of the false pendant and familiarize myself with it, given it's much easier to access than the original. Peron also wants to confirm it is not the original, in case everyone was duped. Apparently, the Neumand family are old rivals of the Dompierre-St-Martin family. There is speculation they may have been involved in Jasper's kidnapping. Were they complicit?

I search the room, focused on my objective. It takes forever. I keep an ear out for noises in the corridor, while my heart feels like it's trapped on a roller coaster ride.

I check the hidden compartments in the bed. I've also checked the dresser, the wardrobe and the garderobe and have come up empty. I keep searching, telling myself it has to be here.

My arm is wedged deep in a cupboard drawer filled with silks when I touch a solid object. I grasp the item and pull it out with careful fingers, anxious to keep quiet. When it comes into view, my heart leaps in recognition. I've located it. I exhale in relief.

I stare at the small jewelry box. It's like a miniature treasure chest. Replica or not, the drawings I was sent don't do the artwork justice.

It's snug in my hand and is inlaid with strange symbols on both sides. The lid is exquisite, with a detailed figurine of a winged maiden perched on top. Her bronze hair flows down her back and over her sliver-tipped wings, which stretch the length of the box.

She stands proud, wearing a long dress which shows off her feminine figure. She holds a sword in one hand and a shield in the other.

Who is she? An angel? A Protector? I shake my head at that. It's a woman … I'm pretty sure the Protectors have always been men.

With the amount of secrecy surrounding Protectors and the pendant, it's becoming clear to me that my employer has neglected to mention a few things. Peron has some explaining to do when I complete this mission, because I have a lot of questions.

I study the small statue again. The maiden's face seems to hold an expression of trust and strength, but her eyes betray a deep yearning. For what?

Then it comes to me … Love. At least, that's what I'd be yearning for if I had to be a vessel of protection for the world. It would be awfully lonely.

I stare at her for several moments, captivated by her beauty. My eyes drop to her long neck. She is wearing a small necklace, with a pendant in the shape of a tree which hangs from a delicate chain. There is what appears to be a genuine, tiny crystal in the middle of it. Wow.

This is an exceptional piece in and of itself, a true work of art. This masterpiece can't be a replica. Not with this level of detail.

I tear my gaze away long enough to check the time on my own necklace. Fifteen minutes have gone by since I left the girls. I've been here too long. Better wrap this up.

I look back at the figurine and feel a kind of bond with this woman. It's as if she's staring at me and trying to tell me something. But what?

I shake myself out of the daze, determined to get back to my mission, and take the required photos with the small device hidden in my bracelet. I imagine Peron will be happy when the images are projected back to headquarters.

Once done, I examine the jewelry box again, searching for a way to open it. I spy a tiny latch, which I undo gently. The lid opens and inside is a larger version of the necklace the figurine was wearing.

The pendant is beautifully crafted and seems identical to the picture Peron showed me. I look for the distinguishing mark on its base, a slight chip it earned when a Protector wore it in battle. This one has a smooth base, as if it has only been taken out of the box to be admired and shut back in each time. It's a replica. I knew it would be, but I'm still disappointed.

A voice jolts me out of my reverie and I hurry to finish taking photos, trying not to fumble as I place everything back as I found it.

The voice gets closer. Closing the drawer as quiet as I can, I look around for a hiding place.

There. Behind the curtains.

I tiptoe to the window with a speed I didn't know I possessed and manage to slip behind one of the heavy curtains mere seconds before someone enters the room. I grab the swaying curtain to still its movement.

Listening to the footsteps, I hold my breath as the person moves closer. They pause and I tense up, my hand trembling on the curtain.

Perhaps they think a breeze came through the open window, because after a moment their steps turn in a different direction. I breathe out in relief, my senses on high alert.

Without warning, the curtain is ripped from my hand. I gasp and look up.

There before me stands Mon Puce. He pushes me further along the window and I stumble, heart hammering. He grabs my arm to stop my fall and covers us both with the curtain, pulling me close.

The door bangs open again. We both freeze.

What sounds like a maid enters the room. She calls out to someone and we listen as more footsteps scurry to join her.

"Ooh!" the second woman groans. "All this work, as if we don't have enough already! These guests are always so demanding, making a mess wherever they please."

"Now, now, Louise, you know the Duchess is quite particular about her parties. The sooner this is over, the sooner things can go back to normal. Let's just make the best of it, shall we?"

Louise huffs and I hear the rustle of material. They must be fetching something for the Duchess.

After a few agonizing minutes, they leave. We wait an extra minute to be sure and then Mon Puce peeks out from behind the curtain. His shoulders sag. Realizing it's safe, I turn on him, ripping my arm from his hold.

"What are you doing here?" I demand. He smirks. The prickling sensation I felt downstairs—and the man I saw—it must have been him.

"What are *you* doing here?"

"That's none of your business Mo—"

His hand clamps over my mouth and he sticks his head back around the curtain. Hearing nothing, I pull his hand away and try to push past him. He grabs me and we struggle for a few moments, almost getting tangled in the curtains.

We hear a squeak in the folds and both look up to see a surprised mouse clinging to the curtain. His little beady eyes are staring at us in fright.

Mon Puce releases me unconsciously. I look at Mon Puce. Mon Puce looks at me. I look at the mouse. The mouse looks at Mon Puce. Mon Puce looks at the mouse.

"Oh, for goodness' sake." I flick the curtain open to walk past. Unfortunately, the mouse loses its grip and falls ... right onto Mon Puce's face.

He freaks out, the mouse freaks out, and I walk out.

Chapter Twenty

I AM HALFWAY DOWN the hallway when someone grabs me from behind. A hand clamps on my mouth again as I'm pulled into another room. I bite the hand and Mon Puce grunts as he releases me. I swing around and sink into a slight crouch. "Mon Puce, this has to stop."

He appears reluctantly impressed. "*Mon chaton.*"

We stare at each other in challenge. He seems to know why I'm here and it annoys me.

I straighten. "I can't say it's been a pleasure, but farewell."

I turn to exit the room, but he grabs me and pulls me around to face him again. I take a step back at his proximity, but he immediately closes the distance.

I glance up at him. "Release me."

"Why would I do that when we've just found each other again?" he asks with a grin.

Although I'm on edge, I know nothing will come of this, so I let myself deflate with a sigh. It leaves him examining my mouth as if trying to solve a complex equation. His expression turns so serious that I find myself staring up at him.

We make eye contact and I see his look become determined.

The next moment his lips are on mine in a fiery kiss that shocks me. I'm frozen for a few moments. Then I come to my senses and force him off.

The air crackles as I slap him for good measure. My hand smarts. I know it's inappropriate to slap a man in my own time, but this is the seventeenth century.

The white imprint of my fingers fade to red on his cheek. He stares at me and looks sad for the briefest of moments. Then, he steps back and gives me a curt bow.

"I apologize, Mademoiselle."

Silently, heart pounding, I turn and walk out the door, feeling his eyes on me—and run into a maid.

"Oomph!" We stare at each other in shock and her face swivels between me and the private bedroom several times before her expression turns to one of accusation. "What were you doing in there?"

I scramble for a viable excuse. Anything to avoid being caught.

Just as I'm sure the game is up, she looks behind me and her expression changes to surprise. Then she blushes.

A possessive hand lands on my shoulder and I tense.

"*Pardon.* The Mademoiselle and I were engaged in a private ... conversation. I'm afraid I was overcome with passion and took no notice of where we ended up."

My face heats while the maid giggles as if they share a secret. I wrench my shoulder free and Mon Puce lets me go. I turn and glare at him and he touches his face, the redness still there.

"The Mademoiselle sadly did not appreciate my advances." He looks crestfallen and I'm sure he's putting it on. Certain I'm free now—and warring between gratitude, exasperation, and an apology that I'm sure he doesn't deserve—I dip a curtsey and murmur, "If you will excuse me."

I steal away before they can stop me and turn a corner, a little short of breath.

I can't believe he tried that. Good job we're not in Astanalle or I'd be expected to push for marriage. For once, I'm glad their morals are looser in the République de L'Aurente.

I move as fast as I can without running, reaching the end of the hallway and slipping down the stairs, almost tripping over my feet.

Most of the ladies are either outside or in the salon and no one seems to notice me.

I check behind me. Seeing the coast is clear, I sneak into the salon as if I've come from outside and start a light conversation with a few ladies. The overall talk turns to the hunt and I struggle to hide my distaste.

I make an excuse and walk outside, breathing in fresh air while trying not to think of the deaths of innocent game—or the kiss that was stolen from me. My heart is still beating a little too fast. I use one of the breathing techniques I've been taught to calm myself, box-breathing.

Gradually, as I stroll toward a flower garden out the front, I feel like myself again. I spy my cousins sitting on a bench among the shrubbery, trying to coax a pretty bird from its branch.

I join them and they make room for me. We admire the beautiful estate.

"Lily, where did you disappear to?" Cherie asks.

"Oh, I had to relieve myself. I had a quick peek at the bedrooms after and got waylaid by a very big cat."

"Ooh that's daring of you. And was the cat dangerous?"

"Hmm. He was scared of a mouse if that's anything to go by."

"Scared of a mouse? How funny!"

"Yes." I smile at the memory.

"Well, we need an adventure too. Let's take a stroll around the chateau. It's quite impressive," says Charlotte.

We agree and start on our walk. The grounds are expansive and well-maintained.

"Oh, this heat is getting to me. Let's retire to the shade of the salon and enjoy a cool drink. Please?" Cherie says, after a time.

Charlotte looks ready to agree.

"You girls go on ahead, I want to visit that small forest for a bit," I say, indicating an area off to the side.

"Be careful. Don't stray too close to the hunt," Char says.

I nod, and they head back, while I venture onwards. A trickle of sweat runs down one side of my face, but I dab it away with my sleeve. This has to be better than the loud overcrowded salon. Or what goes on in private rooms upstairs.

It doesn't take me long to reach the trees and the air cools as I enter their canopy. I sigh at the blessed relief from the sun and the chatter.

The beauty of the sunlight filtering down through the leaves reminds me of my real family and a forest we once hiked in. The soft sounds of nature calm me and I breathe in deeply. A flowery scent wafts toward me, a gentle breeze caressing my face. It's exquisite.

This place reminds me of an old hymn my mother taught me once, "How Great Thou Art."

I hum to myself as I meander deeper into the forest.

I follow a trickling sound to a small creek that looks inviting in the midday warmth. Gathering my too-thick deep green skirts, I kneel down and wash my hands. The water is cold and I pat my face and neck to cool my parched skin. Hat on the ground, I make myself comfortable on the soft earth and watch the life around me. And try to forget that kiss.

I'm conflicted. No matter how good it was, it was unwelcome. Regardless of how attractive Mon Puce might be in society's standards, something is a little off about him. Call it intuition, my imagination, whatever you want. There are too many secrets where Mon Puce is concerned.

A small colony of frogs begins singing, their varied voices blending into a beautiful song. It's so delightful that my worries slip away.

I'm here in seventeenth century Pariseine, experiencing the unaltered beauty of what some would call the Creator's glorious creation. It's so serene, my own private paradise. There must have been a super-intelligent brain behind the ingenuity and design of what I can see here, right down to the cellular level.

How could a random explosion cause everything to function so perfectly, each having its place and purpose in the circle of life? There was nothing random about it. Everything is needed for something. And so am I.

A rustling some meters away startles the frogs. They become silent, their bodies frozen as they float around in a pretense of death. I laugh. It must be a foraging rabbit, as nothing has emerged. The frogs move again but don't sing. Their silence leaves me with a sense of loss.

After a while I hear another rustle and voices float toward me. One strange voice ... and one I recognize. I stiffen.

How did Mon Puce find me? Did he follow me? He's speaking with someone else. Another Relic Hunter?

I might have an irrational trust in him, but there's no way I'm going to be a sitting duck for the rest of them.

Jumping up, I brush myself off and slam my hat back on, moving away with quiet steps.

The voices fade as I hurry away and an excited smile splits my face. I feel like a kid in a candy store who just got away with a big bag of chocolate. Purchased of course.

I laugh at myself when I reach the chateau, huffing like I've run a marathon. I wipe a sleeve across my forehead and it comes away moist. I can't wait to get out of this heavy dress.

When the twins find me, they exclaim over my flushed state and lead me into the salon to press a cool beverage into my hands. Their concern for me is endearing. How thankful I am to have found a new family here. It's a salve to ease the ache of missing my own back in Australia.

We while away the afternoon with light banter, sipping glasses of fresh lemonade and devouring some delectable pastries, before the men return from their hunting trip. I don't see Mon Puce again, thankfully.

Later that evening, having settled in back at my uncle's mansion, I hand him my bracelet and he connects it to a machine that sends the pictures of the jewelry box through the vortex to Peron. Now we must wait for the results of analysis. I ask Uncle Raimond to make me an appointment with Peron so I can discuss some important matters with him, and he confirms he'll arrange it.

Guilt slinks into the back of my mind. Yet again, I've hidden something from Vestige for Mon Puce's sake. They'd want to know about my run-in with a Relic Hunter, but I figure it doesn't endanger the mission. Much. They don't need to know yet.

I tell myself he's harmless. Seriously, what can a guy who's afraid of a mouse really do? I chuckle.

Chapter Twenty-One

It takes Peron a full week before he contacts me through Uncle Raimond for our appointment.

Peron confirms the pendant was a fake but says the jewelry box appears to be genuine. Then he admits it symbolizes the Protector.

"But I thought the Protectors were men. This is a woman. Why would the box portray a woman and not a man? Or aren't you going to tell me?"

The line is silent for a moment. "Lily, the ruling Protectors have always been women."

What?

"But ... but Henry and Alex and Terry and Nick ..."

"Henriette, Alexandria, Thérèse and Nicolette. All women, Lily. It seems they had more of an affinity with the relic, a stronger sensitivity to it. We have kept this fact under wraps to protect the identities of our past Protectors, to ensure potential Protectors will never be targeted."

I'm reeling at this news. A small part of my world view has been blown apart.

Peron interrupts my chaotic thoughts.

"I'm sorry I didn't tell you this before, but it was need-to-know information. Now you're more involved, I can justify enlightening you. However, you must be careful to keep this to yourself. Tell no one. Not even Raimond."

"Okay," I say, feeling small.

"For now, Lily, you need to concentrate on finding Jasper."

Yes, the ever-elusive Jasper. I admit I've been distracted of late and had almost lost sight of my mission.

Peron confirms he will send another agent to obtain the jewelry box from where I found it, to prevent any suspicion from falling on us. They'll swap it with a replica, so no one should be the wiser.

We end the call and I determine to focus more on my mission.

Chapter Twenty-Two

Next day, I decide it's time to figure out the mysterious picture Mon Puce gave me. I can no longer wait until I get back to HQ.

I ask to borrow Uncle Raimond's tablet so I can prepare myself further for my mission. He agrees and I hide the tablet in the folds of my dress as I return to my room.

I haven't used this type often as it runs on magnetic transmission technology, but it seems to operate the same as any tablet back home.

After loading it, I search for a family crest that matches the tattoo in the picture. After a while, I come up with an image matching the symbol.

When I see the name under the crest, I swear my heart stops beating.

Du Fleur.

My mother's maiden name. There must be some mistake.

I search again and again but the only crest that matches the picture is that one. Why did the deceased Valentino have my mother's family crest tattooed on him? Are we related?

I infiltrate Vestige records further, tracing my mother's family tree. Mon Puce, that pesky flea, mentioned he went five centuries back, which would make it the twelfth century. I continue through my mother's ancestral line until I find a woman named Adele Du Fleur in that time period.

My mind is going in a hundred different directions as I struggle to make sense of what this means.

Valentino wore Adele's crest.

Adele was my ancestor back home. She must have had a doppelgänger in the ARK1 dimension, who fell in love with Valentino.

I switch from Earth to ARK1, looking for any Du Fleur's in the twelfth century. I find her after about ten minutes. She was also named Adele and she was born around the same time as my Adele. But whereas my ancestor lived to almost fifty-five years of age, this Adele only made it to twenty-one. She didn't marry and died before she could have any children. Perhaps I don't have a twenty-first century doppelgänger in this dimension after all. As disappointing as that feels, it could be a good thing.

But how on earth did Mon Puce know about my connection to Adele? Does the Vestige Society know?

What kind of sick, twisted fate would have an alternate dimension's descendants of a woman who'd been murdered by an organization, then join said organization to fight their cause? It mystifies me and I wouldn't be lying if I said that it felt like I was betraying Adele.

Did fate make my dad, a Vestige spy, fall in love with Amanda Du Fleur? Dad saw her on a poster advertising a fragrance when shopping for his mother's birthday. It was love at first sight for him. He went to great lengths to discover her identity and procure an invitation to a function she was due to attend.

Their meeting went better than he expected. He always brags that he could sense their mutual attraction.

But it didn't stop there. Oh no. Dad discovered where Mom lived and watched her for a few days. Creepy, right? He blames it on his spy instincts. Whatever you say, old man.

Then he turned up when she was grocery shopping and acted all surprised. He said it must be fate and asked her out. She said yes. A few coffees later and they were inseparable. She was ecstatic when he proposed.

They always laugh when they tell me and my brother—Trick—that story. Mom did eventually find out about Dad's antics. Somehow, she saw past the creep factor and thought it was endearing.

That aside, would they ever have met if Dad hadn't seen that picture of Mom? Would I have been born a Destin, brought into the Vestige family, or would I have ended up ignorant to what could have been?

Would I have ever met Mon Puce and found out about Valentino and his love affair with my ancestor in another world?

Would I have met Marc and the girls?

So many questions. So many answers I want to shy away from. I guess I can be thankful Dad was a creep in his younger years when it came to Mom ... or maybe he was in love. Love can make you do crazy things.

I shake my head and sigh.

I won't share what I've learned with anyone yet. I want to uncover the full story about Adele and Valentino first. I need to know I can trust Vestige, but they seem quite adept at keeping secrets that make them look bad. I have a feeling they don't want me—in particular—to know any of this.

That is, if Mon Puce's words can be trusted.

I delete my entire digital trail, ensuring anyone who checks on what I was doing will think I was searching for cake recipes from the seventeenth century. Interesting use of rose water ... hmm.

I return the tablet and walk back to my room, deep in thought.

Vestige and the Relic Hunter Society are two opposing forces, each believing they are right and willing to die for their beliefs. If I can't trust Vestige and I can't trust Mon Puce ... is there anyone I can trust?

Chapter Twenty-Three

WHEN I'M NOT ON mission, I'm studying under Marc's tutelage.

Despite the increased frequency of painting and music lessons starting out as a sham on the girls' part, I look forward to them. Sadly, I don't share Marc's artistic talent. Thank goodness he doesn't teach needlework. I imagine the needle springing loose, piercing the tender skin beneath my nail, and fight a gag reflex. The image becomes more drastic, the needle launching itself into my eye, absurd and impossible, but vivid enough to make me flinch. I shudder and force my thoughts back to Marc.

I breathe in deep, feeling the tightness around my ribs release, as if an invisible weight has been lifted off my chest.

Marc. Well, the good news is I no longer suspect him of being in league with the Relic Hunters. It doesn't fit. He's a good man. I would have noticed something by now if he wasn't. And he hasn't reacted to any of the hints I've thrown his way. In fact, he's looked downright confused.

We won't go into that.

What I want to know is, what does he think he can gain from being so attentive toward me? Does he like me, or is he after something else?

My mother isn't around to lure him in. She was the model, not me—and the reason for my last boyfriend's attention. At fifteen years old, letting a guy almost take advantage of me only to find it wasn't even me he was interested in, was like a knife to the heart. Being manipulated to be someone I wasn't, clued me in to his motives. And that's when I got my wake-up call about guys.

I soon escaped his hold and cut ties—his interest waned after I put him in hospital. It was self-defense.

Since then, I realized I could never pull off Mandy Destin's flawless vibe, so why even bother? Instead I've kept my heart out of reach.

But Marc ... he's from this era. He wouldn't have even seen a picture of my mother. Does that mean he *does* like me?

Can I trust him?

Today's lesson was easier. Now finished, Marc's fingers dance across the keys, pulling out a light melody that matches the rhythm of our conversation.

"When I was mastering that last piece as a boy, I practiced for so long, I feared I would accidentally summon the composer, Merulo. Or a migraine," Marc says. His smile is depreciating.

I chuckle. "Well, it was worth it, for you are very accomplished."

"*Merci.* If I strike this chord just right, I believe the chandelier may descend in applause."

I laugh at that. I'm discovering that Marc has a good sense of humor. It's nice. When he speaks, his voice resonates with the lower notes of the piano between us.

The door clicks shut—the girls have slipped away without my noticing. My shoulders, which had been nearly touching my ears during our first lessons, now rest easily against the back of the couch. I catch myself watching Marc, and quickly turn to study the pattern of rain beginning to dot the garden path outside. A few droplets hit the window.

"Playing piano, Merulo's music in particular, reminds me of the village where I grew up," Marc says. "I often visit there to stay grounded and remember where I came from. In winter, I bring what food I can to help the poorer households and chop wood for the older folk who have little in the way of family. It's demanding work but rewarding. When I see their happy faces, it warms my heart. Knowing I've made their lives a little easier does too."

Who is this guy? But that explains his muscular figure.

"That's kind and generous of you, Monsieur."

He smiles warmly. "It's my way of repaying a kindness done to me. After my mother passed away, an old neighbor helped me out. I was in a dark place for a while, but Gérard kept sharing his source of hope and joy with me—the great Creator. Everything the old man did declared his love for the Creator. Gérard was always there for me, guiding and encouraging me. Because of him, I came to believe that the Creator is real and has a purpose for me, and my life changed."

His eyes are bright as he looks at me and I debate whether running from the room would be a good idea. I swallow but decide to stay.

"My parents believe in the Creator too."

He smiles wider, revealing a dimple on his left cheek. "Really? That's wonderful. What about you, Mademoiselle? Do you believe in him?"

I lick my lips. How did this conversation escalate so fast? I thought we were discussing music, not the nature of the soul.

"Um. Well ... I've heard the story about a Creator coming into the world in human form. That he took the punishment for our wrongdoings—against him, others and ourselves—our sins. My parents said it was because he loved humanity so deeply, he was ready to do anything to forgive and reunite us with himself. That he invites us into an intimate relationship with him. But I don't know. I'm not sure I believe that. I'm not even sure he's real."

I tense and wait for his response.

Marc considers me for a moment. "I share the same belief as your parents. But I cannot tell you what to believe, Mademoiselle. I will be praying for you. I believe the Creator has brought us together for a reason."

Something in his gaze causes my heart to stutter for a moment. He sees the look on my face and a blush works its way up his cheeks. He clears his throat. "That is, what I meant to say is … ah …"

Marc glances out the window next to him, as he searches for words. Distracted by the tiny butterflies doing somersaults in my belly, I slip into English. "It's okay, really. I understand what you meant."

Marc scrutinizes me and his expression turns to one of surprise.

"You speak Astanallean?" This said in English with a French accent.

"Ahh …" Thinking frantically, I say with a half laugh, "My family was always open to other cultures. My father felt it was important that we learn Astanallean so we could converse freely when we traveled there."

I breathe a relieved sigh when he nods, accepting my words. He gives me a measured look and something in his expression makes me nervous, as if he knew I could speak Astanallean all along.

He breaks eye contact with a secret sort of smile and stares off into the distance. The afternoon sun breaks through the window, creating a sun shower, and the light glistens on Marc's golden hair. "My great grandmamma was Astanallean, so she insisted my mother also learn. Maman taught me the language and as a boy I even lived there for a brief time."

He looks at me quizzically. "But your accent … I can't place it. And some of your words are strange. Who taught you?"

I want to slap myself again. I scramble for a believable answer.

"Oh, a … a traveler from a distant land. I cannot remember where he was from, but my father didn't have the time to teach us himself and this man needed work. Father took pity on him and hired him to tutor us in the language."

All this said in English with my twenty-first century Aussie-American accent. Yep, evidence of the distinction I received in my Olde-Astanallean language class, right there.

I want to dissolve into the ground, but instead of worrying about my complete failure as a spy when I'm around Marc, it's a relief to speak English again. It reminds me of home and I miss it.

As if sensing my thoughts, Marc asks about my family. Remembering Marc is a real person and that I can't build a trusting friendship if it's all based on lies, I find myself telling him about my real parents and brother. Just a bit. He seems to like my unconventional father and I warm up to the subject, making us both laugh with stories of his antics. A thought stops me from sharing too much about my upbringing. What if he realizes I'm not a proper Pariseinné lady?

I become quiet and he breaks the silence with a question about my mother.

"What is she like?" I repeat. "She was the local beauty and it wasn't just external—she's a beautiful person inside too." Here it comes. He'll want to see a picture of her, like every other guy I've told.

I tense in apprehension, but Marc surprises me, his voice low. "So that's who you get your beauty from."

My eyes flick to his in surprise. A deep sense of appreciation warms his gaze. Something about it makes me nervous and I squeak, "Um."

My reaction must throw him off because his face grows pink. He clears his throat and things get awkward for a moment. Then he rubs the stubble on his chin with the back of his fingers.

"Where is your family now, Mademoiselle?"

As if sensing my tension, his eyes burn a hole through a smear of sunburnt orange paint between his fingernails.

I take a breath before replying. "They live in the country, in the town of Mari. You may not have heard of it, but it is many days' ride from Pariseine."

He looks surprised. "I have not heard of it. And I thought myself well versed in geography." He huffs and shakes his head, his firm mouth twisting. "Ironic."

"Ironic?"

"Never mind. What brings you here?"

"My parents sent me to live with Uncle Raimond for an extended sojourn, to have a change in scene and increase my cultural experience."

"And are you enjoying your time here?"

I grin. "Very much."

He seems pleased at this, then stares at the piano keys. "I hope you stay a while, Mademoiselle."

"I do too."

He glances at me over the piano. His green gaze is piercing, as if wanting to know something more. My heart beats faster.

Before I can process the moment, the girls stumble upon us, their chatter filling the space. Marc smiles wryly as they pull us outside to the garden, where we spend the afternoon in high spirits.

That evening, I retire to my room with a light heart. After scribbling memories of the day into my diary, I slip it into a hidden panel behind the bed's headboard. Then I climb into bed and tuck the covers right up to my chin.

When I dream, a man with green eyes appears. His face is hazy, but I'm drawn to him. As he's about to embrace me, something dark and evil sweeps in and cuts him down.

I scream myself awake and lie there in the dark, panting and hot, tears running down my face at the thought of losing him.

Chapter Twenty-Four

Uncle Raimond hands me a missive the next morning, his brow puckered.

"What's wrong?" I ask.

He shakes his head. "Read it in your room."

A cursory glance tells me the missive is still sealed, but the handwriting is not Peron's.

Curious, I hasten to my room and close the door before tearing the missive open. Scanning the contents, my heart plummets.

It's from Professor Crabb.

It seems he has been keeping tabs on my whereabouts and although he's not apprised of the mission, he doesn't believe I am up to the task. Having no confidence in me, he has threatened to send Alyse in my place. He's also hinted that if I come back a failure, he will flunk me across the board and push for my removal from Vestige, claiming I am unfit for this line of work.

On his own he wouldn't have the authority. But he's got the ear of Stefan—Alyse's father. The threat is real.

Unwelcome thoughts assault my mind, setting off my emotions like a string of fireworks.

The shame of not living up to my father's legacy, and failing the organization he poured his heart into, weighs heavily on me. I foresee the uncertainty and trepidation of the unknown, going back to real life and searching for a tedious nine-to-five job.

Even worse, I fight the fear of losing all my memories, having all the people and experiences I hold dear wiped from my brain, as if it were nothing more than a computer hard drive.

Would they implant false memories of the last few years? Maybe I'd believe I worked for a research company and got fired. Or that I was still in school.

Then what purpose would I have? How will I ever achieve anything great if I don't remain where I am?

I can believe Valentino's story now. What would've happened if I'd been in his position? Would I have defected?

Will I?

I crawl into bed and spend the rest of the day in my room, refusing food and guests. I war with my fears and try to formulate a plan that prevents them being realized.

Chapter Twenty-Five

Some days later, I've decided on a course of action. I get Uncle Raimond's consent to take a carriage and a manservant-slash-spy out for a spin. Unbeknownst to him, my real intention is to lure out Mon Puce and discover everything he knows about the nurse and Jasper.

Perhaps I'll make a deal with him—insurance in case Vestige turn their backs on me.

After an hour of riding, checking out a few places he might be without success, I'm ready to give up and call myself a fool. A naïve little girl who's trying to be a spy.

Maybe Crabb is right. Maybe I'm not in the right field of work after all.

I sigh.

Why did Peron bother to hire me? Why did he seek me out?

I'm confused. I'm still trying to work it out when the carriage comes to a sudden stop.

I hear a yelp. I look out the carriage window and almost yelp myself. My driver and I are surrounded by men.

Heart beating, I duck my head back in and try to think. *Be calm, Lily. You can handle this.*

Feeling around for my weapons and making sure they're within easy reach, I open the door and climb down unassisted. Several men move back to give me space, but that doesn't stop them from leering at me.

I shudder and glance at my driver. He is unconscious but still in his seat. We're in the middle of nowhere, in some part of the back country bordering Pariseine. I'm a fool. I should have brought more backup.

I lift my chin. "Where's your leader? It seems I must speak with him."

They all grin and a few jeer as they glance over at the driver's seat. Frowning, I follow their line of sight. A man in dark pants and a white shirt is walking around the horses. Recognition sparks victory in my mind when he looks at me with a smirk.

It ... worked. Somehow, I got his attention and he found me.

I watch as he swaggers toward me. "Well, if it isn't Mon Puce," I say.

He smiles wider. "*Mon chaton*, it seems you were looking for someone. Was it me?"

I blush at his implication, but it is true.

"As a matter of fact, it was."

His men jeer again and a few whistle. He waves them down but he's grinning now and studying me with a raised brow.

I lift my chin higher and ignore my deepening blush.

He looks me up and down. "I must say, my dear, you're looking marvelous today. Rose suits you."

I know he's not talking about my dress, because that is a drab brown, fit for a long dusty ride in the carriage. I huff and turn my back on him to get some space, but all I do is set the men off again. One laughs right in my face and his breath smells like death.

I choke and stumble back, losing my footing.

Strong arms come around me to hold me up. Mon Puce pulls me firm against his chest. I tense, not liking how well I fit within the curve of his embrace.

"Form a perimeter around the carriage and tie up the driver." His deep voice reverberates against me.

One arm still around me, he leads me back to the carriage door, opens it and gestures for me to go in.

Obediently, perhaps stupidly, I move to climb up. He captures my hand to help me and I notice a mischievous look in his eyes.

Nevertheless, I accept his help and slide to the other side as he climbs in behind and shuts the door. He sits opposite and stares at me for a moment with a faint smile on his face.

"Well, Lily, aren't you going to tell me why you want me?"

His look is expectant, so I ignore his innuendo and jump straight to the point.

"Do you know of Jasper Dompierre-St-Martin?"

He hesitates. "I might." He sounds non-committal.

"We believe your society persuaded his nanny to kidnap him for you. She did, but for some reason we suspect she never delivered the boy as expected. Is that true?"

"You want me to tell you our secrets?" he asks with a disbelieving look.

"Given you were so forthcoming about Valentino, I thought you wouldn't mind telling me this too."

He laughs then shakes his head. "You, *ma chérie*,[1] are a rare and delightful surprise. Like a kitten, extremely cheeky."

I smile in response. "Well?"

He chuckles again and considers for a moment.

"What will you give me in return?" His eyes gaze at my mouth for a lingering moment. I swallow.

"If Vestige is as bad as you say they are, I may consider finding another employer."

He looks at me sharply then, his eyes darting back and forth between mine as if to see whether I mean true. He leans forward.

"You would consider an alliance with the Relic Hunters? Or even a defection?"

Shaken in my resolve now that it's out in the open, I want to backpedal.

"Given the right circumstances."

He looks at me as if wanting to hold me to that promise.

"If you mean that, a little information to sweeten the deal won't go astray." He nods. "For you, I will make an exception. I'm sure you understand you cannot tell anyone you heard this from me. Best to keep our meetings secret, yes?"

"Of course. Getting it from you, I cannot prove anything. But what of your men?"

---

1. "Ma chèrie" is an affectionate term meaning "my dear" or "my darling." It is more intimate than "ma chére."

He glowers out the window. "They shouldn't be able to hear us in here, but if they did, they wouldn't say a thing." His voice hardens. Then he takes a deep breath and releases it.

"You are correct that our society enticed the nanny into giving us the boy, Jasper. We paid her a hefty sum. What our leaders didn't realize was that the woman cared for the boy as if he were her own son. She took him as arranged, but did not arrive at the agreed meeting place. When we sent search parties looking for her, they came back empty-handed. I am not sure if she'd learned of our intentions, or whether she hid him for other reasons. She was surprisingly adept at hiding, considering who she was up against. Our leaders were in denial for a while that this woman had outsmarted us. Some of us believe she had help."

I interject, my boldness returning. "Then why didn't she return Jasper to his family?"

"I imagine she couldn't take him back as she'd be in a world of trouble. Kidnapping the first-born son from such a high-ranking, well-established family? It would have meant the end of her career—or her life."

"I guess you're right." I frown. "What about later?"

"Later?"

"From what we've learned, the nanny lived in a run-down cottage for several years, pretending to be Jasper's mother. However, she disappeared again. I believe the boy would have been left on his own."

"A run-down cottage?" Mon Puce is considering me. "Where? And how did you discover that?"

"I'm not at liberty to share that, I'm afraid." I guess he hadn't been watching me as much as I thought when he was masquerading as our driver. Victoire mustn't have told him either. "Consider the fact that I've shared some relevant information with you, as a thank you for your own intelligence." I wink boldly.

He scoffs and shakes his head. "Have you discovered the whereabouts of the boy?"

"No, we haven't. We've come to a dead end." I may like this guy but I'm not about to share my suspicions. I don't want to take the chance that the Relic Hunters will find Jasper or his body before I do. "I take it that means you haven't found him either?"

Mon Puce laughs quietly. "Very perceptive, *mon chaton*."

Is he being sarcastic? And why do I care?

"I'm thinking your people discovered the nanny, which is why she left us a cold trail."

He shakes his head. "Not much gets past you, does it?"

I smile. "I'm right? She was discovered?"

The Flea's look turns serious, if not a little regretful.

"Yes, she was found and interrogated. Like I said, Jasper was like a son to her—a replacement for the son she'd lost to the black plague ten years earlier, which wiped out almost a third of the République de L'Aurente. She'd lost her husband then too." He takes a breath and releases it slowly. "She wouldn't reveal Jasper's whereabouts and instead took her own life to protect him."

Air falters in my lungs. What she must have suffered at the hands of the Relic Hunters. So terrible it drove her to end her life rather than give up the boy she loved.

"You seem bothered by this. I understand. Our methods have not always been humane."

I clench my teeth but manage to hold my tongue and nod.

A knock on the carriage door startles us. Mon Puce opens the door. One of his men stands there.

"What is it?" Mon Puce asks.

"It's time to go." His look turns meaningful and I sense several unspoken words passing between them.

Mon Puce nods. "Gather the men."

The man departs and the Flea turns back to me. "While I would love to continue this conversation, I have other places to be, *ma chérie*."

Assessing me, he holds his hand out. "Give me your neck-lace."

At my blank look, he explains. "For your driver."

His meaning becomes clear, so I unclasp and hand him my necklace.

He raises it to his lips for a quick kiss.

I roll my eyes with a sound of disgust.

With a grin and a chuckle, he slips it inside his breast pocket and climbs out of the carriage. Turning, he bows to me. "Until next time, *mon chaton. Au revoir.*"[2]

I nod and watch them leave, then climb out to find my driver. He's just coming around. I cut his bindings. Once I'm sure he's okay, I make up a story about bandits, pointing out my missing jewelry. After I've spent a full minute lamenting the loss of my gold necklace, he seems to accept my story. Seeing that I'm unhurt, he agrees to take me home.

---

2. "Au revoir" means "Goodbye – until we meet again."

Chapter Twenty-Six

After a rushed breakfast and change the next morning, I'm in a carriage headed to the local parish for Sunday worship with the Therriot family.

I have admitted to myself that I believe in the Creator's existence after all. Therefore, I need to get on good terms with him.

The girls' chatter blends into background noise, like the hum of a distant radio. I mentally ask the Creator to forgive me for all the lies and deceit. He might seem distant, but I don't want to walk into church with guilt weighing me down.

"... Marc ..." The name cuts through the static, my head snapping up so quickly my neck twinges.

"Do you think Geneviève will try to sit next to him again?" Cherie asks with a laugh. "It was so funny last time. He just got up and sat on the other side of the room, without saying a word."

"Well, after the way she's behaved, I would too, were I him," Charlotte says.

"What do you mean?" I ask.

Their eyes sparkle with mischief, lips curling into wide grins as they exchange knowing glances, before turning their gazes toward me.

"Oh, you don't know, do you? Geneviève has been after monsieur Coupier for years, ever since he started tutoring," Cherie says. "I thought they were in love once, but then a wealthy Count pursued her and she dropped monsieur Coupier like a hot brick. He withdrew from society for a while and then came back and seemed to be busier than ever tutoring. I'm sure he took on more than before."

"I think she hurt him deeply," Charlotte says softly.

"Yes, well, she married the Count and they moved away. He died in a freak accident two years ago and Geneviève came back to her family in mourning. Then she bought a nearby property with the Count's money and has been living there ever since. Within six months, she was after monsieur Coupier again, as if nothing had happened."

"She's unbelievable."

"She's terrible, that's what she is. The way she's treated her old friends, like they're beneath her now that she's a Countess. I bet she murdered her husband because he was a bore."

"Cherie!" Charlotte says in a disapproving voice.

I tune out their squabbling and think of Marc. He's a kindred spirit. My compassion wars with something else I can't yet name, but it's an uncomfortable feeling. I'm not given time to consider it however, as the carriage is pulling to a stop outside the parish.

We alight with the help of our footman and follow Uncle Raimond into the building.

After being welcomed by the parish priest, we head to our pew. The stained-glass windows reflect scenes of the Creator—when he lived among humanity, when he fought the dragon and freed its captives, and when he returned to paradise victorious. The morning sun shines through, reflecting a myriad of colors on the parishioners and walls. It dazzles me.

We reach our pew and I sit near the end. There's half a space next to me so I place my small bag there, close my eyes and turn my thoughts inward again, this time pleading with the Creator to help with my mission and keep me from being expunged from Vestige.

"Mademoiselle Therriot."

I flinch and open my eyes. Marc is standing over me, his expression open and ... hopeful?

"Would it be too forward of me to ask for a seat in your pew today?"

I look at him, dumbfounded. "Er—"

Charlotte interrupts. "Monsieur, you must sit here, of course. Come along, Cherie, let's make room."

The girls shuffle along the bench and it dawns on me that I'm holding everything up. Marc must be feeling awkward.

"I apologize, Monsieur." I grab my satchel and move over, making room for him.

Marc smiles and takes the seat next to me. The sleeve of his jacket brushes mine, sending a current across my skin that makes my fingers tighten around my bag's leather strap. His pine scent fills the narrow space between us. I draw a shallow breath and shrink into myself, my spine curving forward as if I could disappear into the pew.

Uncle Raimond must have something important to discuss with him about our lessons. That would explain why he's here instead of his usual pew, sitting close enough that I can feel the heat radiating from his forearm.

"Mademoiselle Therriot, you're looking well today."

"What?" I look at him in surprise and see his eyes crease as if he's laughing at me.

"I said, you're looking well. A little tired, perhaps? Are you not sleeping?"

"I ... I haven't slept well the last few days. My mind has been too full, I suppose."

His expression shifts, concern flickering across his face. My gaze locks onto his vivid green eyes—striking, intense, impossibly beautiful.

He's beautiful.

After a moment I realize he's said something and I've missed it again. My face heats and I duck my head.

"You must forgive me, Monsieur. My thoughts are quite muddled today."

A warm, strong hand covers one of mine and I look up, startled.

"Do not fear, Mademoiselle, I am just concerned for your well-being. Though I would like to know what could be stealing your rest. Perhaps I could be of assistance?"

I swallow hard, but an image of me telling him about my real purpose for being here snaps me out of it. I almost laugh at the prospect. What would he think? Would he try to send me to a lunatic asylum? Then I remember Valentino and horror fills me. Would he be killed like Adele?

I fumble for an answer. "Ah, well you see, it's of a private matter."

The light in Marc's eyes dims and I remember what I learned in the carriage ride over. I study his hand still covering mine and can't bring myself to hurt him. I force myself not to pull away and instead I smile at him.

"I am sorry, Monsieur. I wish I could tell you. I appreciate your kindness and if I can think of anything that might help, you'll be the first to know."

He seems to accept that and smiles. "*Merci.*"

The priest enters then and calls everyone to stand. We do, and the impression of Marc's hand on mine remains long after he lets go.

The congregation is led into a time of singing—something that started in places of worship a lot earlier in this dimension than it did mine. The words of the songs speak of the Creator's love and forgiveness and I get the sense that all will be well. That perhaps he's heard me after all and he's closer than I realize. Encouraged, I join the singing.

Marc is holding a hymnal for me and I'm reminded of how considerate he is given the book is at the perfect height for my eyes. Except it's upside down. Luckily I know this song.

I glance up at Marc and find him gazing at me. The light filtering in through the stained-glass windows casts a golden glow on his hair, like a halo.

"You're an angel," I say, and he beams in response. He looks at the hymnal and must realize it's directionally challenged because he drops it. I bite my lip to keep from smiling as he bends to retrieve it.

A prickling sensation has me glancing across from us. A woman is glaring at me. She looks at Marc then back at me before tilting her chin up. Her upper lip curls. Her voice carries as she raises it, a sharp soprano. It draws attention. Two girls behind her giggle and I realize she's gotten the lyrics wrong. It takes all my effort not to choke on a snort.

She must be Geneviève.

I school my features and concentrate on Marc as he tries to recover. He clears his throat, holding out the hymnal again.

"*Merci, Monsieur Ange,*" I say.

I place my hand on Marc's arm and smile at him, holding his gaze this time. It seems to settle him. He smiles back and a flurry of butterflies swarm my chest. My breath hitches.

I remove my hand and refocus on the singing.

The message that morning is inspiring. It makes me feel closer to this Creator and he sounds kinder than anyone I've ever met. I want to meet him.

"Of all the gods humanity believe in," the priest is saying, "the Creator is the only one who reached out to us first. More than that, he's the only God who died for humanity. Now he sits enthroned, with authority over every created thing, and he shares his authority with those who know him intimately. He's not the angry God so many make him out to be. He's not even interested in judging us—he took our punishment upon himself to prove that. Yes, he performs judgment and justice, because he is Lord of the universe. But what he loves to do is extend mercy, just as he calls us to forgive others and ourselves. Because *relationship*—friendship with us—is what he wants most."

The service ends on a positive note and everyone stands to file out, but the message lingers with me. Marc walks next to me as the girls chatter behind us. He opens his mouth a few times like he's trying to say something.

We come out into the sunshine and Marc still hasn't spoken a word. Before he gets another chance, girls swarm over to us like bees and surround Marc, vying for his attention. With his patience, quiet confidence, and impeccable manners, I can see why the ladies gravitate toward him. Aware of my inadequacies, I find myself backing away, squeezing myself between the bodies pressing in on us. Somehow, I end up behind a tree, peeking out at the scene as if watching a documentary on the behavior of zoo animals.

Then I spy her. The woman who got the lyrics wrong. As she approaches Marc, her eyes become slits that shoot invisible laser beams at the girls. One by one they make excuses and move away. Marc appears relieved. He glances around as if searching for someone.

She moves into his view. His look turns pained and he nods at her before moving to turn away.

She grabs his arm and his jaw locks. He clenches his fist, knuckles turning white, as if he's holding himself back. Suddenly, he looks vulnerable. My feet move of their own accord and I stop in front of them. Both look at me, the woman in annoyance, Marc in what might be gratitude ... or something more.

"Monsieur, there *is* something you can help me with," I say, having no idea what it could be.

Light enters his eyes and he seems to forget the other woman for a moment. His eyes search mine and his expression warms. My heart flutters.

"Monsieur, who is this little girl?" I glance at the demanding woman whose voice drips like poison. She's still clinging to Marc and if looks could kill ... luckily, she isn't part of Vestige.

I smile. "I'm a friend of Monsieur Coupier. We have plans for today, so I'm afraid we're going to have to leave you here."

She sputters as Marc pulls his arm out of her grasp. She grabs it again, like a dog with a chew toy.

"Let go of me, Madame." Marc firmly removes her hand this time, the steel in his voice giving her pause.

He holds his arm out to me. I take it before she can and we walk away at a fast pace.

"My apologies, Mademoiselle. The countess is not someone I wish to renew an acquaintance with." I hear the undercurrent of a growl in his voice as we put distance between us and her.

Glancing back, she hasn't moved, her mouth hanging open in an unattractive way.

"Pfft!"

Marc looks at me as we come to a stop near a pretty rosebush. I cover my smirk with a gloved hand.

"I am sorry, Monsieur, if I overstepped, but I discerned you were in need of assistance."

"And I am much obliged to you." His earnest tone resonates with sincerity.

I smile at him openly. It's like we defeated an evil queen together. "I am sure you would have discovered the fortitude to escape her eventually."

Marc seems to be trying to repress a grin and his dimple shows. Gosh, he's cute.

"I am honored that you think so, Mademoiselle. And please," he says, his voice deepening, "call me Marc when we're alone."

I breathe past a spike of anxiety at the thought of how easily he could break down my protective wall. But there's something innocent about his look. I find it difficult to refuse him, what with the puppy dog expression on his face.

"I will do so, Marc, provided you call me Lily." Nerves aflutter, I look at him with determination. And a bit of apprehension.

His grin appears, brilliant as the sun. "Lily," he breathes.

I can't stop a laugh from escaping and he grins even wider.

Cherie joins us at that moment, asking what's so funny. We both try to marshal our expressions into something neutral, and refuse to answer her. She persists but I give a tiny shake of my head and a meaningful look, and she gets the message. Thank goodness.

It doesn't stop her pestering me that night though, so I spill the beans to her and Char on our victory against the evil queen, and the strange agreement I had with Marc to use first names in private. She and Charlotte tease me straight away, saying it won't be long now before I form a romantic attachment with our attractive and desirable tutor.

I laugh it off and shoo them away. How ridiculous, to become romantically involved because he wants to remove the formalities in our speech. It's just an offer of friendship. At least, that's what I tell myself.

Geneviève fills my mind as I drift off to sleep. Is it an inferiority complex that makes her act all superior? Maybe she felt unloved as a child. Unbidden, sadness fills me. Wounded people carve their pain into others, often without knowing.

Uncle Raimond's face is grave the next morning. He calls me into his office after breakfast to give me the news. I'm being sent back.

Shock sets my gut on a low burn.

Sent back? Why? What does this mean? Have they given up on me?

Alarm bells intone a warning in my head, sending vibrations into my tightening chest.

I pack my bags with shaking hands and say a quick farewell to the girls, telling them I'm headed home for an emergency. I even go off in the carriage, but we stop at a secure point and I walk through a secret tunnel that returns me to Uncle's den.

Anxiety burrows into my churning stomach. I'm tempted to run away. What if I can't come back? I box-breathe to prevent myself from hyperventilating and I'm still doing it when I arrive in the twenty-first century.

Chapter Twenty-Seven

Present Day, United States, Earth dimension

My body hits the landing pad at HQ with a thud. Sam's cheerful face calms me a fraction, but her clear deep green glasses remind me of Marc. Pain shoots into my heart like a poisoned arrow. Disoriented, I push past it, telling myself that Peron will sort everything out and I'll be able to return soon.

Peron doesn't look happy when I arrive at his office. He seems distracted when he directs me to sit. I watch, anxiety threatening to reach boiling point. He shuffles some papers across his desk as if trying to work out what to say.

Finally, he faces me.

"Lily, Professor Crabb has raised some concerning accusations against you. I've got a team investigating, but I get the sense that he wants to eject you from the company."

I open my mouth to object, but he holds up a hand and I fall silent.

"Lily, I'm aware of the conflict between your father and Professor Crabb. I don't believe this is your fault, but his claims are serious and I've been forced to take other measures. Measures I was not prepared to consider until recently."

It's as if thick clay has been molded to my head and shoulders, weighing me down. As my worst fears are realized, the pressure deepens, threatening to crush me into the floor. I can't hear what Peron is saying anymore—his voice becomes faint as a whooshing sound grows in my ears.

Slowly, I look up and notice the clock behind Peron. Although the time doesn't register, the minute hand is almost at the thirty-minute mark.

The clock hand ticks to the next minute. My head pounds and I close my eyes, fighting the urge to throw up.

The whooshing fades. I open my eyes ... and see a different scene.

I'm outside, somewhere I've never been before. Shock reverberates through me. This isn't one of my daydreams.

Confused, I look around. It looks just like the ancient city of Jerusalem, the one in the drawing we were shown last month in class.

I must be dreaming. I must have fainted and now I'm having one of those faint-dreams.

I slump in relief and take in my surroundings. There are people everywhere. Their clothing confirms I'm not in present day Jerusalem. Surprisingly, I'm wearing the same type of garment other women are wearing.

I'm unable to understand the excited chatter around me. I guess they're speaking Aramaic, which I haven't learned yet. Still, I try to look inconspicuous.

Someone pushes past me roughly and I fall against a tree. I push off to get my balance and rub my sore arm as I look up—and find myself staring at a mesmerizing life-size image of the *Arbre de vie*. The Tree of Life. It sparkles in the sun, flawless, like a mirage.

The clamor below draws my attention. People are gathering around a man who is riding a young donkey. I allow my curiosity to lead me down the hill toward the throng. When I reach the edge of the crowd, someone thrusts a palm frond into my hands. Others are holding them too.

I push toward the front and see others throwing the palm fronds on the dirt path ... right where the colt is headed. Copying them, I throw mine onto the ground and look up at the man riding toward me. The fabric of his long, belted tunic ripples in the breeze, adorning skin roughened and bronzed from years laboring under the sun. People shift closer to him like flowers turning toward light. Then his gaze finds mine and time stops.

He seems to recognize me. His eyes—first clear as morning sky, then deep as fertile earth, suddenly aflame—peer into my soul. I see understanding, compassion, eternity in them, as if he's reading every tear-stained journal page I've never written. The crowd disappears. Something warm trickles down my cheek before I realize I'm crying.

Then he smiles a secret sort of smile, as if we share a joke, and nods in acknowledgement. Who is he?

Heart hammering, dizziness threatens me again. I close my eyes and take a steadying breath. When I open them, I'm back in Peron's office. The Aramaic chatter has stopped but Peron is still speaking.

What?

Disoriented, I look at the clock and it's in the same position as before—not even twenty seconds has passed.

Black spots fill my vision, a warning ringing in my ears. I slide off the chair into and fall into silence—out before I hit the ground.

Quiet.

Murmurings, like a drop on still water sending ripples across a lake.

The ripples intensify as the murmurs become more insistent.

Someone is shaking me. Calling my name.

I come to, feeling like I'm waking from deep sleep, and crack open my eyes to see Peron's worried face.

"Lily? Are you all right?" He checks me over and seems relieved. "You scared me for a minute."

Becoming aware of my surroundings, I let Peron help me up into a sitting position on the floor. I guess I fainted.

"But it was so real," I blurt out.

"What? What was real?"

"The *Arbre de vie*. The man," I say. I must sound stupid.

"What man?"

"He … no, never mind," I say.

Peron waits for me to explain, but then he glances down and frowns. He picks something off my sleeve. "Were you in the greenhouse earlier?" He sounds perplexed.

My eyes follow his and impossible as it seems, there's a green leaf in his fingers.

"The palm frond?" It couldn't be. Could it?

"The what?"

"That's impossible. It was just a dream … or something."

"Lily, you're not making any sense."

Peron looks around, then reaches for something on his desk. He turns back to me, a glass of water in his hands. "Here now: sip, breathe, then tell me. From the beginning."

I look at him, befuddled.

"Sip," he says.

Shakily, I take a few sips of water.

"Breathe."

I take a few deep gulps of air and calmness settles over me.

He puts his hand on my shoulder. "Now, tell me about the *Arbre de vie*, the man, this plant. What happened?"

After a hesitant start, I tell him what I experienced. "It felt like I was there. It was like he knew me," I finish.

Peron has gone still. I look up and his face is flushed. I can see excitement in his eyes, maybe even a yearning to ask for more.

"Do you think I'm crazy?"

He's staring at me with an odd expression, but seems to come to his senses after a moment. "No, no, Lily, you are far from crazy. You've just had an important vision. Let's keep this between us for now, all right? I need to do some investigating first."

He helps me up slowly, then calls his secretary in and tells her to take me to the sick bay to get checked out.

I leave in a daze, more bewildered than ever.

Chapter Twenty-Eight

I AM DREAMING. I know I'm dreaming because I'm not me. I'm someone else.

I'm walking down stone steps and through a room with amber interior. It's the entryway to a house. I exit a door and find myself outside and looking down more stairs. Taking them two at a time, I walk across the gravel to a waiting coach.

Someone calls out my name before I can climb in.

I turn back and see a modest-looking manor house. An elaborately dressed man is running after me with a gleeful look on his face.

"Marc, my boy. You did it again!" he says.

"Did what again, Gustav?"

"The Society News! You're the main feature. Look!"

He shows me the paper and I grimace as I read about how influential and famous I'm becoming. It goes on to mention the King's acquisition of one of my paintings. For someone who's not high-bred that makes me an exception in society.

"See?" Gustav cries. "Now all the other wealthy families will want to throw their daughters at you in marriage. This is wonderful boy! You can take your pick!"

Wonderful. Just what I need, more unwanted attention.

Yearning fills me, a longing for a woman untouched by Pariseinné society. Someone not affected by society's views, who sees me for who I am.

I sigh, as I wave goodbye and leave Gustav chortling and mumbling about his luck in being the benefactor of a rising star.

My thoughts turn to one particular woman and hope flutters in my chest. I climb into the coach and signal the driver to move.

The carriage lurches forward. When will she return? I'm tempted to travel to Mari just to see her again, but I've been restraining myself for fear of appearing the fool. It would be too forward of me. Wouldn't it?

"Lily," I whisper.

I wake with a start at hearing my name. My heart is beating fast. I have a moment of panic as the word "arrhythmia" flashes across my mind.

Box-breathing, I wait until my heart slows to a normal rhythm.

It must be because I'm dreaming of Marc ... of being Marc. That's weird.

I sit up and put my head in my hands, groaning.

What is going on with me? My head aches and I'm conflicted and confused.

I think I miss him. I must miss him if I'm dreaming about him missing me. And then there's Mon Puce, who I'm starting to like in spite of my decided aversion to the bad boy types ... and whose real name still eludes me.

I might go crazy if I can't go back to ARK1.

My mind goes haywire, overwhelmed with everything that's going on in my life right now—the threat of eviction from Vestige, my inability to find Jasper, and the threat of never seeing those I care about in the seventeenth century again.

Failure.

Loss.

Humiliation.

Whimpering, panic rises to the surface of my brain like a tsunami, threatening to overcome me.

My breathing quickens.

My head hurts.

I climb out of bed and walk around the room, breathing deep and slow into my diaphragm until I can calm down to a functional state.

"Creator, please help me."

Chapter Twenty-Nine

A FEW DAYS LATER, still in doubt as to my future, I'm having one of my silent crying episodes in a toilet cubicle during lunch. Two colleagues enter the bathroom talking about the recent attack on Japan.

I'd forgotten about that. It seems so long ago, but not as much time has passed here as it has in the seventeenth century.

I grab some toilet paper and dab my face as I listen.

"An operative named Kae was abducted. Sounds like they brutalized him," one girl says.

"Really? That's terrible. I mean, he would have been trained for interrogation, but you always hope you won't ever need that training."

"Tell me about it, babe. Poor guy, when our agents managed to find him, he'd been beaten so bad they had to rush him to hospital."

"Oh my gosh."

"Yeah. He was in intensive care for a while. Thank goodness he survived. They moved him back to the Unit when he was released, so they could brief him."

"It was the Relic Hunters, right? I wonder what they were after this time?"

I don't hear the reply. The door swings shut on their way out and all I hear is my own erratic breathing.

I come out of the cubicle, my thoughts spinning.

Kae was the first guy to make friends with me when I interned at the Japanese Vestige unit. He was so friendly. He made an effort to include me. I would get constant invites to karaoke nights with him after my first experience out on the town, Japanese style. Karaoke there is more intimate, more tech-savvy, and more socially embedded than at home. It was fun and Kae said we sounded great together. He begged me to form a team with him for a karaoke battle at his favorite club.

I smile at the memory. The reigning champions at the time were full of themselves and he wanted to knock them down a peg or two. I'd relented as they did need to get off their high horse, and Kae celebrated all night long when we beat that duo.

Kae. I have to see if he's all right.

I wash my hands and race back to the dormitory to check the time. It's not too late, he should still be up.

Turning on my computer, I set up V-Chat, Vestige's video chat technology.

I bite my nails as I wait for the program to load. In a moment of self-awareness, I stop and inspect my nails and gasp. Darn it, I should have used my herbal anti-nail-biting concoction. On second thought, maybe it's best I didn't. The last time I wore it, I still went for my nails in a moment of anxiety-ridden weakness and almost choked on the vulgar-tasting stuff.

I need to come up with a better plan. For now, I sit on my fidgety hands. Then I look at the computer again and wait.

It takes a few minutes.

I release a breath I didn't know I was holding when Kae answers the call with a *"Moshi moshi."*[1]

My screen registers the video feed and shows his face. I have to school my features when I see the scars and bruises visible through the BB cream.

"Kae! How are you? I just heard … are you all right?"

"Hey Lily-san,[2] it is good to see you. You look good." His voice is croaky. "How are you going? I thought you were on assignment?"

I shake my head. "I was, but I'm back now. I'm okay. Getting there, I guess. But what about you? What did the Relic Hunters do to you, Kae? Are you all right?"

---

1. "Moshi moshi" means "Hello."

2. "Lily-san means "Miss Lily." Adding "san" to the end of a name is a way of showing respect in Japan, and is gender-neutral (e.g., Mr, Miss, Mrs, Ms).

Kae looks down and takes a breath before meeting my gaze. "I will be. I am happy to be rescued." He tries to smile and fails.

"I'm so sorry, Kae." I can't stop the tears. It seems they did some serious physical and psychological damage. I move out of the camera's view to wipe my face.

"I guess you're lucky they couldn't destroy your animal magnetism—or your fabulous hair," I say as I come back.

His lips curve upward. "Yeah, but now I have real battle wounds. Scars make me look dangerous, right? Maybe I catch eye of beautiful, rich woman."

I force a chuckle. "You betcha! What woman could resist you now?" We smile at each other.

"I am glad you called, Lily-san."

"I had to check in on you. I don't know what the Relic Hunters wanted but I'm glad you're alive and recovering."

"*Arigatou*.[3] I have wanted to contact you, but thought you were on assignment and unreachable."

"Oh? What's up?"

"Lily-san, the Relic Hunters were trying to find out who the Protector is. As if I would know. But they got my phone and went through my photos. Lily-san, you were in them. Remember the night we won karaoke? I kept it on my phone to remember our victory. I did not think it would fall into hands of our enemies. I am sorry." He looks down, as if ashamed.

"Kae, it's all right. Don't worry about it. It's not your fault."

He doesn't look convinced. "Lily-san, I am sure they guessed you are with Vestige. They asked many questions about people in my photos. I did not give them much, but I think you are on their radar now. I have put you in danger."

"Kae, there's no need to apologize. I'm fine. I'm just glad you're all right now." I won't tell Kae about Mon Puce, but I'm positive that's how he got my picture. The thought doesn't sit well with me. The Relic Hunters must have a mole at Vestige, probably more than one—which means they have access to our time travel technology.

---

3. "Arigatou" means "Thank you."

Kae continues. "Lily-san, you need to be careful. There is more." He stops to cough and I tense up in concern for him. He swallows and appears to be in pain, but then he faces me again, his expression tightening. "The Hunters took much interest in you, Lily-san. Something is going down. You need to stay off their radar. If they find you ..." he struggles to get the rest out, as if remembering something terrible. "I do not know what they will do, but I do not think it will be good."

He peers at me through the camera, his face serious. "Promise me, Lily-san. Promise me you will be careful."

"I promise," I say.

Given I might not be at Vestige much longer, it should be easy to keep my word.

After hearing from Kae, I hide in my room and go without dinner. My emotions are in turmoil and I'm angry with the Relic Hunters. If I ever go back, there will be words between me and the Flea. Maybe even Justice will make an appearance.

I look at my baton with affection. I'm sure she would appreciate the exercise.

Chapter Thirty

I AM WOKEN BY the sound of my stomach rumbling. That's a first.

Five-oh-three AM glows on my bedside clock and I moan.

Still, I crawl out of bed, muscles protesting as if they'd had a long workout the day before. Throwing on some clothes and freshening up, I head to the cafeteria. At least I won't encounter Alyse. She loves her beauty sleep.

Unfortunately, I run into someone else I wanted to avoid. Jason.

He sees me and calls my name before I can back away. I wave and grab breakfast. He's still eyeing me with unspoken expectation when I turn and face the tables, so I walk toward him. He gets up and pulls a chair out for me.

Oh.

Still, I let him seat me. "Thanks."

Jason drops back into his seat with a quick, bright smile that doesn't quite reach his eyes.

I start eating but catch him stealing glances at me between adjusting his collar for the third time in the last minute.

I stop, uncomfortable. "How have you been, Jason?"

"Good. How about you?"

"Good."

"I'm glad to see you, Lily."

I smile and take a bite of my omelet. It gets stuck in my throat and I gulp some water to help it down. I sense Jason wants to ask me something, but he doesn't push. I'm grateful. I'm not sure yet what I want. I'm mid-mission but could be expelled soon. That's a sure-fire way to cut short any relationship at Vestige.

If, by some miracle I get to go back to ARK1, I'll have to sort out what I feel for two other men. Three is too overwhelming right now and it's unfair to Jason.

After a while, I break the silence again. "How's your latest mission going?"

Jason's eyes light up. "I've been training for a three-month stint in Mushiactal. It's this dimension where blue stick-creatures live in giant toadstools. Luckily, they're not dangerous—we think—and they produce a valuable substance Vestige need."

"How interesting." I smile.

"It is, actually. Vestige uses the substance to perform safe mind-wipes on citizens who are caught in the wrong place at the wrong time. An injection, and they lose the last thirty minutes of memory. I'm going as a diplomat to come to a more profitable trade agreement."

The mention of mind-wipes sets my nerves on edge. I glance at the clock—I have a meeting with Peron this morning. I need to get my thoughts in order before then.

"Hey, I've gotta run—got a meeting with the boss."

"Oh, sure. Better not keep him waiting." Jason gives me a wistful look.

"All the best with your mission, Jason. I hope we can catch up after." He perks up at that and guilt slides down my throat, leaving a nasty trail.

After getting myself together, I take the elevator to Peron's floor for our meeting.

The elevator doors slide open. Peron is standing in his office, talking with the man from last time. Alyse's dad. What was his name? Stefan?

I step out. The man glances at me through the glass wall, his eyes assessing me, and I can't stop an involuntary shiver. I pretend indifference and walk to a stuffed orange sofa and sit down.

Grabbing a magazine, I shuffle through the pages, wondering what they're talking about. I glance up. Stefan seems to be arguing with Peron over something. I watch as his face goes red. Then Peron says something that shuts him up.

Peron glances at me and I look down. I wait another ten minutes until they're done, but don't look up when Stefan leaves.

The boss calls me in after another minute. When he indicates, I end my salute and take a seat, my stomach twisting uncomfortably.

"Lily, after much consideration, the Board has decided to allow you to return to your mission."

The weight falls off me like ballast from a hot air balloon. I breathe out in relief and lean forward to thank Peron, but he stalls me with a hand.

"Don't get too excited, Lily. Wait until you hear what else I have to say."

Dread beats in my chest. I sit back slowly.

Peron sighs. "Professor Crabb has been making things difficult, but new information has come to light that confirms I was right in giving you this assignment, Lily. However, I need to make concessions, so I'm sending someone with you this time to appease Professor Crabb and all who have joined his crusade."

"Okay." Who will join me?

"It might be good to get you out of the spotlight anyway," I hear him mutter as he leans down and rifles through a desk drawer.

When he sits up, his expression is apologetic. I know who he's sending.

I shake my head. "No. Please. Anyone but Alyse."

"I'm sorry, Lily. It was the only way to convince the Board to give you another shot."

Of all the unfair things, now this too? She'll ruin my small taste of paradise. She'll turn everyone against me. Plot the whole way through to thwart my plans and make me look even more incompetent. She'll manipulate Marc ... even Mon Puce, if she meets him.

I consider resigning as Peron speaks again.

"Alyse has been given explicit instructions not to let her personal agenda get in the way of this mission, Lily. She knows it's unprofessional and her neck is on the line too. You must work together. Perhaps this will be a chance to resolve your differences."

Yeah, right.

Peron continues to talk but all I can think of is Alyse sabotaging my mission.

"Lily? Are you even listening to me?"

"What? Oh. Sorry, sir."

"I know she's made things difficult for you here. I'm not sure why the Board tolerates her childishness, but she's had some success and she's got the backing of one of the Board members, as well as Prof. Crabb, so I didn't have much say. But look on the bright side—you'll have help locating Jasper. She'll be driven to find him before you do. And all of us will benefit from seeing this mission completed, regardless of who finds him, right?"

"Right."

Glumly, I accept Peron's decision and resign myself to the oncoming battle.

I see Alyse on the way to my dorm. She smirks at me but doesn't say anything.

Why am I so affected by her? I need to get tougher. At least where we're going, she won't have her posse to back her up. Maybe she won't be as bold.

My movements are sluggish as I pack for my mission, my earlier joy smothered by the trepidation of having Alyse join me.

I hope I'm ready for this.

CHAPTER THIRTY-ONE

1629 A.D. République de L'Aurente, ARK1 dimension

THE GIRLS ARE DELIGHTED at my return. Questions about my family soon turn to curiosity when Alyse steps out of the carriage.

"Who is this, Lily?" Charlotte asks.

"This is my cousin, Mademoiselle Alyse. She'll be staying with us for a while. Alyse, these are Mesdames Charlotte and Cherie Therriot."

The girls accept Alyse in their friendly way and Alyse reciprocates. "Lily has told me so much about you. I feel like we're family already."

I stare, totally floored, watching this new version of Alyse—polite, polished, even sweet—charm the girls like it's no big deal. Who is she, and what has she done with the real Alyse?

How long will it take before her true colors start showing? Maybe she'll surprise me and actually grow a heart. Or maybe—just maybe—we can figure this out and stop acting like mortal enemies.

I'm given little time to wonder as Uncle Raimond motions us in and leads the way to his study for a rundown of our first mission together. I'm even more uncertain as I consider the prospect of spending a lengthy time with Alyse in a carriage, but we accept our mission and have a quick dinner before heading to our rooms for an early night.

The carriage rocks and jumps with an irritating stubbornness as we traverse the rough roads, heading toward La'Ristante, in the region of Nemmes. Our mission is to locate Monsieur Bernard, the previous owner of the seaside cottage in La'Ristante. We're hoping he at least met and remembers Jasper. If he's not Jasper himself.

The journey has been a silent one, as Alyse and I keep to ourselves and consider our approach.

I'm still taken aback by her different persona. She's been acting as if nothing horrible ever happened between us. I don't trust it. I don't trust her.

Nevertheless, it's better than back home, so I turn my thoughts to our mission. Will we have any luck today?

After a stopover in a half-decent establishment last night, we've been traveling for hours. Now we're itching to get out and move about. We've agreed to search independently so we can cover more ground. Our unspoken need for separation from each other doubtless contributed to that idea.

Thirty minutes later, we arrive at our meeting point and exit the carriage, stretching our sore limbs in the deserted area. It feels amazing after being cooped up for what felt like years next to Alyse.

We consult our maps and head off in opposite directions. At last.

I grin as I wander over green fields toward a small township. The air is fresh and I pass a few cows, stepping over a cow patty here and there with a liveliness I haven't felt in a while.

I feel so free—being back in the seventeenth century, enjoying the unspoilt countryside away from Alyse. It's like my shackles have been removed and I can relax. For a moment, anyway.

When I reach the town, I consult my list of Monsieur Bernards who are recorded as living in this area. There's a few. I rehearse my cover story as I head to the first location.

Well, that was an unfruitful day. Or perhaps fruitful if I consider the four names I've crossed out as not being the Bernard we are after. Three of the men were pleasant enough but the wrong age, and one was of such a disagreeable nature, he wouldn't have stooped to inhabit a run-down cottage, even in his barefoot days.

Disappointment reproaches me for my failure as I head back to the meeting point. I hope this doesn't go against me. As much as I hate to admit it, I hope Alyse had better luck.

Twenty minutes later I find out she didn't and I can tell she's unhappy about it. Our day was spent running after dead ends.

Our bodies betray our exhaustion as we climb into the carriage. I try to lighten the mood. "Well, that's one area down. We can start on another tomorrow."

Despite Alyse's expression curdling the air, she concedes. I brace for a verbal onslaught that, astonishingly, never comes.

The next day after two more knock-backs, I stop for lunch in a small establishment, ignoring the stares that demand to know why a woman is walking around and eating alone. It may not be proper, but they're not going to remember my face and I can take care of myself. At least they're not above serving me for a coin.

Halfway through my meal, a small group of men enter and I perk up. I recognize one of the men. The one who helped us fight the Relic Hunters a while back. What was his name?

I'm racking my brain for a moment until he looks straight at me, almost as though he was expecting to find me here. His name slips back into my memory: Alain.

I smile and he nods at me. He speaks to his men and they head to a corner table while Alain walks toward me.

"Mademoiselle, a pleasure to see you again."

"You also, Monsieur. I hope you have been well?"

"Indeed, and you?"

"*Oui.*"

"May I join you for a moment? I feel awkward standing over you to speak."

"Oh, yes. Of course, please sit."

Alain sits opposite with an assessing glance. His nearness puts me on edge, but I'm drawn to him at the same time. Not in a romantic way, just … I don't know, like something is pulling at me, connecting me to this man. My dad would joke that it's a pull of destiny. Not because of my destiny, but my surname. One of his dad jokes.

I consider Alain. His unique silver eyes are kind, but wary. "It's nice to run into a familiar face out here," I say.

"It is. May I ask what you are doing here on your own?"

"I do have traveling companions. I'm investigating the disappearance of a particular gentleman, but don't seem to be having much luck."

"Hmm. Perhaps I could be of assistance?"

My appreciation for this man increases. This would be the second time he has helped me.

"I would like that. I need to find a man named Bernard, a Bernard who owned a seaside cottage in La'Ristante. So far, none of the monsieur's I've located share this particular past."

"And why are you looking for him?" he asks, raising an eyebrow.

Something about Alain makes me want to trust him, so I divulge a little.

"He might know of a boy who grew up there about thirty years ago."

"Is he a relative of yours?"

"No. But it's important that I find him as soon as possible."

Alain leans forward and my unrest increases. It's weird, but if someone told me Alain had a static shield around him, I wouldn't be too quick to dismiss the idea. Maybe he's one of those people who get electric shocks wherever they go, and he just attracts electrons like there's no tomorrow.

"Mademoiselle, why is it so important that you find this boy?"

"He was kidnapped as a child and his family wants to find him. He stands to inherit an estate of some consequence."

Something flickers in his eyes. "Perhaps he died. A man due such a legacy would have returned to his bloodline by now."

"It's possible he doesn't know. He was young when he was taken."

"What was the boy's name?"

"Jasper Dompierre-St-Martin."

He goes still and his look becomes distant.

The buzzing increases, uncomfortable in its intensity, nearing breaking point. I sit back, trying to put distance between myself and Static Man, relieved when the sensation lessens.

Alain sits back and his expression becomes shuttered. "What if it's not safe to go back? What if finding him puts him in danger?"

What a strange question. Does he know about Jasper?

"It is vital that I find Jasper. I hope to the Creator that he's still alive and well."

Alain takes a deep breath. "I will be on the lookout for you then. How can I reach you if I find anything which may help your search?"

Pleased, I tell him where he can reach me. He nods, as if familiar with the general location.

"It was a pleasure to run into you, Mademoiselle. I must rejoin my men now."

"And you. I appreciate any assistance you can provide."

He nods then stands and heads to the corner table.

I finish my meal in light spirits and wave to Alain as I leave. He nods again with his silvery assessing look.

The afternoon provides more opportunities to cull my list and I head back to the meeting point in a more thoughtful frame of mind.

We find another layover that night and set out the next day to repeat the process in a new town.

After days of endless setbacks, Alyse and I are feeling defeated and a touch teary-eyed. It's weird that we've managed to collaborate with a semblance of harmony. Alyse's continued agreeableness has left me quite bewildered.

Our carriage ride home is quiet. We've exhausted a large region and had no bites at all. It's like Monsieur Bernard just disappeared. Maybe he sailed to another country or moved to the other end of the République de L'Aurente. Maybe he changed his name. Or maybe he died after all.

My one hope is that Alain might find something. I can't help the niggling feeling that there's something he isn't telling me.

I'm mentally rehearsing my report for Peron, aiming for something polished and professional, when Alyse suddenly dissolves into tears. Loud, ugly sobs shake her as she buries her face in a handkerchief.

I freeze, staring, my mouth agape. She's really crying. Like, *really* crying. As the handkerchief turns into a soggy mess, I realize this isn't just dramatics.

Awkwardly, I reach out, barely brushing her shoulder with my fingertips. Comforting Alyse? Yeah ... way out of my skill set.

After some moments, she speaks.

"I'm so jealous of you, you know."

What? No way. She's got the whole package: a squad, the fame and recognition, looks that kill *and* she's loaded. Doesn't she have everything?

"What do you mean?" I ask.

"I am under so much pressure. You're lucky, Lily. Your dad was a top agent at Vestige and he's always encouraged you to do your best. My dad is nothing like that. He might be on the Board, but he's hard on me. I can barely meet his expectations. I know he'll be angry with me after this mission. I wish I had it as easy as you."

Wow.

Okay, so I didn't realize her father was like that, but still. At least she has the backing of someone who has power at Vestige—given he's on the board of directors.

Besides, I'm stressed out too and it's all because of her.

I sigh and try to be the bigger person. "I'm sorry you are under pressure from your father, Alyse."

But my situation is worse than hers—she hasn't had to undergo constant bullying and it's not like she'll be ejected from Vestige if she fails.

I notice her wince. I'm still patting her shoulder, quite forcefully now, so I remove my hand.

"I am fortunate to have a great dad," I say. "We can't choose our fathers, but we can choose who we become." And how we treat others. "I'm under pressure too, but I'm trying my best to get through it."

She sniffles in response and scowls out the window.

I leave her to her thoughts and focus on my own. Is that why she always bullied me? She was jealous of my dad?

I'm not sure how I feel about that. I guess in the end, she's as much at the mercy of her circumstances as I am. Perhaps her upbringing trained her to threaten those who have what she wants.

My guard drops a little, though I question the wisdom of it. I can't forget everything she's put me through, but I'm relieved Alyse was open with me. Maybe this can be the foundation of a better relationship.

Chapter Thirty-Two

THE DAY AFTER WE get back home, thick gray clouds smother the sky, and the cold seeps through my clothes. I've had about ten hours of sleep to recover from the journey, so I throw on extra layers until my shivering stops, and head downstairs.

I spend a quiet morning catching up with the girls, while Alyse is stuck in Uncle's study. She's on a call with Professor Crabb. Last night, I found out that the deal for me to come back here includes her being the one to share our mission details.

They don't trust me anymore—I'm officially on thin ice. And knowing my so-called "frenemy" is the one reporting on our assignment? It's messing with my head big time. If we discover anything major, I can already see her swooping in and taking all the credit.

Right now, Alyse holds all the cards, and she could ruin my reputation without even trying. I grit my teeth, biting back a scream. I want to punch a wall or, honestly, just break down and cry. But instead, I pour everything out in my diary when no one's around. It's not much, but it's the only thing keeping me from falling apart.

Marc arrives, bringing me back to the present, and a stupid happiness overwhelms my turbulent emotions.

When our eyes connect, his smile is brilliant ... it takes my breath away. I forgot how gorgeous he is.

He steps closer, and suddenly my heart is racing like it's got a mind of its own. His hand finds mine—warm, steady—and the spark that shoots through me is electric. He lifts my hand, presses a soft kiss to it, but doesn't let go. And just like that, the world stops spinning.

"I am glad to see you again, Mademoiselle."

The golden stubble that tickled my skin a moment ago looks good on him. Then again, everything does.

"And I you, Monsieur," I breathe.

Marc's gaze is intense, like he's drinking me in, and my hand tingles where his skin touches mine.

We part, and I struggle to catch my breath. I can't stop staring at him—when he's not aware—and I keep telling myself we're just friends.

It's like I haven't seen him in ages. Something has changed but I can't figure out what. He's different. Or maybe I am. I don't know.

We all agree to stay indoors by the fire for today's lesson. I huddle closer to Charlotte on our shared chaise lounge as Marc talks. My eyes flick to the door. Marc hasn't met Alyse yet, and I'm dreading the inevitable. A childish thought keeps poking at me, that she'll nab him before I can blink.

I shake my head. Whatever that means. It's not like he's mine or anything.

The thought sends a sharp pang through my heart, and my mine recoils, trying to block it out.

I refocus on Marc. I should be listening, but my mind jumps to the mission and I worry. What clue am I missing? What do they think of me back at home? I feel like a failure. I haven't found anything of real value yet. Can I still be thrown out? If I do get to stay with Vestige, will I be trusted with anything worthwhile ever again? Or will I be relegated to a boring desk job back home?

I picture the hot dusty outback and all at once find a new fondness for the cold.

I sigh and glance at Marc again, finding his eyes on me. He appears concerned but focusses back on his notes.

Wouldn't it be nice to stay in this time and place, this dimension, and have nothing more significant to do than learn under the tutelage of this magnificent man?

Yet, if Alyse and I somehow do find Jasper, we'll have to return home. That means I'll never see Marc again ... or that pesky Flea.

Out of nowhere, sadness threatens to overwhelm me.

Our lesson continues and I struggle to rein in my emotions. Cherie laments about the dismal weather when our lesson is over. She jumps up and heads off to help Cook bake some pastries as Marc leans down to pack his satchel.

Char has a strange expression on her face as she watches Cherie leave. I can't be sure, but when she glances back at me and Marc, she seems to be calculating the situation.

She stands with an abruptness that startles me. "I am going to help Cherie."

I rise, ready to offer my services, but she shakes her head at me with a meaningful look at Marc.

My gut flips. Char throws back a winsome smile as she exits the room and I sink back into my seat by the fire.

Not sure what to do with my hands, I grab a book off the table and pretend to be interested in it.

In my peripheral vision I see Marc straighten. He moves toward me and I swallow hard. The room is quiet, apart from the cracking and occasional spitting of logs on the fire. I hold my breath, waiting.

"May I sit with you a moment, Lily?"

I look up startled. His use of my first name feels intimate.

As he waits for my response, I notice that the chandelier behind him is causing a halo effect on his golden locks. That's the second time now. He's got to be an angel.

"Angel!" It bursts out from my stupid mouth.

"What?"

"What?" I say back. I can tell my face is going red.

He seems uncertain. "Umm ..."

This is so awkward.

"So ... you ... you look like an angel."

He stares at me and his face grows pink.

"The light is framing your hair," I rush to explain.

It takes a second before my words make sense. "Oh." He laughs.

I laugh with him like a schoolgirl. It's hysterical. I want to sink into those golden locks—no, I mean the floor—and disappear.

I look down and grimace.

Marc comes to sit on the seat next to me. I'm hyper aware of him as the couch sinks with his weight. His arm brushes mine.

I don't know what to say ... I don't know what to say!

Anxious, I fight the urge to chomp on my nails. Where are my Skittles when I need them? Or those berries?

"I need something sweet and red," I mutter.

"Are you hungry?" he asks, overhearing me.

"I could do with something sweet right now," I say.

Marc smiles. "I can't give you red, but I do have something sweet." He pulls out a small paper bag from his breast pocket and opens it. He offers it to me and I look inside to find some type of yellow sweet. That'll have to do.

I reach in and take one, popping it into my mouth. He watches as if fascinated while I taste it. My eyes widen. It's some type of tasty sherbet lemon.

"You like it?" he asks.

I nod with enthusiasm and he chuckles. He takes one and puts the bag away in his pocket.

We suck on our sweets for a while in silence and I grow more at ease. As I finish mine, I glance at him to find him gazing at me with a soft smile on his face. He's so close, I can see the light green specks in his eyes. They look mysterious in the firelight and I'm mesmerized by their beauty. His pupils dilate and I am drawn to the black depths within.

Marc takes a sharp intake of breath. He's staring back at me. I've moved closer to him ... oops, a little too close. I wanted to see his eyes in more detail but despite the awkwardness of the situation, I can't bring myself to move back yet. I watch as he seems to struggle with himself. His eyes drop to my lips and my heart pitter-patters like spring rain.

My stomach clenches and I have this crazy urge to grab him and kiss him like I've tried so hard not to think about doing.

The clock strikes three and we both startle, leaping apart as it chimes the hour.

The spell broken, I look at the clock, as if it were a strict chaperone. Then my already-warm cheeks heat up enough to rival the fireplace. Perhaps I should thank the clock.

I can't believe I almost kissed Marc. I can't be getting involved with a guy who'll be dead centuries before I'm born ... and who's not even from the same universe. Ugh. Creator, help me.

Marc clears his throat, gets up and walks to the window, commenting on the weather as if our almost-kiss never happened. I'm thankful he's preserving my dignity, like the gentleman he is. But I still feel like an idiot.

"I was reading a passage from the Creator's Great Letter this morning," Marc says. "It was from James 1:27. It resonated with me, so I memorized it."

He's pretty serious about the Creator. I give him a look of encouragement and he continues.

"It says, 'Pure and genuine religion in the eyes of our Creator is to care for orphans and widows in their distress, and refuse to be corrupted by the world's values.'"

"Does the Creator's Letter really say that?"

"Yes Lily, it does," he says with a smile. "I believe the Creator speaks to us through his Letter. He was showing his heart for me, and he reminded me of how he took care of my mother and me when we lived in the village."

"Oh." I shift to angle myself toward him.

"He also impressed on me that he is my provider, so I will always have more than enough, and I need to help others who are in need as I was. I want to follow his example of giving out of love. Just as the Creator sacrificed for mankind, so I want to give out of what I have to help others."

He pauses and I smile at him, enchanted. It's not like he doesn't already do this, from what he's told me.

Marc goes on. "I would like to teach some of the poorer families from my old village for free when I can. I hope one day to have a sizeable enough income, to set up a fund that will better support their needs."

My smile falters. I feel inadequate. He's like the male version of Mother Theresa.

I shake off my reservations. "Marc, you are a remarkable man, to think of doing something like that. If it's in your heart, you should do it. Imagine what you could change by lifting those people out of poverty, even giving them the gift of literacy." Passion ignites my spirit, driving me to join him by the window. "Education is a wonderful way to do this. Equip them with the power to change their future." I reach his side, my fingers catching his almost instinctively. The warmth of his hand wraps around mine, and for a second, I forget to breathe. Our eyes meet—bright with excitement, but something else flickering beneath it. We grin, caught in our shared understanding ... and something else unspoken.

I force myself to focus. I want to do something good with my life. Maybe the Creator is as good as Marc says he is and he has a plan for me too. My parents would agree. What about Marc's parents?

"I'm sure your mother and father would be proud of you if they saw the man you've become, Marc."

Marc's gaze shutters, the spark in his eyes gone. His smile doesn't quite reach his eyes. "*Merci*, Lily. I hope so. Although I never knew my father, I hope he would be proud too."

"You never knew him?" I ask, surprised.

"No. I carry my mother's family name. She never told me who my father was."

"I'm so sorry, Marc."

I guess this news hasn't been shared with society. They might not look so favorably upon him otherwise. "Thank you for trusting me enough to share that. It must have been hard, not knowing who your father was."

"At times."

There's more he's not telling me. I want to know. "Can you tell me what it was like for you, growing up?"

His golden brows smooth out as he pauses to reflect. "I grew up in a nearby hamlet, which was peaceful, but everyone worked hard. My mother received money every month until I was nineteen. She wouldn't tell me where from, though I asked her many times."

He sighs. "After a while, I gave up asking. The money allowed us to live more comfortably so I couldn't complain. I witnessed the hardship of some in my village who were often forced to go without meals, and I couldn't be content while they struggled, so I helped them."

I'm sure he did.

"I was also fortunate enough to receive tutelage from a kind old neighbor who became like a father to me, and his guidance saved me from making many foolish decisions. His name was Gérard. I mentioned him before. Do you remember?"

I nod, my appreciation growing for this man, Gérard. I can hear the respect Marc still holds for him, as he describes all the things he did for Marc's benefit. Perhaps he was a retired scholar or something.

"In return for Gérard's tutelage, I would chop wood for his fire and handle tasks he no longer had the stamina to complete. That's how I began helping others in the village, actually. The older folk caught on and Maman encouraged me to lend them my 'youthful strength.'" Marc smiles at the memory. But then his smile fades. Shadows crowd his eyes as he tells of how his mother passed away from an illness, and how his world was thrown into chaos. He'd had to reinvent himself. He began working as a music and art tutor, given that's where his talents lay. His reputation and fame grew through word of mouth.

My eyes burn and I blink fast, breathing past the ache in my chest. "I can't begin to understand how hard that must have been, Marc. But you've broken out of a mold that would have limited other men. You should be proud of how far you've come." I place my free hand on his arm and squeeze it gently. "You are amazing."

Marc's expression softens. He inhales, as if breathing in the weight of my words. His eyes search mine as if trying to hold onto the moment, like what I've said has penetrated him deeply.

"Thank you."

I squeeze his arm again. "You're welcome."

Marc's story has touched a cord in me. I can't help but let my defenses slip. He's real. Tangible. Here. And I'm in danger of falling for him. Hard.

Marc pulls me from my thoughts when he asks about my life. I tell him what I can, and he listens—really listens. Like my words matter.

Not only is he gorgeous to look at, but he's kind and sincere. He even likes my modern thinking.

Maybe, just maybe, he won't reject me.

We talk quietly until the girls come in, bearing delicious hot pastries.

As I climb into bed that night, I realize Marc has become a good friend. Someone I can trust. But he's from a different time and place. I shouldn't let our relationship go any further, even if I want it to.

I wish Marc was the missing Jasper Dompierre-St-Martin. Not that he'd been taken from his family, but that he could be restored to a wealthy home and people who will open their loving arms and hearts to him. And then he'd be "in the know" in Vestige terms, and maybe we could have something together.

I roll over and stare at a picture on my wall in the dim lamplight.

From what I can gather, Marc lives with his patron who is often away, so he's alone most of the time. My heart aches for him and I wish he were with me so I could hug him. Platonically, of course.

I sigh. It's impossible. The missing son would be twice Marc's age.

My thoughts turn to Jasper. Who is he now? Is he even still alive? Yawning, I reach up and blow out the lamp, lie back, and pull the covers up to my chin. After some time, my thoughts swirl with the onset of sleep.

When I nod off, my dreams are filled with visions. Visions of a man with a blurred face and a remarkable pendant that glimmers in the sunlight.

Chapter Thirty-Three

LIFE SETTLES BACK INTO a steady rhythm, and there are no assignments for a week as we mull over our next steps.

Alyse spends the time in Uncle's den, catching up on some physical and intellectual training. I use the time to sort through the chaos in my mind and get it back in the game.

One morning, Charlotte sees me sitting alone on a window seat, gazing outside. She comes over and hugs me.

"Dear Lily, I think Monsieur Coupier might be wanting one of these from you." She winks, indicating our hug.

"Charlotte!" I say in shock. She laughs but becomes serious, describing how absent-minded he was while I was gone.

"He looked crestfallen when he learned you'd be away for a time, but he hid it rather well after that. Very stoic of him." She chuckles. "I'd catch him staring out the window or at the places where you'd sit during lessons, and when I'd ask him a question, he wouldn't even hear me. I've had to repeat myself countless times."

"There must have been something else on his mind," I say, ignoring the warmth blooming in my chest. A noise outside has me looking out the window again. My heart stumbles, then races, when I recognize Marc's carriage.

"And here he is." I don't like Charlotte's tone of voice, so I ignore her on principle.

She leaves to greet our tutor while I feel frozen in time. He disembarks from the carriage and sprints up the stairs with the grace of a mountain lion.

Throat dry, I'm still staring at the top of the stairs when I hear a deep voice. "Mademoiselle Therriot."

I turn to see Marc standing in the doorway. Something about him seems different. He carries an air of determination, a slight smile on his face and a promise in his eyes as he stares at me. The pull feels magnetic and I find myself staring back at him. I almost don't see Charlotte standing next to him.

Realization kicks me into action. I stand and brush myself down, hiding my blushing face.

The book I wasn't reading has fallen to the floor, so I turn to retrieve it. A strong hand reaches down and picks it up before I can.

I swallow hard.

Marc's quizzical stare brings me out of the daze I've stumbled into. He hands me the book with care and I take it, hand trembling. What on earth is going on with me today?

"*Merci*," I croak.

"Well, are we going to the greenhouse, or aren't we?" Cherie enters the room with eagerness in her voice.

We murmur agreement and follow her to the giant clear dome Uncle built for his wife, back when she was alive. It's beautiful to look at and I'm glad for the change of scenery—and for some warmth to combat the winter chill.

I'm also grateful Uncle built a side entrance connecting the greenhouse to the house, so we don't have to venture outside.

Marc removes his coat and leaves his satchel on a chair near the door. His navy shirt compliments his lightly tanned skin, fitted tight against his broad shoulders and strong arms. I swallow again.

We enter through the side door and the tropical air warms me instantly. I move to stand with the twins, facing Marc.

"Today Mesdames, I will be using flowers to teach you how to create the dispersions of light and shadow on a plant through art."

While the topic is interesting, I struggle to focus. I'm hyper-aware of Marc's nearness, of the heat radiating off his arm as he moves to stand next to me, pointing out a pretty blossom with a deep rose hue that must rival my face right now.

This is not good. I have a mission to fulfill. Peron would call this a major distraction and a risk to Vestige, and Dad wouldn't be pleased. On top of everything else, I can't fail Dad.

I come back to the present with an exhale as warm drops of moisture bead on my skin. Cherie asks a question, which Marc answers. He gestures with his hands ... such capable hands. What would it be like to feel them holding me?

No. I shouldn't think like that.

I force myself to snap out of it and try to observe with indifference. There is paint under Marc's fingernails. He must be painting elsewhere. I wish I could see his private work. It would be so enlightening.

I want to know more about Marc Coupier.

He glances at me, catches my expression, and pauses.

"Are you all right, Mademoiselle?" he asks.

"Have you been painting?" I say, feeling put on the spot. My dress feels restrictive and uncomfortably warm.

Marc's eyes widen as if he's been caught with his hand in the cookie jar.

Charlotte pipes up, "Oh, Monsieur, she's right. You have green paint on your shirt cuff!"

Marc checks his cuff and his eyes widen even further. With a faint blush, he unbuttons and rolls up his sleeve to hide the evidence. "My apologies, Mesdames. I must have missed it. It's quite warm in here, isn't it?"

I stare at his strong forearms as if I've never seen a man's forearms before. With effort, I tear my gaze away and notice the others staring at him. They're waiting for an explanation. Marc seems to realize this.

"Yes, you are correct. I have been painting. Sometimes I get so caught up in the subject that I do not notice the details that need attending to. I apologize for my improper appearance. I hope it does not offend any of you." His eyes search mine in earnest.

"On the contrary, Monsieur. It's wonderful that you have such a passion for art and creativity. This shows that you are an artist in the truest sense."

Marc's face goes from "Whoa, what?" to "Phew, that was close," and settles into something undeniably pleased.

I bite back a smirk. "I hope one day I have the privilege of seeing some of your works," I say.

Marc gives me a long look. "It is my great wish that one day you will see them all."

We gaze at each other and the tension grows unbearable. Cherie interrupts and asks to be included in the invitation too. Marc smiles at her with a non-committal look, and I can breathe again. Whoa.

Charlotte gives us both a knowing smile but remains quiet. I appreciate her maturity, because it rattles me that she can be so observant.

We move on to another plant and Marc quizzes us.

Distracted, I brush the end of my hair against my upper lip, catching some of the perspiration. I find Marc staring at my mouth and look away, faking interest in a nearby plant.

The lesson continues for some time, with Marc including me so frequently I'm starting to feel like his sidekick. After another twenty minutes, I develop a small headache. The girls' animated chatter grates on me, though Marc seems to bear with it graciously.

I drop behind the group a little and slip away quietly. The surrounding foliage muffles their voices in a satisfying way. It's peaceful.

Some of the flowers have grown entwined around an arched frame, so I don't even need to bend over to inhale their sweet fragrance.

After a few minutes, the girls' voices become loud again. Exasperated, I turn—and immediately regret it. My face collides with solid muscle, and I stumble back, heart kicking into overdrive.

Marc stands right there, close enough that the heat of him lingers in the space between us. His eyes lock onto mine, concern flickering there, along with something else—something that sends a thrill down my spine before I can name it.

The girls have trailed behind him, but their chattering fades as I return his stare.

I am mesmerized by the strength of his character—and his appearance, let's be honest—so I don't hear the question he asked me. He repeats himself.

"... are you all right?"

I shake my head to clear it.

"Sorry. I am fine, except I have a small headache."

His light frown creates soft turrets in his golden eyebrows.

"I just need some air," I mumble. I spin around, looking for an exit. I take one step but am stopped by a firm, gentle grip on my arm. The twins stop talking and the room goes quiet. I turn back, surprised at his boldness.

Marc's mouth moves as if he wants to say something but can't find the words.

He steps closer. I search his face. A jolt hits my stomach at the deep intensity in his green eyes.

A look of determination crosses his face and he closes his mouth. He's studying me in a way that makes me shiver in pleasure. His eyes roam my face, leaving waves of heat in the aftermath. I take a sudden breath, craving more air, and Marc's eyes drop to my mouth.

Desire flares inside me and I'm shocked at the force of it. His eyes reconnect with mine and echo my own hunger. I watch, paralyzed as his head moves toward mine, his lips parting. His breath is a caress. I tense in anticipation.

A giggle bursts out from Cherie, breaking our connection.

Realization slams into me. I turn my head, my face glowing red enough to stop traffic. I grimace, my feelings mirroring that of someone who accidentally "liked" a year-old photo while deep-scrolling an ex's social media.

Marc clears his throat. "P-Prepare for our—uh—our next lesson. Music."

The girls look smug as they pass me. My face gets hotter.

Marc lets go of my arm, and I don't waste a second. I dart after the girls, my steps quick and desperate, like I can outrun the thought of being alone with him.

His stare burns a hole in my back all the way to the music room.

"I can't believe he was about to kiss you. Oh, how romantic!" Char falls backward on my bed, arms and legs splayed in an unladylike fashion. It's eerie how she echoes my thoughts—not that I'll ever admit it out loud.

"Nonsense. You were imagining things."

"Oh posh. It's obvious he likes you more than a friend, Lily. How can you not see that?" Cherie is serious. "Haven't you noticed he lights up whenever you enter the room? And he always gravitates toward you, like you're the sun and he's the moon!"

She says "mooooon" as she falls backward on the bed to join Char and they both end up in a fit of giggles.

I can't help but laugh at the beloved twins. "You two are hopeless romantics."

They both flash me a grin that's pure mischief.

"Yes, and you love us." Char says.

I groan. It doesn't help that I'm on assignment and I can't stay. I don't know what was wrong with me today, but I don't have time for romance. It's a tangled web that'll only end in heartache.

I breathe a deep sigh, dejected. How unfair. Why couldn't I have met Marc in the twenty-first century?

I gather my wits and tell myself, "I am determined. I'm on mission: Operation Jasper. I can do this."

I ignore the fact that I lack conviction. I can't fall for him.

Chapter Thirty-Four

I REMAIN DETERMINED THROUGHOUT the rest of the week, even when Marc hints at something more than friendship. His confident attentiveness makes it extra hard to stop being so aware of him.

I'm relieved when Alyse and I have a brainstorming session with Peron on our next steps. We throw every idea we have onto the table and by the end of the session we've got some proposals—but still no plan.

I catch myself biting my nails, so I sit on my hands. Alyse looks like she could kick something. Peron must notice, because he says he'll discuss our ideas with the Board. Then he shows us an illustration. Alyse and I jostle each other, straining to see the artwork on the screen. Peron explains that it's of an earlier Protector.

She appears to be floating. The pendant is depicted at the base of her throat with light blazing out of it. Connected to that light is the Creator's forefinger, as if the light is pouring from his hand, through his finger into the pendant. It reminds me of Michelangelo's *The Creation of Adam*.

A shiver races across my skin, a whisper of something electric in the air. It's not just me—Alyse stiffens beside me, her breath hitching, eyes flicking toward mine in quiet confirmation. Whatever this is, we both feel it. Still, there's only so much time I can spend with her before I become like a jittery squirrel on espresso. When our session ends, I make my excuses and leave Alyse to continue with other studies.

Exiting the den, I climb the stairs to ground level. It's almost midday. Sunlight spills in through a tall window. I walk over and soak it in, the warmth prickling my skin after being in the dank cellar for hours this morning. It's a gorgeous day. The blue sky beckons me outside.

My stomach signals it's time to eat, spoiling the moment. I turn away but something in the garden catches my eye. Something that flickers. Something bright.

Intrigued, I ignore a grumbled protest and head outside.

I walk over to the edge of a small forest, wondering if I imagined it.

There it is again. I squint against the sudden light but keep walking.

When I reach the overhanging trees I maneuver around a huge trunk, picking up my skirts. The sun's rays grow faint as I wander further in to search.

A broken twig and half a footprint alert me that someone has been here. Probably the gardener. I sigh and straighten. As I consider heading back, two hands grab me. A breath later, I'm pulled behind the tree, out of sight of the house.

Panic lashes out like a sharp knife, but my reflexes kick in. I slam my head back, expecting to hear a nose breaking. Instead, someone grunts. Then chuckles. Twisting, I see who it is and want to scream in frustration.

"Mon Puce," I say. He flashes a confident grin and studies my face, but I launch into him.

"What are you doing here? No, scrap that. How could you work for an organization who beats up innocent people? I thought you said the RH aren't like that, but I guess someone was telling me fibs."

Mon Puce looks taken aback by my outburst. "I'm sorry, Mademoiselle. I'm not sure what you're referring to."

"Your buddies beat up my friend and almost killed him. In twenty-first century Japan."

He looks uncomfortable. "Oh. That."

"Yes. That." I wish I had my trusty baton with me. Justice would enjoy a good swing at his head. Wouldn't you, Justice? Yes, you would.

"So was it all a lie? Do you have time travel tech?"

"Sadly, no."

"Then who's the mole, Mon Puce? Which of your men has infiltrated Vestige?"

"I'm not going to answer that question," he says with a smile.

Oh, he's infuriating! I frown and move to walk back to the house, but he grabs my arm. "Wait."

"What for?"

"This." He tugs my arm and I lose my balance. He catches my fall, pulling me against him, and his back hits the massive tree trunk. Startled and disoriented, my free hand lands on his shoulder blade. I glance up. His face is so close, his minty breath caresses my mouth. He stares at me for a second, then moves in and kisses me.

I'm immobilized, my heart hammering wildly. The kiss feels urgent and he pulls me closer, one hand moving to the back of my head. I don't know how long we stand pressed together like that, but the need to breathe forces me to pull back, and he lets me go. We're both gasping for air.

I stare at him, shaken by his kiss. Then without quite knowing why, I give his face a delayed, resounding slap.

"That ... that can never happen again," I tell him as I step back clumsily. What am I saying?

He doesn't answer, doesn't even touch his pink cheek, just stares at me.

"Why do you keep staring at me?" I ask with a little more force than necessary.

Sadness flickers over his face so fast I almost miss it. "Because you're beautiful," he says softly.

My heart misses a beat. This is dangerous. I suck in my bottom lip and try not to notice when he stares at my mouth. If I'm not careful, I could end up falling for him and that bothers me more than I'd like to admit.

I search for something to change the topic, trying to get onto safer ground. Then I remember: Adele.

"I found Adele was my ancestor, in my own world. Is that what you wanted me to know from the photo you gave me? The one of Valentino's tattoo?"

No response.

"If not, you might want to add that to your history books," I say in a snarky tone.

He doesn't look surprised. I scowl. "Did you already know?"

"I suspected," he replies.

"What else do you suspect?"

One side of his mouth hitches up at this. He's like a hot model. Creator help me.

"I suspect we'll be seeing each other again soon," he replies. "Fare-thee-well for now, *mon chaton*."

With a bow he steps away from the tree and slips away.

"Lily!"

Charlotte's call has me turning toward the house.

I look back. Mon Puce steps into the shadows, the darkness crowding him in until he vanishes like smoke.

I slump, then shake my head and breathe in deep. It doesn't help much.

I walk back to the house in a daze. That's the second time he's kissed me and my slaps don't seem to be much of a deterrent. I'm going to have to watch myself with him in future. I can feel my resolve weakening and I'm not sure how I feel about that.

When I glance back at the tree, I see no unnatural shadows, no glimmer of light. It occurs to me that he was going to talk to me about something, but that didn't eventuate.

"Stupid. Stupid." I shouldn't have gone off at him until he told me what he came to say. It could have helped the mission.

As I head inside the mansion, I pick at my nails in anxious frustration and call out an acknowledgement to Char. She responds from one of the drawing rooms, so I divert my course, my hunger forgotten.

Sometime later it occurs to me that Mon Puce managed to break through the safe perimeter of the estate.

How did he do that?

The thought bothers me.

Chapter Thirty-Five

The thing I have been dreading, happens. My nemesis-slash-frenemy, Alyse, meets Marc.

It's not like I wasn't already stressed, what with my diary going missing. Now this.

It was foolish to hope they might keep missing each other. I don't know why I'm so hung up over this, but I kind of hoped he'd stay a part of my story, hidden away until I could face what was going on between us.

No such luck.

Marc arrives right after lunch, and we exchange a heated look that makes me blush. He walks toward me with purpose, but Alyse blocks his path and pulls Cherie along to make introductions.

My smile slips and I look down. How long will it take for Alyse to ruin my reputation?

A footman taps me on the shoulder and hands me a letter. Relieved to have an excuse to exit the room, I slip out to read the missive. Anticipation lifts my spirits. It's a request to meet Mon Puce. Guess I'm going to find out what he came to tell me yesterday.

I locate the footman and give him instructions to deliver my reply. He leaves to do so and I pause. What excuse can I find to prolong my absence from the others?

Coming up empty, I sigh. The urge to bolt is strong, but I steel my emotions and take slow, measured steps to the drawing room.

Marc is unpacking a parcel, the introductions finished, so I slip in beside Charlotte.

Beginning the lesson, Marc calls us over to the portrait he's set up. I stay focused on the painting as he gives us some pointers on some modern art. Looks renaissance to me.

I glance to my left. Alyse is staring at Marc like she hasn't seen a man before.

Everything in me wants to throw myself at her in a takedown worthy of Brazilian jiu-jitsu. I even find myself in a ready stance before I realize what I'm doing, and that Marc is watching me. I straighten and avert my gaze, tucking a strand of hair behind my ear.

It comes as no surprise when Alyse flirts with Marc. Doesn't even miss a beat, does she? Straight off the bat, she's all over him like the measles.

I hide my disgust and decide to ignore her.

I will get through this.

I was starting to wonder if I'd ever see the end of that lesson, it dragged on for an eternity. I think I aged a few years.

I give myself a shake as Marc packs his things. I move to make my escape, but I'm stopped by his soft voice.

"Mademoiselle Lily, may I have a moment of your time?"

Slowly, I turn back to Marc with a fixed smile, not meeting his eyes.

Alyse stands. "Oh, Monsieur Coupier, I have so many questions after today's revelatory lesson. Would you mind?"

She steps between us and I see his jaw tighten. He clears his throat. "Of course, Mademoiselle. How can I be of service?"

I give up and leave the room.

Charlotte catches up with me and puts her arm through mine, walking with me.

"You know, Lily-chère, Monsieur Coupier spent a great deal of time today looking at you. I wonder if he noticed anyone else in the room at all."

I splutter in response. "I think you're imagining things, Charlotte."

She stops, halting me. "Lily Therriot, you need to open your eyes and look at what is staring you in the face."

Chapter Thirty-Six

I AM BACK IN the game, ready to play my part in the next big mission. Well, an unofficial mission. I'm going to meet Mon Puce, as arranged.

Given the location of our meeting, I dress in men's apparel. Then I slip outside and take one of Uncle's horses under the cover of darkness, departing with the hush of a cat burglar until I'm enough of a distance away to let my steed canter toward town.

This time, I've brought Justice. I smile wickedly.

When I reach my destination, I slide off my horse and attach a fake mustache to my upper lip. Then I walk my horse over to the tavern, handing the reins to a waiting retainer. I flick a coin his way and it disappears into his pockets with incredible speed, before he leads the panting beast away with soothing words.

I turn and head into the tavern. Tinny music is playing and the crowd is a little wild. I can't see Mon Puce anywhere. Disappointed, I keep to the edges and make my way toward the bar, holding my breath against the feral odors that assault my nose. Sweat, urine, and beer do not mix well.

That Mon Puce should request we meet here is not one of his finer ideas, and I'm grateful for my disguise as a man. I might look slight but at least my appearance won't tempt any of the mongrels in this bar. I hope.

I shudder and check that Justice is still swinging from my hip. She bolsters my sense of security, at any rate.

When I reach the counter, I hand the barman a coin. "Hot brandy. And hold the fleas."

He pockets the coin and gives me a look, then prepares a warmed-up brandy. He indicates a door to his left as he hands over my drink. A man is guarding the door and he nods at me.

Holding my drink, I push past some eager patrons and head to the door. I take a sip without thought. The alcohol is a little cheap tasting but goes down smooth.

I reach the door, the guard looks me up and down, then knocks and pushes the door open.

I nod in thanks and walk in. What's with all the subterfuge?

The door closes behind me and shuts out most of the noise. I take a bigger sip and walk toward a desk, looking around the empty room.

"You made it."

I spin and brandy sloshes over my hand. Mon Puce is leaning back against the door, arms crossed over his chest, a smirk on his face.

"Nice outfit." His eyes roam over me in a way that is far from pure.

I take another gulp of brandy, hiding my discomfort ... or nerves. I'm not sure which.

"Whcrc's my nccklacc?"

"What necklace?"

"The one you took. I'd like it back, thanks." Given it doesn't even belong to me.

"I forgot to bring it."

"Bring it next time. Now, why did you want to meet?"

He doesn't answer. In the silence, I swallow more brandy.

"Reluctant to give me your intel?" I raise my chin.

He smiles. "Why do I need a reason to see you?"

The room is looking foggy and I'm a bit dizzy. Ignoring that, I grab Justice with my free hand and unlatch her from my belt. I'm still angry about Kae.

I walk over to Mon Puce, trying to keep my balance. He stretches and shrinks before me. I shake my head.

"You need anod ... anodder ... annn ..." Annoyed, I poke out my tongue. Not at him—I'm trying to see if it's as swollen as it feels in my mouth. But it's hard to see. I sigh, frustrated.

The Flea's grin looks a mile wide, his face stretching to the side. So weird.

I shake my head again, raise my baton and finish what I was saying. "Mmm-meeting with Justice!"

There. I said it. Feeling proud, I swing my baton at his head. "For Kae!"

The baton goes through his head. One of his heads. Hold on, why does he have so many heads?

I swing again and still don't connect. Serious now, I drop my near-empty glass onto the carpet, where it adds to the myriad of stains already there. Then I grab Justice with both hands and try to hit Mon Puce.

It's like he's a ghost! I hear him laughing under his breath and his grin seems to get even wider.

"W-what's gone on? Gone-go-on-ing?" I try to pronounce the word and he laughs. Indignant, I point the baton at his face. One of them, anyway.

"You d-dare! I'm seriousss ab-bot thhhis!"

He raises several of his arms and one of them knocks my baby out of the way. I lose my grip and she falls to the ground. "Justice!"

I rush at one of him and he moves like the Flash in a DC comic, all of the fleas twisting around. He grabs me from behind and pulls me back against him. I thrash about, desperate.

Why am I so clumsy? Why is he so strong?

The rooms spins and my stomach gurgles in protest.

His mouth is right by my ear. "Lightweight," he says, his breath tickling my skin. "What am I going to do with you?"

Without warning, I'm swung up and held in his arms. That makes me dizzier and my head falls against his shoulder. It catches on my hat, pushes it off, and my hair tumbles out.

I groan, the light stinging my eyes. What is happening?

Something soft touches my forehead. Did he just kiss me? No, I must have imagined that. What I'm not imagining is my stomach threatening to erupt volcano-style into my throat. It's becoming intense.

I dry-heave and hear a curse. We're moving too fast and then I'm on a chair with a big jug on my lap, and Mon Puce is holding my hair back and rubbing my back. The dry heaving continues for a few minutes and dies down. Thank the Creator. I could have puked on Mon Puce.

Wait, that's a great idea! I turn around and try to force it up onto him, but he pushes my head around with another curse. "Are you deliberately trying to vomit on me?"

I stop pretending and giggle. He sighs.

Sensing the nausea has passed, I sit upright and Mon Puce gets up. He goes to the door—there are two of him now. Each opens a door and I hear him murmuring. He shuts the doors, turns and watches me for a minute, both of him leaning against a door with his arms crossed.

Another knock sounds. He opens the door and accepts something. Then he's back at my side, removing the jug and holding a drink to my lips. I'm not sure I can trust him, but when I realize it's water and that it tastes fresh, I gulp it down like my mouth was a desert and the drink was the first rain in years.

"Easy now. Not all at once, or you might really be sick."

He pulls it away and I grab for it, but then his face is there—just one now, thank the Creator. I look at his face up close and his expression seems tense. I poke him in the cheek and giggle again.

He chuckles and I touch his face again, light stubble tickling my fingertips.

Without meaning to, I start exploring his face with my fingers and my eyes. I smooth over his eyebrows and he quirks one up. I giggle again.

I don't know how long this continues before I notice the change in his gaze. Something dangerous sparks inside of me and my breathing becomes shallow. My fingers reach his lips and I freeze.

"I'm thirsty." I say the first thing that pops into my mind and yank my hand away. It works to dispel the moment.

Sighing again, Mon Puce holds the water to my mouth and I take another swig. Maybe a bit too much. I cough and he pats me on the back. I hiccup, and it makes me giggle again, until I'm a hiccupping, giggling mess sliding down the chair.

Then he's there, lifting me up and carrying me to a day bed I hadn't noticed. He puts me down on my side and then sits on the floor beside my head, his back against a wall. I stare at his profile. My hiccups fade and everything goes dark.

My eyelids unstick and my blurry surroundings become clear before I realize where I am. I push myself up slowly, my skull throbbing.

Mon Puce is gone. I scold myself for drinking the brandy. A wasted opportunity. Now I'll have to wait until I see him again before I get any intel.

I check my hidden watch and find I've been here about two hours.

I make a disapproving noise and try to stand, relieved I'm not dizzy anymore. I walk over to the desk.

There's a scribbled note next to a drink and a plate of potatoes smothered in gravy. The note says to consume slowly, so of course I want to gobble it down, but after a few bites I stop.

I test the drink and am amazed at how clean it tastes. Where did he get the water? Must be a well nearby. A secret one? He's one resourceful man.

Maybe it wouldn't be so bad to work with him. Maybe we could help each other out.

I mull this over as I fill up on water and another potato. Then brushing myself off, I pick up Justice from the chair and clip her onto my belt. My head pounds again and I wince.

I feel for my mustache and straighten it, pushing it back in place. Turning I collect my hat from the desk and stuff my hair back into it, slamming it down hard so it can survive the ride back.

Ugh. I have to ride back. My stomach is queasy at the thought.

I need a plan. If Mon Puce has left, I'll swing by the stable and collect my horse. Then we'll try a slow walk, even if it takes till morning to get home.

I walk over to the door and find it locked.

Huh?

Jiggling the lock doesn't work, so I knock a few times. Nothing. Would the window on the other side of the room be a viable escape route?

I'm halfway across the room when the door opens behind me.

I swing around. It's the guard. He surveys the room, sees my picked-at food and eyes me off.

I must look presentable enough because he steps into the room. "You'll find him outside." He jerks his head toward the entry to the establishment, so I thank him and brush past.

I keep to the sides again and take a hesitant breath when I exit the tavern. Ah, there's nothing like fresh, free-range air. Except when it's mingled with unpleasant odors from a tavern. I wrinkle my nose.

There's no sign of Mon Puce as I move down the steps. I wince, my brain still feeling like it has its own heartbeat. I head to the stables, and after a quick discussion and another coin toss to the stable boy, my horse is returned.

My mare brushes her nose into my palm. She's beautiful and I'm grateful for the ride. A walk on my own two feet would be nice, but unsafe.

I lead my horse out and spot Mon Puce leaning against a low, wooden beam of the veranda that wraps around the front of the tavern. Was he there before? I stop and call out to him, still wanting intel. In the same moment, Alyse bursts from the front door and runs down the steps.

"Mon P-lyse!"

They both look at me like I've grown two heads.

"*Mon Police?*[1] What, you have your own now? Where? I'd like to see—" She stops as she notices Mon Puce.

He straightens, quietly assessing her, while she looks a little bug-eyed.

"Er—"

"Friend of yours?" he asks me.

---

1. "Mon Police" means "My Police."

Gosh, darn it. Why couldn't he pretend like we didn't know each other?

Alyse now realizes two things. One—Mon Puce and I know each other. Two—she's just given away that she's not the man she's dressed as. Her voice is a little too high for that.

She squints at me in the light from the tavern and stables, and her eyes widen when Mon Puce walks over to me.

"I'm glad you're looking better," he says.

"You didn't tell me you had such handsome friends here, Lily. Why didn't you introduce us sooner?" Alyse's voice is a mix of accusing and sultry as she walks over, and I know she's referring to both Marc and Mon Puce.

"Mademoiselle, a pleasure," he says to Alyse before he turns to me. "Will you be all right to travel back?" In one stroke he has dismissed her. I'm finding it hard to come to terms with the fact that he hasn't flirted with her. Doesn't he flirt with every woman?

"I'll ... be fine. *Merci*, Monsieur. I'd best be off."

I climb onto my horse, my queasiness returning at the sudden movement upwards. I teeter for a moment, unbalanced, but two hands grip my waist to secure me.

"I'm okay. I'm okay. *Merci*."

His hands slide down slowly and I frown, wondering if he took the opportunity to touch my cheek. And I'm not talking about my face.

He's smirking again and I open my mouth to give him a piece of my mind, but he stops me.

"Shall I send one of my men to escort you home, or shall I take you myself?"

"Neither will be necessary, thank you."

"Oh, I think it is. There's enough room for both of us on that horse, and you need someone to anchor you in or you might slide off during the ride."

"You shall do no such thing." I blush at the thought and am glad for the semi-darkness.

"Pity."

I ignore him and notice Alyse is staring at us in shock again. For the first time ever, she appears uncertain. Well, that's something.

"Good eve to you both," I say. I move the horse forward, but Mon Puce grabs the reins and stops me. Well, he stops my horse.

"*Je suis désolé*,[2] Mademoiselle, but you are not in a fit state to ride on your own. If you won't have me then I propose one of my men escorts you both, and that you share a steed."

The steel in his tone stops me from arguing. Much as I'd hate to share a ride with my arch-nemesis, at least it would be more appropriate than sharing with the Flea.

I sigh and look at Alyse with a cocked eyebrow. "Well?"

She doesn't look too enthused either but she agrees. I move back and he gives her a boost in front of me. She seems to enjoy that and I roll my eyes.

"Hold tight to her." Mon Puce says, his voice brooking no argument as he looks at me.

"Davide," he calls. One of his men appears out of the shadows from behind the stable. Mon Puce speaks to him and gestures to us. The man—Davide—nods and goes into the stable while Mon Puce ties Alyse's horse to mine.

Mon Puce looks hard at Alyse. "Ride carefully with her. Take it slow, or you might end up with bile on you."

She makes a disgusted noise and he grins.

I shake my head but am grateful he's given Alyse incentive to be kind to me, even if it's only for her own sake.

Mon Puce's grin fades a little as he sets his focus back on me. He moves closer. "My man will follow you both and ensure you get home safely. Remember to hold tightly to your friend here. I don't want to hear about you falling off your horse, understand?"

"Fine, whatever." I'm embarrassed and annoyed that he's talking down to me, like I'm a child.

He leans closer with a serious expression and grips my ankle. "If I hear anything about you falling off, I will come steal you away." One side of his mouth lifts then, so I'm not sure if he's joking. I swallow.

"I won't fall."

Our staring contest is broken by Davide riding out of the stable.

---

2. "Je suis désolé" means "I'm sorry"

Mon Puce steps back and I can breathe again. Alyse urges our horse forward. Hers follows placidly at the gentle tugging of the rope. The Flea's man follows us out.

I look back for a moment. Mon Puce stands there with a sad sort of smile.

"Why were you there Alyse? Did you follow me?" I break the silence around twenty minutes later.

"I don't know what you mean, Lily. Why were you there anyway? Enjoying a secret tryst?"

"I don't know what you mean, Alyse." I throw her own words back at her. I'm glad her hair is stuffed into her hat, or I'd be choking on it by now.

"Fine. I intercepted your little love note with that exceptional gentleman. Seems you've been keeping secrets, Lily."

"Love note? Don't be ridiculous."

"Looked like something was going on between you two from where I was standing. Hmm ... I wonder what Monsieur Coupier would think if he knew. Or perhaps he wouldn't care."

Guilt creeps in. "Alyse, nothing is going on with either gentleman, though it's none of your business. And why were you going through my things?"

"You've been acting suspicious. I needed to know if you could still be trusted to fulfill the mission. Can you blame me?"

Blame her? Yes. Yes, I can. However, she's made a good point. I'll need to be more careful around her in future.

The ride continues with me fielding more of Alyse's questions about tonight and making non-committal responses. At least she thinks it's something other than Vestige business. That's a good thing, right?

We eventually arrive home and I'm exhausted. I tumble into bed and sleep it off.

When I wake the next morning, I need to let off some steam. I head to Uncle's secret training den where I take out my frustration on a punching bag that reminds me of Alyse's face.

Chapter Thirty-Seven

THE NEXT FEW DAYS sees me fighting hard in Uncle's basement, the cracked and pockmarked walls my haven as I wrack my brain on how to find Jasper. I pummel a punching bag and practice martial arts with some of Uncle's men to let off some steam.

On the third night, after collapsing from exhaustion, I have a strange, vivid dream. A red brick warehouse stands stark against the sky. It feels familiar, pulling me in, insistent. I hear "Jasper" whispered in the wind. I try to move away, but the ground shifts beneath my feet and the warehouse is in front of me again. An idea curls inside me like a certainty I can't ignore—Jasper could be there.

The following morning, I can't get it out of my mind. I call Peron and ask for his opinion. He surprises me by suggesting I find out where it is. "If it's real, you should go and check it out," he says.

The tension eases in my shoulders, like a weight has been lifted. I have purpose again—until Peron says, "Take Alyse with you." Some of the weight falls back on.

I shake my head and use V-Map—the Vestige online map service, made available in every dimension we've discovered—to look for warehouses matching the one in my dream. The sooner I locate Jasper, the sooner I can separate myself from Alyse.

After hours of searching, I finally found it. It's real. The rush of victory fills me, lifting me like I'm walking on air. For the first time in what feels like forever, I smile. A real smile. And for once, I'm actually happy.

The warehouse is a three-hour ride away. Has Jasper been that close, all this time? Is he still alive?

I share the intel with Peron and we loop in Alyse. She looks irritable but doesn't say anything, so I write it off as another Alyse-ism.

The next day, we set off with a few guards on the premise of visiting a relative.

I second-guess myself throughout the journey. What if nothing's there? Will Peron trust me ever again? I have to remind myself that even if nothing comes of this, at least we're doing something. That's an improvement, right?

I hope so.

After an angst-filled ride, we arrive at the warehouse, which looks abandoned. We leave our horses tied in a copse of trees nearby and ready our weapons. Then we creep toward the building. Though if anyone were here, they would have seen us by now.

We move as one unit, using hand gestures before we enter, and split into three groups. It's dim and cool inside. Weak beams of light filter through a few high windows. The smell reminds me of a farm I often stayed at as a child.

A quick assessment shows the warehouse is empty. Alyse shoots me an annoyed look but I strive to ignore her. Hey, at least we're safe.

We search the building, rummaging through the jumble of old, busted-up farming equipment, bales of hay and empty jars.

What did they use the jars for? I inspect each object with a keen intensity. Searching for something, anything, to explain why I dreamed of this place. A clue of Jasper.

After a couple of hours, I can see on everyone's faces what they won't say out loud—that this was a wasted day.

Confused and feeling let down myself, I turn to say we should finish up and head back, but my foot catches on something. I stumble, my feet tangling beneath me, and throw my arms out to grab an empty crate. It helps to slow the momentum, but the crate topples. I hit the ground with a crash, rolling to lessen the impact.

Shock and pain reverberate along my side and I lie there, dazed and coughing in the dust that was disturbed by my fall. Pierre—one of our men—calls out "Mademoiselle!" He runs over and helps me sit up.

I glare at whatever just tried to take me out—but then, something glints beneath the mess of scattered hay. My breath stills. Nestled there, barely visible, is a latch.

A latch? My pulse quickens.

I crawl forward to move the hay aside, wiping away the heavy layer of dust covering the area. The line of a trapdoor emerges. Excitement bubbles inside me and I catch Pierre's eye. We try to open the latch, but it won't budge.

He calls out to the team and the men run over, Alyse right behind them. Pierre grabs a tool off his belt and after a minute of grunting he manages to break open the latch. Louis steps in to help, and with a mighty heave, they pull up the trapdoor.

The door slams backward onto the floor and we step away, covering our faces from a cloud of dust. A gaping dark hole awaits us, a few cobwebs around the hinges.

I look at the team and see hope reflected in their eyes. We pull out our flashlights. The beams illuminate stairs leading down into some type of cellar.

"Louis, stand watch," Pierre says.

Louis nods and the rest of us follow Pierre down into the room. Alyse gasps. This is not an ordinary cellar. It's more like a secret treasure room. Every place I shine my flashlight, I see relics—timber crosses, silver swords, a bronze chalice, a few dusty leather-bound books, some old jewels.

Pierre sends a comm back to the house to bring an excavation team over. Alyse rushes over to the jewels like it's Christmas morning, while the men look at some weaponry.

I shine my beam along the wall and something catches my eye. I scan it again. There. I hold my breath and step closer. With gentle but shaking fingers, I pick up a small jewelry box from a shelf and wipe off cobwebs and dust.

It's silver, inlaid with similar symbols to the tiny box I found back at the Neumand estate. The woman on top wears a crown. Her long dress was once coated in azure paint, but I can see where it has been worn away over time.

I can't believe it. Another jewelry box. Why here? How?

I brush my fingers across a tiny latch on the box. The lid springs open.

Inside is a silver ring, entwined in a filigree pattern, with a gem that is ultramarine in color by the light of my flashlight. It's beautiful. I pick it up and slide it onto my finger.

Light erupts from the ring and fills my vision. I stumble back, falling hard on my behind. I barely manage to keep hold of my flashlight and the box.

The light fades. All sound vanishes as the world holds its breath.

I'm in a royal court. A woman in a dark blue dress sits on a throne. She wears the ring but is talking to an aide, her face in profile. She's like a ruler in every way. Then she turns her head and locks eyes with me, sending shockwaves through my entire being.

She's the spitting image of Mom.

Before I can work out what this means, the vision changes. I see a man fighting a group of Sentinels. He has a wicked scar on his inner right arm. He faces me then and all I see are his eyes. Silver eyes.

Recognition floods me: Alain.

"Mademoiselle!" Someone is shaking me. The vision fades and I open my eyes. Several flashlights blind me. I squint my eyes shut and turn my head away.

"Ugh. Get that light out of my face."

"Désolé, Mademoiselle."

I turn back, feel around for my flashlight, then wave it around. The concerned faces of my team look back at me.

A chill makes my skin prickle and I'm aware of two things. One, my butt hurts, and two, I'm sitting on the dusty dirt floor in the hidden room.

Pierre and Andre help me to stand up. Andre grunts and my paranoia sets in. Have I eaten too much this week?

"You know, many people say I have a slight build," I say in my defense.

"It's not you, Mademoiselle. It's my elbow," Andre says as he rubs it.

"Oh, I'm sorry. What happened?"

"I busted it in the training room yesterday."

"Sorry, I wasn't referring to that. What just happened here?" A twinge of guilt tells me it was my high kick that connected with Andre's elbow yesterday. But I can't dwell on bygones, given the current situation.

Pierre answers my question. "You were sitting as if in a trance and you were unresponsive, Mademoiselle. Are you unwell?"

"I ... was thinking. Deeply. I needed to concentrate. Sorry." I decide to keep the visions to myself, relieved when they seem to accept my weak explanation.

Louis signals from above. "We have company."

"That must be our excavation team," Pierre says. "They arrived faster than I anticipated."

Alyse rushes up the steps. Bet she wants to take the credit for this find.

The men and I follow. When no one is looking, I tuck the box with my flashlight into a hidden pocket in the folds of my dress.

Alyse screams. The men glance at each other, alarmed. We all draw our weapons and rush up the stairs.

Alyse is being strong-armed by a masked man, a knife to her throat. It's a Sentinel. Louis looks ready to fight him.

"No one move!" the man shouts.

I hear a rush of feet behind me and spin to see more than a dozen masked or hooded Sentinels run in through another entryway. They fan out and I swallow, unease trickling down my spine.

"What do you want?" I ask.

A man on my right speaks. "We're here to stop you. Either you come with us, or you die. Be assured that no one is getting out of here alive unless you are in our custody."

The air is electric and my heart pounds.

"Bring it!" I yell and attack the man closest to me. My men plunge into the mass of swarming anger and prejudice, and the fight begins in earnest, everyone growling or grunting.

I punch, block, spin, kick, duck, twist and elbow my way through crazy after crazy, dimly aware of Alyse whimpering. Justice saves me more than once, but things are kicked up a notch when a Sentinel pulls out a sword. It glances off Justice and I jump back. My wrist narrowly escapes a blade that could slice me open.

Pierre leaps in front of me. "Get out of here!"

What? Then I see he's got a sword. In that case ... I look around and block the blow from another weirdo, jamming Justice where it hurts. He goes down, howling.

Alyse has managed to get out of her captor's hold. I run toward her, intending to help, but she pulls out her weapon and disables him in a flash.

"Let's get out of here!" I yell. For once, she agrees with me.

We run toward a less crowded exit and fight our way outside.

There's a Sentinel with our horses. We race toward him and Alyse and I attack together. He goes down, knocked out cold. We turn to untie our horses.

"It's okay, darling," I say softly to my mare. She seems a bit jittery but calms as I stroke her.

I climb on, grab the other men's horses by their reins and lead them back to the warehouse. Alyse frowns at me like I'm crazy.

"Go, if you have to. I want to help the men," I tell her.

She hesitates, then shakes her head and rides off. I watch her for a moment, but the groaning of the man we took down spurs me to action.

A blood-spattered Pierre runs out of the warehouse. He sees me riding toward him and looks relieved. He sprints over and climbs onto his horse.

"Andre and Louis are coming. They're bringing the leader as hostage," he says. "Where's Mademoiselle Alyse?"

"She headed back on her own," I say. "Didn't want to stick around, you know ... in case ..."

He nods and considers me. "You stayed."

"*Oui.*"

"I don't know if that was stupid or brave. But I appreciate you getting the horses."

We smile and he shakes his head. We're interrupted by a screaming Sentinel who runs out and throws an axe at us.

We jostle the horses back and a whoosh of air blows the tiny hairs on my face as the axe whizzes past my head. The Sentinel runs toward us. Heart hammering, I turn to face him, ready to jump off and fight. Pierre holds his hand out to stay me.

The man reaches us and somehow Pierre's foot lands in the man's face. He goes down and I slump forward on my horse gasping and laughing and crying. I almost died, and Pierre took out my would-be killer like that.

A few minutes later, we hear a shout. Andre and Louis approach, dragging a bound man between them. They look battered but alive. I sigh in relief.

We head back in one piece and I almost feel sorry for the bound and blindfolded Sentinel. What's in store for him? Vestige are going to want intel on the Sentinels and I'm not sure I want to know how they're going to get it. But they can't be as bad as the Sentinels.

I glance back at the warehouse. Was that one of their hideouts? Headquarters? I guess we'll find out.

I keep an eye out for Alyse but we don't catch up with her. She must have been in a mad rush to get home.

By the time we arrive at the secret tunnel, we're all smiles and joking around. The men lead the hostage in and soon we exit the tunnel and enter Uncle's basement.

I walk up the stairs and sneak past a few maids to get to my room. Wasting no time, I clean up and realize I'm still wearing the ultramarine ring. I inspect it. In the light of day, it looks like lapis lazuli. Carefully, I remove the ring and place it back in the tiny jewelry box, which I wrap in a silk shawl. Then I hide it under a loose floorboard.

I call for a bath. After a luxuriating rest in the warm tub, I dry off and dress, giving my dirty and torn clothes to a trusted maid who's part of Vestige.

I head to the kitchen for a bite to eat and run into Charlotte and Cherie. "Where's Alyse?" I ask.

"Isn't she with you?"

"No. She left early after we visited our relative."

"We haven't seen her. Who was her escort?"

"Never mind. I'll go check her room."

I don't find her in her room. Or anywhere in the house. Or the garden. She must be with Uncle.

I head back down to the basement and Uncle stops me. "Good, you're here. I was about to send someone to get you. Where's Alyse?"

"She's not here? With you?"

"I thought she was with you."

Dread starts a drumroll and courses through me like roiling black smoke, making it difficult to breathe.

Chapter Thirty-Eight

Alyse didn't make it home.

Uncle's expression is grim. "Something must have happened on her way back. Pierre mentioned she rode off on her own after the attack."

"Yes, but oh—this is all my fault!"

"How is it your fault?"

"It was my idea to go to that warehouse. And I didn't stop Alyse from leaving first."

"We gained a hostage and a horde of treasure. Mademoiselle Alyse is a trained agent. She chose to ride off and leave you there."

Uncle calls the men in and instructs them to search for Alyse. I offer to join, but he stops me.

"I don't want to be searching for two mesdames now. I'd rather know you're safe here, Lily."

So I stay. I stay and imagine all the horrible things that could be happening to Alyse right now.

I shake my head to dispel the images and fall back on my bed, glaring up at the darkening sky. Why do I care? Why am I worrying like this? Alyse is a manipulative bully. Maybe she ran off for a break from Vestige ... or from me.

And still. We've been on a pretty good streak of normalcy these days. Bit of a stretch to call her a friend, but she was more colleague-like.

Now I feel responsible for her safety. Yet it's out of my hands. Uncle and his men are searching for her, so I must trust them. Trust she'll come back in one piece. Trust that her father and the Board won't threaten my job. Or my life.

Hours turn into days with no sign of Alyse. My trepidation grows and with it, guilt. I close my bedroom window and draw the curtain shut against a darkening sky, the heavy air pregnant with trouble.

This is all my fault. If I hadn't had that dream, if I hadn't thought it might mean something, if I hadn't told Peron ... on and on my thoughts go, threatening to crucify me.

A loud crack of thunder jolts me. The curtain lights up, before returning to darkness. It feeds my ominous feelings.

I climb into bed and pull the covers over my head, trying to block it out.

I become a shut-in as one week progresses into the next, fighting dark waves of depression and guilt. Fear too—that I will be removed from my post because of this. Uncle calls off the search, planning to tell the Vestige board that Alyse is missing. Presumed dead or a deserter.

The girls are confused at my behavior, having been told Alyse is visiting a dear friend who went into labor the day she went missing. That she was called away during our trip.

Uncle must be fed up, because he pulls me out of my room and takes me to his office. There, he force-feeds me and tells me to snap out of it. After a long lecture, I start to pull myself together. It's not all my fault. I have to believe that.

At his insistence, I drag myself upstairs to see the girls, who've been worried about me. They take one look at me and rush over to hug me.

"Don't you ever scare us like that again, Lily!" Char says. "Our père forbade us to enter your room. We were starting to wonder if we'd ever see you again."

"I'm sorry. It was selfish of me," I say. My behavior was unhealthy. Another reason I'd have counselling on offer for Vestige agents if I were in charge.

I spend an hour reassuring them I'm all right. That I won't keep hiding away or going without food. Their friendship is like a balm to my weary soul.

Then they tell me I have a secret admirer. That surprises me.

They bring out a beautiful vase of the prettiest flowers I've ever seen: roses in a kind of arctic blue shade, mixed with white lilies. They hand me a sealed letter from the admirer.

"Oh, read it for us, will you? Please? Please?" Cherie says.

Uncertain, I open and read it to myself first to make sure there's nothing embarrassing in the contents.

Relieved but intrigued, I read aloud a poem about not giving up and trusting in the Creator and those around me to help when I'm overwhelmed. It's encouraging, but unsigned.

The girls try to guess who could have given it to me. I admire the fine script and wonder myself. It could be Marc, but how would he know what I've gone through?

My musings are interrupted by a maid, who says Uncle has asked for me again. I leave the girls and head back down to the basement, pocketing the letter for later consideration.

On arriving, I'm told Peron has called to speak with me, so I take his call on the V-Screen. I'm surprised when he asks for my updates from the time Alyse arrived here. Not sure why, I oblige and give him a quick run-through.

Then he tells me that there are inconsistencies between my updates and the reports Alyse had been giving them.

"Inconsistencies? How? What do you mean?" I ask.

"I believe Alyse has been fabricating information to give the Board ammunition against you. I had a feeling that might be the case, given that her accounts of you were out of character. But I haven't been able to convince the Board that we need your official statement."

I sit in stunned silence. Why have I wasted the past two weeks worrying about someone who was trying to sabotage me behind my back? No wonder they all think I'm incompetent.

"Lily, don't be too concerned yet. I'll revise our reports and see how the Board reacts. Though now I'm wary of Stefan Georges. I suspect he's behind the Board pushing for this to be your final mission."

My stomach churns as blood rushes to my face. A sense of injustice grips me.

Peron must see my inner turmoil ... or at least my red face. "You know Lily, I believe there are higher powers at work. I believe they have a different plan for you. You might be surprised."

I let out a quick laugh and squeeze my eyes tight, pinching the skin between my eyes. "I hope so, Sir."

I am facing the cliff edge in my choice of employment. If I don't want to bow in defeat, my only option is to believe the Creator has a bigger purpose for me. Perhaps the Creator will turn things around. If not, there's always a job with the Relic Hunters—although that would mean never seeing my family again.

I skip over that thought in case I lose my resolve. Instead, I look at Peron on the V-Screen.

He confesses that he hasn't told the Board Alyse is missing, expecting there will be an uproar. "I'll give it a few more days. Maybe we can still avoid all hell breaking loose."

I sag into my seat and breathe a bit easier, grateful to delay the inevitable blame. Given what Alyse has been telling them, it'll be the final straw to remove me from Vestige forever. And maybe from the world.

I can almost feel the pitter-patter of microscopic feet as agitation crawls up my diaphragm toward my throat. My fingers curl and I wish I had claws. With my short nails I can't even scratch the desk. I stop short from pounding it and breathe fast through my nose instead.

My anger at Alyse's deceit is red hot. If she were here, I would strike her down in a heartbeat.

The hateful emotion is halted by the thought that her actions may have caught up with her. Maybe she has got what she deserved.

My conscience reminds me of what my parents have always taught: follow the Creator's teaching and forgive.

I don't want to forgive Alyse. Not even a little. But an annoying little voice reminds me: holding a grudge is like locking yourself in a cage, and bitterness? It's poison. Do I really want to let her live rent-free in my head and ruin my life? Ugh. No.

With a deep sigh, I let it go—well, I try. Forgiveness is supposed to set you free, right? So, I close my eyes, take a shaky breath, and send up a silent prayer for strength to forgive her.

When I open my eyes, Peron is studying me, his brow furrowed. The silence is heavy.

I need to shift gears—fast. My mind lands on the Protector's jewelry box and the ring I found inside. Turning to the V-Screen, I finally confess to Peron what I found. "I took them with me," I admit.

His eyebrows shoot up. "That's ... unexpected. Where are they? Can I see?"

"They're in my room." I leave for a moment and go up to my room to get them.

Back in uncle's basement, I unwrap the box and show Peron, along with the ring.

He leans close, his nose filling my screen. I tell him about the vision I had of the queen.

Peron leans back and stares at me for a moment while he considers what I've divulged.

"You know, Lily, I've heard rumors of a Protector who became a queen in the ARK1 dimension. It was during the Middle Ages. From memory, there was a war or a plague of some sort in our Earth dimension. The Vestige elders at the time felt the pendant would be safer where you are now."

"So they brought it here?"

"So I've heard. A Protector was chosen soon after the pendant arrived with its keeper. She later married the king. It was returned to our dimension upon her passing, once things were safer."

"Wow. You know what's super weird, boss?"

"What?"

"In my vision, the queen looked identical to my mother."

That gives him pause.

Now I feel silly. "Perhaps my mind wanted me to see something comforting or familiar. Maybe my mind was exhausted and made it all up." I laugh.

Though it didn't seem that way.

"But then how did you know she was a queen?" asks Peron.

"Well, the figure on the jewelry box wears a crown."

"Touché. Hold on. Let me do some quick investigating."

I wait while Peron uses his super access to get into the Vestige vault of secrets, as I like to call it. After about fifteen minutes of twiddling my thumbs (okay, picking at my nails), Peron comes back on screen.

"I've got it. The pendant was taken to the République de L'Aurente around 1340, right after the Hundred Years war began in our dimension, and before the Black Plague. A protector was chosen, by the name of Éléonore … I can't find a last name. She was sixteen years old and reigned as Protector from 1341 to 1402."

I calculate. "Sixty-one years. That's a long time."

"She married King Claude—they would have been powerful allies—though it is said she was quite beautiful so that could also be a reason. She survived her husband by fifteen years. Then the pendant was taken back to France by its keeper."

"What about the ring she was wearing?"

"Hmm … it doesn't say anything about a ring here. I'll need to do some more investigation."

"I'd like to know more about her genealogy too, if you can. Please."

"Of course. You've got me intrigued, Lily. Never fear, I won't stop researching this until I find something solid. You can be sure of that."

"Thanks, boss."

"No need to thank me, Lily. You've just made my job more interesting. I'll need you to send me the ring and box though. And keep this to yourself. Let's be discreet until we know what we're dealing with. Agreed?"

"Agreed."

We finish the call and I send him the artefacts through the V-mail express, my nickname for the time travel tech we use to send items through the multiverse.

On my way back to my room, I stop. "I forgot." I groan. I didn't mention the vision of Alain and my previous run-ins with him.

Forget it. I'll tell Peron next time. For now, I'll do some serious reflection.

Sitting on my bed, I trace the calluses that have formed on my palms since arriving at Vestige. Each one marks a lesson learned, a failure overcome. Am I truly stronger, or just better at hiding the trembling?

The priest's words echo: "With the Creator, all things are possible." I consider this, then whisper my name—"Lily Destin"—testing how it feels in my mouth now. Different. I can still be a klutz sometimes, but something's changed in me.

A certainty settles in my bones: I am made for this mission. Chosen.

My fists curl with purpose as I kneel to pray. For my soul, for Alyse's. If the Creator has a plan, I need to see it soon.

Chapter Thirty-Nine

The sky is starting to lighten outside when I'm woken by someone shaking me. My eyes snap open and I see one of the Vestige maids. She's smiling but a little frantic.

"What is it?" I say in a raspy voice.

"It's Mademoiselle Alyse. She's alive!"

What?

"She arrived back on the property a few minutes ago, alone. Come."

Throwing off my covers, I grab a dressing gown and race out the door behind her.

She leads me down to Uncle's den.

Uncle is already there, wearing his bedclothes, along with two of his men. They must have been on duty outside, as they are fully dressed and don't look like they've just been woken by a shocking discovery.

I move closer. Alyse sits on a couch facing the men. Greasy strands of blonde hair hang like a curtain over one hollow cheek, the other mottled purple-yellow where someone's knuckles found their mark. Dirt crusts the beds of her bitten-down nails, and her collarbone juts sharp against skin that's lost its luster. When our eyes lock, something flares in her—a spark in the ashes—and her spine uncurls until she's no longer cowering but facing me.

"Lily. I must speak with Mademoiselle Lily. In private," she says. Her desperation pushes through the veil of fatigue lining her face.

I make eye contact with Uncle. I can tell he's concerned, but he gives me a slight nod. He motions to his men, who withdraw and close the door.

Surprised at the gratitude spreading through me at Alyse's recovery, I step toward her. She looks lost and forlorn and so unlike the Alyse I know, that I chide myself for not wanting to trust her.

"Alyse, I'm glad to see you. We thought we'd lost you. What happened?"

"It was the Sentinels. They captured me on the way back."

I gasp. How did she survive?

Alyse licks her dry lips. Her grimy hands twist on a cup of water. "They ... they tortured me for two days until they realized I couldn't help them. I don't know why they held on to me for so long after that, or why they let me live, but I found out something, Lily. Something you need to know."

Something in her tone draws me closer and I crouch down before her, looking into her eyes.

"What is it, Alyse?"

"I found him. I found Jasper."

What? For a moment I'm stunned. Alyse leans forward, spilling water on her skirt. She grabs my wrist with a grubby hand. There is something else mingled with the dirt under her fingernails. My nose wrinkles with the stench that wafts from her at this close range. I swallow my aversion.

"What do you mean, you found Jasper?" I ask.

Her expression looks severe for a split second before she ducks her head. I must have imagined it. She releases me and reaches into the folds of her rumpled and soiled dress, pulling out a crumpled piece of paper. With shaking fingers, she hands it to me.

I take it and unfold it several times. A diagram drawn in red-brown ink.

No ... a jolt shocks my system. It's blood.

I don't recognize the image at first, but then it starts to make sense. It's a warehouse, not unlike the one we explored. This one is closer to the sea. I know, because I remember riding past it the day we found Jasper's previous house. It was perhaps a couple of miles away.

"I know where this is. And you say Jasper is there?"

"The Sentinels have him. But they haven't found the necklace—yet. You have to save him, Lily!"

"How did you find this out?"

"I heard the men talking when they thought I was still passed out. They took me there one day and I heard them talking, saying he was there."

Something doesn't feel right, but I look up at Alyse and her eyes beg me to believe her. Everything in me wants to.

After what she's gone through, I have to give this a shot. It's worth the risk. I don't see why she'd jeopardize the mission with everything that's at stake. There has to be a level of trust if we're to see this out.

"How many Sentinels were there?"

"About four, not including the men who brought me there."

I refold the paper and nod to her. "I will find him," I say.

Alyse seems to deflate and gives me the first heartfelt smile I've ever seen from her. It makes her look pretty.

I call Uncle back in and he orders one of his men to carry Alyse to her chamber, where a warm bath and hot meal await. She looks exhausted and I know she'll be sleeping for the next few days.

When they're gone, I stop Uncle. Seeing my look, he closes the door and turns to me, eyes questioning.

"I have one more mission and I'll need a few men."

"What did Alyse say?"

"She said she knows where our target is being kept."

"Where?"

I pull out the folded paper and watch his expression change from disquiet to realization.

He looks at me again. "Are you sure about this?"

"I am," I say. I hope I'm doing the right thing.

After another searching look, Uncle nods. "I'll have men ready within the hour. I'll brief Monsieur Davies." He means Peron.

"*Merci.*"

"Be careful."

"I will."

Chapter Forty

An hour later, I've had breakfast and am dressed and ready in Uncle's den.

He enters, trailed by five men, and gives us instructions about our covert rescue mission. We check our weapons then make our way down the tunnel to a waiting carriage.

The day is gloomy, and a light chill wind is blowing. It makes me eager to fight.

The bumpy journey is a quiet one, save for a few jokes between the men. Several hours later, after a quick pit stop and stretch, we pull into a secluded area about 250 meters away from the warehouse. This warehouse is painted light blue. It's newer and larger.

I swing my arms and do other stretches to become more limber. The men roll their shoulders and heads, gearing up for the snatch-and-grab we're hoping the mission will be.

I draw in a steady breath, forcing myself to focus. Jasper being here changes everything. It makes the risk feel bigger, heavier. This isn't just about getting kicked out of Vestige. It's about something far more important.

If the Sentinels have the pendant, if they figure out how to control it, or if they find the Protector and control them, then we're all doomed. Countless lives hang in the balance, even history itself.

I won't let that happen. I'm going to put a stop to this, once and for all. This is my destiny. I can feel it.

Movement from the men signals it's time to leave. We get into position and stake out the perimeter for fifteen minutes. Then, one by one, the men run toward the warehouse, using the nearby trees as cover.

I follow behind and we station ourselves by the north and south entrances.

The man standing closest to my entrance, Xavier, goes in. We wait until he comes back a few minutes later, giving us the all-clear. We slip inside and I take care not to trip over the unconscious bodies, courtesy of Xavier.

We head through the passageways, scanning rooms as we pass, but find them all vacant.

All is quiet as we cover ground until the entire south side of the warehouse has been checked, upper and lower levels. There's no sign of Jasper. Or anyone, for that matter.

Perhaps our other men will find him. Xavier gives us a signal and we nod, agreeing that we need to continue through to the other half of the building. He creeps up to a heavy wooden door and listens behind it. We hear a muffled sound and go on the alert.

With a great shove, Xavier pushes open the door, but there's no one inside. We walk through a long, narrow corridor to another door. There are clear sounds of fighting on the other side.

We're in Sentinel territory, so I reach for protection Justice can't provide—my Vestige Zapr pistol, a sleek, wire-free taser manufactured to look like an old-fashioned gun so it blends in. Uncle gave it to me before I left the house, saying it's a new product Peron would want me to have at a time like this.

Xavier shoves the door again and it bursts open. Inside, three of our men are fighting off about twenty Sentinels.

We rush in to join them. Quick and quiet, I knock out ten Sentinels with my Zapr. It fires like a laser but stuns like a thunderclap. I wince in sympathy as the last man goes down. Around me, jaws slacken and eyes widen. Xavier looks my way, his face a mirror of the others. Yet his lips are parted, not in horror, but in something close to awe.

Together with my colleagues, it doesn't take long for us to knock out the rest of the Sentinels.

When the dust settles, we check in with each other. Joseph has a cut above his elbow and Jean must have been punched in the face, but other than that, we're all good.

I look around and my heart sinks. There's no way Jasper is here, not unless there's a secret compartment in the walls. Disappointment and hurt war with my anger at Alyse, but a sound draws my attention to a railing above us.

A lone figure in a dark cloak stands watching, slow clapping as if mocking us.

I'm tempted to use my laser on him, but I only have twenty shots left. No point using it if he isn't attacking us.

"Bravo," the man says. "You do not disappoint. Though bringing the devil's weapon was *la triche*."[1]

Whatever. I raise an eyebrow at him.

He chuckles. "Well, well. If it isn't our *petite* Protector. We've been waiting for you, Mademoiselle."

What? I look at the others and see furrowed brows and clenched jaws. Jean's hand freezes mid-reach for his weapon.

"Don't try to hide it. We know you are The One. Believe me, your friend could not have lied when we made her hurt."

What? Alyse told them I was the Protector? Then sent me to my doom. She set me up! That lying, scheming—

"Oh, this is sublime! You believed her, that we had something you needed? Well, no matter. You will help us find it. Then *we* will be the ones in charge." The Sentinel gives off Darth Vader vibes.

"What are you talking about?!" I say. "I'm not who you think I am. Alyse was lying to you. She'd say anything to save her own skin. And I will never help you locate anything that can give you power."

His persistent use of the plural dawns on me. An uneasy feeling settles in my stomach.

"This is a trap," I say to no one in particular. Then I feel stupid for pointing out the obvious.

"*Oui*, Mademoiselle Destin."

---

1. "la triche" means "cheating"

Destin? My hands sweat and I grip my gun tighter. Alyse gave them my real name. Her betrayal runs deeper than I thought. It was foolish to come here.

The sound of running footsteps has me looking around.

More men than I can count swarm onto the floor from every direction—I'm guessing two hundred.

My men and I put our backs to each other to face the growing circle of danger around us. This is my fault for listening to Alyse. I hope to the Creator these men don't die for my mistake.

"Bit much, don't you think?" I call above.

"We don't know what your powers are, Mademoiselle. We aren't taking any chances."

The irony of this is not lost on me as I take note of my situation.

We're surrounded.

At a whistle from the cloaked speaker, the Sentinels rush toward us.

Chapter Forty-One

THEY SWARM, A BLUR of movement and chaos crashing toward us. My body reacts before my mind can catch up. Every instinct drilled into me over the years takes over, sharper, faster than ever before. No hesitation. No fear. Just action.

Blows rain down, each strike a test, but I meet them head-on. Justice is an extension of my body, every parry and counterstrike fueled by sheer force and calculated precision. I twist, I lunge, my muscles burning with the effort—every ounce of martial skill I've mastered surging through me in perfect rhythm.

The Sentinels' movements are deliberate, coordinated, relentless. My blood turns to ice. This isn't combat. The Sentinels are stalking prey.

I grip my weapon tighter, forcing myself to move, but my mind betrays me, flashing through faces I may never see again. My family. My friends. The people who have come to mean everything. A hollow ache follows—the sorrow of words left unsaid, love unspoken. After so much angst, I've found a place to belong.

Something rises in me, a determination to survive this. My resolve hardens. Empowered, I surge forward. And the battlefield swallows me whole.

We fight, we push forward, but for every soldier we take down, two more rise in his place. The odds are suffocating. And in the back of my mind, a thought lingers, unshakable—I don't think we're making it out of this alive.

Overcome, I use the laser gun, aiming to get more than one Sentinel in each shot. The tide seems to slow for a moment until

I am clicking empty rounds. I slip the gun back into my waist-band and the men and I get in formation, backs to each other.

We fight with renewed energy, giving it our all.

A slice to my arm burns like fire and I cry out, shifting to kick the offender in the chest. He falls back and takes a few men with him. They scramble to avoid being overrun by the men behind them, who press in to take their place.

The circle grows tighter and tighter around us. We keep fighting, but even I can see our time is running out.

Jean dies first, a sword in his chest. He staggers back, face pale, before falling. I watch, horrified as he bleeds out within seconds.

"No!" I yell.

A knife slices my cheek, missing my eye, and I redirect my focus on the imminent threat before me.

Mourning Jean's loss, I fight back with such ferocity that the Sentinels coming at me start to backpedal, alarm on their faces.

A kick in my side halts me. I stumble, gasping for air.

The Sentinels come at us with greater force than before. Joseph and Augustin fall. Xavier's back is to me now, with César on our side. Three of us against an army of Sentinels.

Only a miracle can save us.

Bodies have piled up around us and the new Sentinels are stepping on them to reach us, which elevates them. We manage to push back, stepping on unconscious or dead bodies to even the height, as we dodge and move in almost impossible ways to spin away from the attack coming at us from all sides.

Tiring, I sense Xavier and César also fighting exhaustion ... as are the Sentinels. Desperate, I renew my efforts to protect myself and the men, but my movements are slower, uncoordinated. A laugh in my ear has me turning to my left and I shove a man back.

A fist comes from my right. I don't see it in time to dodge. Pain explodes in my temple and my head snaps back. I collapse onto the bodies beneath me. I can't move or breathe for several moments as black dots appear in my vision.

I hear my name being called. Someone throws himself over me to ward off the blows raining down on us.

No. I can't let someone die for me. My vision clears when air enters my lungs, and I try to shove them off. The stench of blood and sweat on the ground has me gagging.

"Don't move, Mademoiselle. Let me do this for you," Xavier says in my ear.

"No—please," I mumble.

I hear the clashing of swords end when César falls next to us with a grunt. His eyes fade and stare vacantly at me.

My heart breaks for these men, men who trusted me, men who fought with me, men who died for me. Whimpering, I again try to push Xavier off me, but the Sentinels stomp on him, laughing. He grunts in pain and a cheer goes up from our attackers.

A whistle rings out.

Xavier rolls off me with my next shove and I struggle to sit up.

The Sentinels have stopped fighting and are eyeing me like I'm the prize. One man licks his lips in anticipation.

I look over to Xavier. He is lying face up, struggling to breathe. Blood oozes from a wound in his chest. Panicked, I reach my hand underneath and find a knife in his back.

"No, please, Monsieur," I say.

Xavier's eyes find me. "Dés ... désolé ..." Blood bubbles from his lips.

"No, it's not your fault, Xavier." My face is wet with tears and a sense of helplessness threatens to overwhelm me.

How could we lose like this?

After everything I trained for, everything I hoped for, to end up at the mercy of the Sentinels is my worst nightmare.

Even if I survive this day, I don't know how long I will last under their torture.

With a final struggle for air, Xavier breathes his last and his eyes flutter closed. His chest deflates with the departure of his spirit.

The truth of my situation crushes me. I can't hold it in anymore. A scream tears out of me, years of pain and betrayal pouring into the sound as it bounces off the walls. My anger burns hotter, fueled by Alyse's lies and the lives she sacrificed today for her own gain. She might've been tortured, but I bet the Sentinels went easy on her when she sold me out—when she gave them something they wanted more. Smart move, making herself part of the plan so they'd let her walk free.

The thought leaves a bitter taste in my mouth, and I'm left gasping for air, trying to swallow the rage threatening to consume me.

"I'm disappointed, Mademoiselle. You fought exceedingly well today, I'll give you that. But where's your power?"

I stare up at the cloaked man, furious and silent.

"Don't tell me you're not The One?"

A calmness settles on me as he waits for my answer. After the way my men have sacrificed themselves today, how can I do any less? I will not be like Alyse.

I pull the knife out from under Xavier.

"I only have whatever power the Creator gives me," I say.

He seems to consider me a moment.

"Apparently it's not enough. Perhaps you're not the Protector after all."

I stare back at him, trying to see his face beneath the hood. It's hidden in shadows.

His voice sounds annoyed when he speaks again and I detect a slight accent that wasn't there before.

"Well, if you're not The One, what use are you to me?" He indicates to his men surrounding me. "Finish her."

Relieved to be spared from torture, I stand with calm acceptance of my fate. Who am I to expect anything less? May death be swift.

The Sentinels charge at me with a deafening roar. I swing the knife, cutting through two of them before it's knocked from my grip. Pain explodes in my arm as a sword slices deep, blood spraying everywhere. The burn is unbearable, but I choke down the urge to collapse. Adrenaline surges through me, keeping me on my feet.

I throw everything I've got into the fight, but there are too many of them. They close in, overwhelming me. Spit flies as they attack with wild, frenzied rage. A blow to my head leaves me stunned. For a moment I can't see—I can barely breathe—and I slip to the ground.

I'm tossed around like a rag doll, their kicks and stomps landing with relentless force. A blade finds its mark, and the fiery pain cuts through me. I welcome it, ready to join my men in eternal rest.

Then someone yanks my hair, snapping my head back, and a fist crashes into my face. Pain explodes like a bomb in my skull. My vision blurs, blood drips down, and I feel my life slipping away.

CHAPTER FORTY-TWO

A YELL RINGS OUT from one of the entrances and I'm dimly aware that no one is attacking me.

Swords clash as I lie broken and bloody, in so much pain that even breathing hurts. I can sense death is close. I'm on my last breaths now.

My vision goes dark and I remember the Creator, the God-man on the donkey who acknowledged me in the vision. A longing for him, to be with him in the afterlife, fills me.

Creator, please save me. Forgive me for my offences against you.

I remember the Lord's Prayer, which I learned at Sunday School as a child. The phrase "as we forgive those who sin against us" sticks with me. I need to forgive Alyse. Again. This time, it's easy. Who would have thought? But with my life at an end, I see how futile it was to hold onto. I release it with my final breath.

Creator, I forgive her.

My limbs grow weightless, and I drift upward, watching my crumpled form below become smaller, stranger—an empty shell of broken flesh that no longer contains me. I'm pulled higher, faster, until I'm immersed in darkness. I feel a moment of panic.

The darkness is pierced by a single pinpoint of light. The light grows and fills my vision, unspeakably bright.

Waves of comforting light roll into me. A pure and undeserved love embraces me.

My pain has gone. Instead, a peace that defies understanding leaves me buoyant. I stare into the brilliant, blinding light before me. It cleans me and makes me whole.

I sense an all-knowing, all-loving Presence standing inside the light. Waves of his unconditional love flow into me, healing my heart. I weep uncontrollably.

Then I hear a voice.

"My beloved child, it is time. Will you accept me and what I have done for you? Will you embrace the destiny I have written for you? I will be with you always, even beyond the end of time itself."

I am overcome by his goodness. "Yes Creator. I believe in you. I accept your plan for me. Thank you," I gasp. I feel his pleasure increase in response.

Just like that, my spirit is pulled back into my body. The pain has gone.

"Mademoiselle!"

I blink my eyes open and find myself in the arms of Alain, his unique silver eyes regarding me in wonderment.

Clashes of battle echo around us. I glance past Alain to see his men forming a protective circle. Beyond that, massive warriors are taking on the Sentinels, but there's no time to process it. Alain's voice pulls me back to the moment.

"You were dead and now you're alive. Your wounds—they've healed."

Wait. What?

I raise my arm and see dried blood starting to crust over smooth skin. My arm is whole and unblemished. I wave it around and then notice something else.

Alain's shirt has been ripped open and a gold necklace is swinging free. It's familiar, like a pocket watch or locket, with the emblem of a tree engraved on it. A steady thrum begins in my chest.

"Let's get you out of here, Mademoiselle."

Alain lifts me in his arms and surprise lights up his face. "You are weightless." He shakes his head, bewildered, and moves toward an exit. His men move with us, maintaining a barrier.

The tide has turned in the fighting. The giants look like warring angels. They plow through the mass of bodies, not killing them but knocking them out.

Shadowy figures hover over some Sentinels, and the giants spear them. As the shadows dissipate, the men flee in fear. I blink, wondering if I imagined it.

Alain jostles me as he runs, and I look down. The necklace grabs my attention again. I feel ill at ease, like I'm on the verge of something.

A gunshot shatters the air and Alain stops. He looks at me as if to apologize, but his knees buckle and we fall. I hit the ground hard, Alain falling on top of me. Blood trickles from his mouth and I realize he's been shot.

The necklace hangs on top of me. A buzzing grows in my ears, so intense that I grimace.

I roll us over until I'm leaning over Alain. There's a scar on his right arm and I remember the vision from the ultramarine ring. It must have been trying to tell me something. Am I too late?

Alain's men scramble around us to form a new circle, facing outward. Their expressions flicker with alarm, but they hold their ground, their shields rising—higher, stronger, the gold gleaming in a way that demands attention.

Even from the underside, I can see the intricate craftsmanship, the delicate patterns that speak of something ancient, something powerful. I want to study these shields, to understand their purpose, their origin.

But there's no time.

My gaze drops, shifting to Alain's ashen face, where reality crashes back into focus. His eyes are closed. He looks like he's teetering on the edge of death.

"Alain! Alain, please wake up!"

There's no response. My throat is dry as I hold two fingers under his nose, fearing I'm too late. A puff of air, barely there but there nonetheless, reassures me.

The necklace hums, softer than before. My eyes are drawn to the golden casing.

On impulse, I reach forward, heart pounding, and open the clasp with trembling fingers.

CHAPTER FORTY-THREE

It's the Arbre de *vie*.

Alain has the *Arbre de vie*. Is Alain the Keeper?

Resting on a delicate platinum chain within the case, the bronze, silver and gold branches sparkle on the Tree of Life pendant, the gem almost glowing from within.

The sensation of something yanking on my belly catches me off guard. I experience a moment of panic when I sense a physical pull toward the pendant. My stomach is queasy, battling the tug between my belly and the vessel.

I can't comprehend how I can see it. Only those with the blood of a Dompierre-St-Martin can see the pendant while it's worn by the Keeper. Either I'm related, or Alain—Jasper?—is dead.

Panicked at the thought, I check him again, relieved to find he's still breathing—though it's faint. A red patch spreads over his chest. Tearing my jacket off, I press it against his wound to stem the flow. The humming is growing louder and getting uncomfortable.

A scream to my left is the only warning before a small band of Sentinels attacks. The barrier around us holds—until a sword pierces through. One of Alain's men collapses, and the others scramble to seal the gap. But it's too late. A Sentinel slips inside. The opening closes before more can break through, but the barrier buckles inward as Alain's men strain to keep the circle intact.

The Sentinel freezes, shock flashing across his face as he sees I'm alive and unharmed. His eyes shift to Alain, and a sinister smile creeps across his lips. He raises his sword and lunges straight for me.

On instinct, I fall forward to grab the *Arbre de vie*.

The moment I touch it, a wave of power explodes from the pendant in a bright light. The repercussion is so powerful it throws us both backward into the men surrounding us.

I lie there, stunned, hearing moans from the others who were knocked down.

Something shiny glimmers within my peripheral vision and I roll my head over to see the *Arbre de vie* rising in the air on its own.

My skin prickles.

Shouts of surprise from other men are drowned out by the intense humming, which now hits a fever pitch so piercing that I slam my hands over my ears. Sweat tickles my brow and my head pounds.

As if tugged by a leash in my gut, the *Arbre de vie* glides toward me, hovering above me. I reach up to swat it away.

As my skin connects with the pendant, my hand freezes.

The heavy thrum beating against the walls of my heart dims. The buzzing and screaming quieten to a soft hum and I relax. I breathe in and out, and the nausea dissipates. Feeling a release in the connection, I pull my hand back.

I stare at the pendant, mesmerized. Time seems to grind to a halt.

Without warning, the *Arbre de vie* hurtles toward me at a blinding speed, giving me no time to react. The moment it touches my chest, the chain slides around my neck like a living thing and fuses itself together. I gasp, tensing up.

A surge of power fills me, electrifying in its pure intensity, yet warm and pleasant. It reminds me of the light I sensed when I died. It's the Creator's presence. I close my eyes in bliss.

As if to acknowledge my unspoken thought, I hear him in my heart.

"Daughter, you are my treasure. I love you and have great plans for you."

Tension melts from my shoulders. His joy intertwines with mine, a quiet harmony. My lips curve upward without conscious thought.

The clamor of battle fades into silence, replaced by the caress of a gentle wind. I open my eyes to find everyone around me shrinking away below, their mouths hanging open.

I look down at myself. *Oh.* The *Arbre de vie* has lifted me off the floor and I'm hovering in the air.

Wild exhilaration surges through me, making me believe anything is possible. Power hums in my veins, potent and alive. I feel invincible. Yet, beneath the thrill, I know this strength is not mine alone—it's a gift, entrusted to me with purpose.

The pendant hums, warm against my skin, like the embrace of an old friend who has found me again. Like the Creator designed it with me in mind, to be an extension of who I am. The Creator ... he's so real. I sense him with me now, protecting me. A laugh of pure joy escapes me.

The room is bathed in a radiant glow emanating from the *Arbre de vie.* My hair floats around me, caught in a soft, ethereal breeze. The men stare at me, their expressions a mix of awe and disbelief—or terror. One of Alain's men crosses himself, as if confronted with something divine—or something otherworldly.

Seriously, they're eyeballing me like I'm an alien.

The warriors stand tall at the back of the room, watching me. I know it then—they are angels, sent by the Creator to help me. They smile. One even salutes me.

I chuckle at that, and he winks.

A sudden pain in my center has me folding in on myself, crunching myself into a ball as it expands. On instinct, I throw my limbs out and the pain leaves me with a whoosh of power. Everyone in the room is knocked off their feet.

I sense the Creator's light flowing through me like a steady, brilliant white river. Then the light fades and I float down to the ground, sensing the flow still within me.

None of the Sentinels are moving. The angels are gone. So is the cloaked Sentinel.

My hair settles. I sense that something deep within me has been unlocked and set free—freeing me to grow and fulfill my destiny.

I crouch beside Alain and touch him with intention, asking the Creator for help.

Power shoots from my fingers and I know Alain has been healed. He takes a deep breath and opens his eyes.

"It is not yet time for you to meet the Creator, my friend," I say. "Monsieur Jasper Dompierre St-Martin, your family has been looking for you." His eyes widen.

Some of his men have come around. They scramble toward us, relief evident in their postures when they see their leader alive.

I leave them to help him up while I stand and look out at all the bodies. Something tells me the Sentinels will be out for a while.

Moving forward with purpose, I cross to the center of the huge room, scanning for the bodies of my men. There—Xavier. I move over to him, sensing the Creator hasn't finished yet. Leaning down, I place my hand on his wound, murmuring a prayer. I feel his life return before he takes a breath.

"Thank the Creator," I say. Xavier opens his eyes. I smile, but he looks at me with reverence. It troubles me.

"I saw you," he whispers. "You died. Then you came back. You manifested."

What? I stare into his eyes and understand. He had an out-of-body experience. Was he here in spirit the whole time?

Skin prickling, I help him up. He kneels before me, a little uneven given the bodies we're positioned on.

"You brought me back. Thank you."

"Thank the Creator, not me."

"I thank you both," Xavier says. He finds his sword and holds it before him, narrowly missing someone's arm where the tip touches the ground. He bows his head.

"Protector. My life and my sword are yours to command."

I stumble back. I don't know what to say. I blink a few times. Then I see Joseph, so I bend down, touching him almost without thought as I try to come to terms with what's happening.

Joseph gasps. I look down, surprised. He's alive before I even asked the Creator to save him. His kindness leaves me in awe.

Joseph stares at me in wonder, so I move on before he can say anything. I find Jean, César and Augustin, and repeat the process until they're all breathing and well. I move on to Alain's men, finding those who were killed and touching them. They're easy to identify—each has a green piece of cloth tied around their upper left arm. A marker, perhaps to help them identify each other in battle.

When I'm done, I straighten and take a step back. What's happening hasn't hit me yet—I'm just going with the Creator's flow. I look down at my fingers, struggling to grasp how the Creator's power could flow through such small hands.

The pendant is heavy against my chest. I pick it up to inspect it. So intricate. It must be a point of connection to the Creator, for he still feels close. My heart warms in response.

I look around, thankful for the Creator, and for these brave warriors who fought with and for me.

Alain and his men are wide eyed, still processing the miracles they've witnessed. My colleagues appear to have accepted it with ease. Having brushed themselves off and helped each other up, they've found some vacant floor space and are now kneeling before me. Alain and his men do the same.

I step back and start to protest but Xavier speaks again. "We hold to the Vestige creed and recognize you as the Creator's Protector of worlds. May we serve you with honor, great Protector."

The sound of assent from the men flows around me and I'm forced to face what I've been avoiding.

I, Lily Destin, am the new Protector.

Chapter Forty-Four

Alain, Xavier and the men give Uncle a full account of the events. Then they're given clearance to repeat their stories to Peron and the entire Vestige board. Although the technology seems to unsettle them, Alain and his gang are sworn into Vestige.

I am left reeling when the Vestige leaders give a majority vote in favor of accepting and recognizing me as Protector. Pending in-house testing, of course.

We all break to clean up, while Uncle sends a retrieval team to capture any Sentinels still alive at the warehouse. Then I have another session with Peron.

He explains he'd set the record straight about Alyse while I was headed toward our "rescue mission," though not all were willing to accept it at the time.

However, now we know she sent us into a trap, both she and her father have been suspended and imprisoned at Vestige. They'll come under intense investigation. It doesn't look good for either of them.

I have mixed feelings when I hear that Alyse has already been sent back to the twenty-first century.

Peron then tells me Alain has had a blood test and the results prove he is the missing son.

He congratulates me on a successful mission—finding both Jasper and the pendant—while he studies my necklace on screen with keen interest. I know he's going to want to see it in person soon, but I'm not ready to return yet.

"Please, Peron. So much has happened. I just need a week to say my goodbyes and come to terms with the idea of who I am."

"Well, after what you've achieved you deserve a break, Lily. You can have it. And I would love to give you more time, but for your safety, it's imperative that you come back soon. It won't be long before our enemies know who you are, and there will be those who seek to use or harm you. Besides, you will need to undergo testing with the pendant before the Board can officially proclaim you as the Vestige Protector."

I'm a bit overwhelmed, but that last comment makes me especially nervous. It's the second time Peron has mentioned it. "Testing?"

"Unfortunately ... yes. Stefan Georges is of the opinion that we need to validate your manifestation. Despite his suspension, he holds sway over enough board members to get it enforced."

That's just great.

Alain is waiting for me when I exit the communications room.

"Mademoiselle Therriot, may I have a moment of your time?"

"Certainly."

He smiles, his silver eyes shining a little brighter, and he leads me into a vacant sitting room across from Uncle's office.

We sit and he removes the golden necklace he's wearing.

"I believe this belongs to you now."

"Are you sure?" I ask.

"Very."

With some hesitation, I take the necklace from him, admiring the fine case. It's as beautiful as the *Arbre de vie.*

"Thank you."

"You are most welcome, Protector."

I'm still getting used to that title. I don't even know what I'm supposed to do as Protector. Peron said he'd fill me in when I returned to HQ on Earth. Guess I'll have to wait.

Alain smiles and I relax. "You know, I always felt uneasy around you," he says. "Now I know it was the *Arbre de vie's* power when you were near. It must have sensed you."

Well, that explains how I felt around him, too.

"I've been keeping tabs on you ever since I discovered you were searching for me."

I look at him in surprise, but he continues.

"When I heard you were near that warehouse, I was concerned. My men had already noticed the shady activities of these ... what are they called again?"

"Sentinels."

"Ah, yes. Sentinels. I had my men stake out the area, and they alerted me when you and your men entered the building. I was on my way to see what was happening when we ran into some warriors." He wets his lips. "I've never seen men as tall or built as they are—and their clothes and armor were so bright it was hard to look at. I was more than a little daunted, I admit. But they seemed friendly, so we spoke."

"You spoke to them?" I ask with excitement.

He nods. "Their leader told me to come with them as a matter of urgency—that we needed to fight with them to save the Protector." He laughs a little. "When he said 'Protector,' something about that word struck me. I remembered what *mon père*[1] told me as a boy, when he gave me the necklace. He said I was keeping it for the next Protector."

"You remembered that?"

He makes an affirmative sound in his throat. "Yes, it is strange, but I did. It was enough for me to believe the giant, and my men and I followed them. Imagine my surprise when we arrived at the same warehouse I was already heading to." He raises his brows and I smile.

---

1. "Mon père" means "my father"

"One giant was already there," he continues. "I overheard him say, 'She needs us now, Michel.' The leader turned back to me and asked if I was ready. I said yes and we all rushed in."

He shakes his head with a grimace.

"I was not prepared for what we found in there. The bodies, the blood. You, fighting for your life."

Alain stares at me, looking grim.

"Thank you for coming," I say. "If you hadn't been there with the *Arbre de vie*, we wouldn't be having this conversation right now."

He dips his head in acknowledgement. Then opens his mouth, hesitant.

"What?"

"Those giant men ... they were angels, weren't they?"

I smile, remembering. "Oh yes."

He laughs, his eyes filled with wonder. "Incredible."

Before Alain leaves with his men, they all swear fealty to me—again—and I want to squirm. I head upstairs as they leave.

A maid hands me two letters, which I carry to my room. The bold strokes on both alert me to the sender. Mon Puce.

I close the door and open the first letter, which the maid told me arrived while I was out.

I scan it and my happy thoughts plummet.

According to the letter, the Relic Hunters had noticed increased Sentinel activity around the warehouse and suspected there could be a Sentinel mole at Vestige.

Great. It might have helped to know this beforehand, but everything worked out in the end. At least the team Uncle sent to the warehouse has captured most of the Sentinels.

All but one: the cloaked leader.

Unease settles in my gut. Because of him, the Sentinels now know my identity and have confirmation of my role as Protector.

I shiver. Could this leader be a mole? I can't ignore the fact that he was hiding his identity. I chew on my lip.

I should tell Peron. But that means revealing more than I'm ready for—my involvement with the Relic Hunters, the secrets I've been keeping. I doubt that'll go over well.

No. I need another plan.

Maybe I'll bring it up with Uncle instead. Plant the idea, let him put the pieces together himself. I feel myself nodding, and with it, my breath comes easier.

My eyes land on the other letter. The maid said it had arrived that very hour.

It doesn't say much, but it's enough to stall me. Mon Puce sends his congratulations on hearing that I have manifested as Protector. He regrets missing the fight, but he's glad I'm all right.

I huff. I shouldn't be surprised he knows. I wonder which of Uncle's men is a double agent. I should get that investigated.

His letter finishes with:

My offer still stands. See you soon, mon chaton.

I can't stop a smile. "What cheek."

CHAPTER FORTY-FIVE

I observe an emotional scene as Alain—Jasper—is restored to his family. Clean-shaven, the resemblance is uncanny.

Alexandrine, Jasper's aunt and the late Comte de Dompierre-St-Martin's sister, embraces him and sobs.

His younger brother, Étienne, stands back with an uncertain expression, having been born after Jasper disappeared.

They invite us into their luxurious home.

We're introduced to Marguerite, Alexandrine's younger sister and Jasper's youngest aunt. She soon has everyone laughing with stories of Jasper's childhood pranks.

The room goes quiet when Alexandrine tells us how the Count and his wife mourned Jasper's loss for many years. The grief-stricken parents refused to accept his death and never gave up hope that one day he would be discovered.

In fact, their will dictated that the title and estate wouldn't pass to Étienne until his fiftieth birthday.

Now restored to his family, Jasper will be granted his rightful lands and title. I have a feeling he'll let Etienne continue to manage the estate. I can't see Jasper giving up his ways yet. Perhaps I should drop a hint that he should watch Etienne's cash flow like a hawk.

Still. *Mission accomplie.*

Oh, who am I kidding? I can't take credit for finding Jasper. He found me. Or maybe it was destiny after all.

I say my goodbyes an hour later, promising another visit. I have a meeting with Peron to get to.

I'll be seeing more of Jasper anyway. Now he's a Vestige agent, he and his men will be undergoing Vestige training at the Therriot estate.

Underground, of course.

The excited gleam in Peron's eyes is noticeable as I look at him through the video screen.

"Lily, my little Protector," he says.

"Peron."

"Before I get into the good stuff, I need to tell you that Stefan Georges has been dismissed from his role on the Board. Due to the gravity of his actions, his memory has been wiped."

"Wh-what?" I stutter in shock. Something I have always feared has happened to Alyse's father, the big man on the Board. This is crazy.

"He was conspiring to falsify a manifestation of Alyse becoming Protector."

"What? Oh."

"Yes—and about your missing diary. One of the maids found it in Alyse's room after she was taken back to headquarters. It's with the investigation team now."

"Huh?" I don't know which is worse—my embarrassment that my personal thoughts are now being read by the investigation team, or the sting of learning Alyse was cheating and hoping to use my discoveries to get ahead with the Board.

I cough. Fat chance of that. If she could find clues in my cringe-worthy ramblings, she's a better spy than I gave her credit for.

Thank the Creator I didn't mention the Relic Hunters. I'm still not ready to share that detail. Maybe I never will be. Though I might get asked who Mon Puce is, given I did reference him once or twice. Not the best decision I've made.

I think it's time I graduated from keeping a diary. Too dangerous in this line of work.

"Yes, it's unfortunate but I'll make sure you get your diary back as soon as possible," says Peron, bringing me back to the present.

"Um, yeah. Thanks." I am going to burn it to ashes. They'd better not have made copies. If they did—well, I don't want to think about that.

Heat rushes to my face, and I shove the thought away before it can get any worse. I change the subject. "So does that mean I won't need to undergo testing anymore?"

Peron shakes his head, his lips pressed together in a grim line. "While Stefan may have been dealt with, his influence over certain board members will take longer to dismantle. I'm sorry, Lily."

This sucks. "Fine."

"The good news is that the evidence from your diary supports the case being built against Alyse and it helps to prove your innocence." Peron scratches his chin, oblivious to my inner torment. "Perhaps it's fortunate that Alyse is due to have her memory wiped tomorrow. She'll be assigned to a desk job where we can keep an eye on her from now on."

I feel a moment of pity, but this could be a good thing for her. At least she'll be away from her father and his demands. Maybe now she can enjoy some serenity.

"Thanks for taking care of everything, Peron."

"It's the least I could do, Lily. And now—what I really wanted to tell you. Did you know that your manifestation reflected the power of Françoise?"

"Françoise?"

"Yes. She was the one who reigned as Protector from 1409 to 1470. There are records of her hovering and flying and she's been depicted as having the wings of an angel, to represent her ability. Perhaps you will take after her."

"Oh, that's cool." I *had* wondered if that would be my power but hadn't said anything in case it sounded pretentious.

"Yes and that's only the beginning. I've discovered something that will help to confirm your role as Protector, Lily."

"What is it?" I lean forward.

"Do you remember Da Vinci's scroll? The one you retrieved in Astanalle?"

Oh, not the scroll again. I ignore the sinking feeling. "You mean, the one I ruined?"

"Yes!—Er, well that is, yes." Peron clears his throat and looks awkward for a moment. "Lily, let's not worry about that now. It's all in the past. We managed to decipher the message, despite the scroll's appearance. It's the message part I want to tell you about."

He grabs an item from his desk and waves it.

"This is a copy of the contents of the scroll, Lily. I've obtained permission to share it with you. Of course, once you complete the tests here and prove on a scientific basis that you are the new Protector, I won't need to seek permission anymore. You'll have access to everything you want to know." He grins.

Well, that's generous of Vestige. Lucky for them I don't have an evil agenda. "Okay. So what does it say?" I clasp my hands to stop from picking nervously.

"Well, it's a riddle of sorts. I'll read it to you."

He clears his throat again.

> "Green fronds before Him
> The future coming King
> When the last Protector appears
> She will find the deep blue ring
> He'll see her heart and if she be worthy
> She will return from Him."

My skin tingles in awareness and revelation.

"Do you see it, Lily?"

I jerk my head forward in a nod. My mind shouts.

"Lily, you told me about your vision. How you saw the Creator when he walked the earth. You found the lapis lazuli ring. You died and returned." He pauses. "Did you encounter the Creator again?"

I look at him for a moment, swallowing, then nod.

"Tell me." He leans forward, his nose almost pressing against the screen.

I describe our encounter, including what the Creator had said. Peron sits back, silent for a moment.

"So, he is real. I tried to believe, but this ... this changes everything. And he let you return." His head dips, shoulders rising with a quiet chuckle. "It's not lost on me that you are the one who was sent to retrieve the scroll. This must have been his plan all along."

My mind is still reeling from the prophecy, but something bothers me. "Peron, you read 'last.'"

"What?"

"Last. You said, 'when the last protector appears.' Does that mean ... does that mean I'm the last one?"

He looks at me, hesitates for a beat. Then he sighs. "Lily, it does look that way. Our best scholars are looking into it but we're still not sure what it means. To be the last, to not have a Protector again ... I know we haven't had one in 400 years, but why have another now, only to be the last? We don't know yet. I'm sorry."

He pauses, his mouth opening as if to say more, but he doesn't.

"Please go on," I say.

Peron licks his lips. "I have made an observation, Lily. An incomplete observation and I don't have a theory yet, but at least it's something." He leans forward and steeples his fingers. "I've been researching your family history, and I've found something quite fascinating. Do you want to hear it?"

Do I? Feeling like I'm about to step off a precipice, I nod.

"Yes, please."

"It's from your father's line, the Destin family line. Alexandria, the first Protector, had a daughter who married into the Destin family. You, Lily, come directly from that genealogy. So, if you are in fact the last Protector, it seems to have circled back from the offspring of the first. Closing the loop if you will."

What does this mean? Is there any significance? Who am I?

I have to find out.

Chapter Forty-Six

I walk in on Marc tutoring Charlotte and Cherie the next day. Seeing them together like that, realization slaps me upside the head. I don't want to leave the life I've found here. I don't want to leave these people. I'm happy. I'm finally happy.

Of course I realize that *now*, when I'll be departing in a couple of days. When I've run out of time for … I don't know what exactly.

Pressure builds in my throat at the thought of leaving.

I study Marc's profile. He hasn't seen me yet, but I'm overcome by his presence. Not just by his firm jaw, his steady hands as he crafts something in paint, or by any other physical qualities he possesses.

There's something solid about his character, his honesty, his gentleness and overall goodness. Even the steadiness with which he looks at me, his eyes showing the truth he hasn't yet said.

He's the type of guy who holds doors open, not because he's old-fashioned, but because he's got manners with a capital 'M'. He's become more than a friend. Marc gets under my skin in a way even Jason couldn't.

Someone else affects me too, someone who shouldn't. I frown, conflicted and unsure.

Marc notices me then and the brilliance of his smile washes over me. His face burns into my memory like a photograph I'm desperate not to lose. What if I never see him again?

My throat tightens further and I turn away, leaving the room before he sees my tears.

I've almost reached my bedroom when Charlotte catches up with me.

"Lily, what's wrong? You ran away so fast and monsieur Coupier looked so upset. I had to stop him from dropping his paints all over the floor in his effort to come after you. What are you doing to the poor man?"

"Oh, I'm … *pardon*, Charlotte, I felt unwell. Please give him my apologies." I keep my back to her, hastily wiping my face.

"Of course, Lily. Go and rest. I'll tell Cook to send up something that might help you feel better."

"*Merci*."

"I do hope you feel better soon, Lily, not the least because the monsieur has invited us to his benefactor's manor to see some of his paintings."

"What?" I stop. "When?"

"This afternoon, after our lessons. Lily, is there something else I can do? You seem upset."

"No. *Merci*, Charlotte. I just need time to rest. I'm sure I'll feel better by this afternoon."

"All right. I'll come by and check on you later."

"*Merci*."

She pats my arm in a maternal way. I glance at her. Her eyes soften at the corners, and she tilts her head slightly. I can't bear the gentle knowing in her gaze.

My smile feels tight as I turn to take the final steps to my room. Charlotte is aware I will be returning home in a few days. She just doesn't know how far away home is. Or that I may not be back.

The door latch clicks behind me. My vision blurs, the bedroom swimming into watercolors as something hot slides down my cheek, then another, until my sleeve is damp where I press it against my face.

The sooner I accept this, the sooner I can get over it.

I manage to get myself sorted out and cleaned up by the time we're due to take our trip to Marc's home.

Charlotte, true to her word, is a wonderful support. I feel strong again by the time we arrive at the estate where Marc lives with his patron.

It's just like the manor house in my dream.

I look around in amazement, wondering if my dream was in fact a literal night vision, rather than a symbolic one.

We exit the carriage and Marc joins us from his, just as his patron, Gustav Remy-Charles, rushes out the door. I know it's him. He looks so familiar, right down to his flamboyant outfit. I'm sure he looked like that in my dream.

"Whoa," I whisper.

I shouldn't be surprised anymore when I see impossible things.

Gustav introduces himself, confirming my suspicion.

He looks blissful to be meeting acquaintances of the famous Monsieur Coupier, and more so, the first ladies Marc has ever invited over. He studies each of us with a keen eye, as if trying to guess which lady has captured Marc's heart.

I look away at that thought.

Three days. Three more days until this dream ends. Three more days of caring. Then it must stop.

I ball my hands into tight fists, wishing my nails were long enough to pierce my skin and give me something else to cry about.

After our introductions, Gustav leads us to a display room where we get to see Marc's long-awaited paintings—amazing scenes of nature, hills and village life.

To say they're excellent is an understatement. He's a genius and his works show his appreciation and care for creation and those around him.

Gustav is speaking jovially with Cherie, Charlotte, and an older woman hired as our chaperone for the afternoon, when Marc takes my elbow with gentle fingers and leads me away.

They don't seem to notice. One side of Marc's mouth lifts in a secretive sort of smile as he looks at me. "Would you permit me to show you another painting, Mademoiselle Lily?" he asks in a soft voice.

I look up into his clear green eyes and see the promise of something.

"*Oui.*"

He searches my face and his smile deepens. He steps back and holds out his elbow. My lips turn upwards in response and I take it.

Marc leads me carefully up a stairway into another part of the house. He catches the attention of a maid so she can follow us.

"I keep a copy of my favorite painting on a scroll in my satchel for when I'm away from the manse, but the one I'm about to show you is a better rendition."

"It must be very special."

"It is." Marc looks at me for a moment, then asks the maid to stand outside the door of a room. He draws me inside.

"If you feel in danger at any time, Mademoiselle, you can call for help and Adélaïde will rush in to assist you or call for further aid if needed. *Merci*, Adélaïde."

I look at Adélaïde. She bobs in acceptance and we smile at each other. I'm sure she knows he won't try anything untoward. He does close the door, but not altogether.

"Why go to such lengths to show me this painting, Monsieur Coupier?"

"'Marc,' please. You are the only person I can share this with, Lily."

"Oh? How intriguing." The way he's behaving is making my heart speed up. I take a slow breath to calm it.

Marc grins and captures my hand in his. With a gentle tug, he leads me into another connected room. This time, he leaves the door halfway open.

The smell of paint permeates the air, distracting me from his hand for a moment. I smile in anticipation. I'm surrounded by white canvases, some empty, but most covered in drapes.

Marc releases me with a lingering look. Then he weaves through his works. He moves paintings away from one wall as he speaks. "I dreamed of you the other night. You were like a warrior angel. Beautiful and magnificent."

"You did?" I blush.

"*Oui.*" He stops, staring out a narrow window as if remembering. "I shall never forget." He glances at me. "There's more to you than meets the eye, Lily Therriot. Of that, I am certain."

"I'm sure I don't know what you mean," I say, trying not to smile.

"Well then, let me tell you a story," he says, as he continues moving paintings to the side. He must have hidden this picture far back behind all the others. I'm tempted to lift the drape off the canvas nearest to me to see what hidden gem lies underneath.

"When I was a boy, I saved a damsel in distress."

"Really? That's sweet."

"Yes, and I found I couldn't forget her. I painted her that same night and all that week, again and again until I felt I had captured her likeness. I always hoped to find her again, even made annual trips to search for her, but I never did find her ... until recently."

"Oh?" I refuse to accept the jealousy that pokes at me. I smile instead.

He selects a moderate-sized painting, lifts and carries it over to an easel, drape firmly in place. Setting it down with care, Marc walks around to the side of it.

The corded muscle in his neck is more pronounced as he prepares himself.

"Whenever I felt alone or depressed in the past, I would pull this out and remember our encounter, and feel cheered again." He looks at me, his eyes intense. "She was my first love. She left a lasting impression, and no woman has ever been her equal in my eyes."

He beckons me over, but my feet feel stuck, as if they're in heavy blocks of cement. At his expectant look, I swallow and drag them over, the weight of discovery bearing me down.

Geneviève. It must be Geneviève. She stole his heart. He couldn't bear to be near her after what happened and found solace in her portrait instead. But why show *me*? Blinking rapidly, I take a fortifying breath.

I reach his side, wanting to run from the room but forcing myself to face the inevitable. My eyes burn and my mouth twists. This will help me cut ties and face reality.

Marc pulls off the drapery and looks at me. I can only look back at him, delaying the cruel truth I must accept. He smiles, shifting his head in a motion for me to look down at the painting.

I brace myself and clench my teeth. Sluggishly, my eyes drift down and to the right. Toward the girl I hate.

The scene is dark, at night. My first thought is that she's wearing men's clothes. Strange.

My second is that there's a red mark on one side of her mouth and blue and yellow streaks on the other.

Is that a mistake? I bend down to look closer.

No ... no mistake. I look up at her face and recognition slams through me.

Wisps of hair fall around her face, shrouding her in mystery as a breeze lifts her ponytail to the side. The moonlight brings the planes of her face into clarity. She's beautiful.

I feel a sense of camaraderie with her. She looks like she has a world of secrets and has just divulged one of them.

A weight lifts off me, but my face turns crimson. And then I'm confused.

It's me.

On my bumbled mission to retrieve the Da Vinci prophecy in Astanalle. How—?

"I don't understand," I say.

"Her name was Lily too. She gave me this."

I straighten. He holds out his hand and turns it over, letting a necklace drop and hang from his fingers.

A silver pendant swings at the bottom of the chain as he dangles it in front of me.

"My necklace!" I say, before my brain catches up with me. "Oh. I mean, what a charming necklace."

He looks at me, eyes bright, like a man who's just won the lottery.

Stupid. Stupid. Stupid.

"It is you. I knew it!"

"What? I don't know what you're talking about. You know what? I need to go. I remember I have something urgent to attend to," I say and move to flee.

He grabs me from behind and pulls me flush against his chest. My breath falters and I push down the joy streaking through me. He cannot know. I'll be in so much trouble.

Nuzzling my ear and sending tingles down my spine that make me breathless, he whispers, "I have waited for this moment since the night you left. When I saw you again after so many years, looking as if not a day had gone by, I knew the Creator had answered my prayers."

"I ... it's not me. I don't know who she is, but she's not me."

"Don't lie to me, Lily. Don't rob me of this joy in finding you at last." His breath is warm on my ear and I want to swoon. Could he really be that boy? I can't believe it, yet I do.

This is too much for me. For the sake of Vestige—and Marc's own safety—I must try. At least once more.

"But if she met you when you were a boy, wouldn't she be much older than you now?"

"I don't care."

His response is so fast, I'm taken aback for a moment. It's hard to concentrate with the way he's holding me, and my thoughts are muddled.

"But you only knew her for less than an hour and she would be near her third decade by now. So you see, it can't be me, for I'm not yet eighteen." It occurs to me that I've just given away my real age, but what's one year's difference? Still, I stiffen at my deceit.

His laugh sends soft wafts of air that tickle my cheek. It drives me crazy for him. I barely manage to maintain my composure.

"Oh Lily, how could you know we only met for such a fleeting time, unless it was you?"

Crap. "I ... I ... but I'm too young to be her!"

"That is true, but I'm willing to have an open mind about how that is possible." I hear happiness in his voice. "All I care about is that I finally found you again and you're perfect."

I give in. "I'm not perfect. The picture tells you that. I had Skittles all over my face!"

He tightens his hold on me and sighs though his nose, sounding content.

"You were a mix of endearing and feisty. The way you defeated William? Well I was impressed. You'll have to show me that trick sometime."

I smile, my embarrassment fading away with my surprise at how easily he's accepting this. "It's called mixed martial arts. I guess I could find time to show you."

Marc chuckles. "I hope so." He rubs his clean-shaven face against my cheek, nuzzling me again. My legs feel weak.

Then he pauses. "Skittles—are they the strange colorful sweets you had?"

"How did you know they were sweets?"

"They tasted delicious."

What? "Eww gross! They fell out of my mouth onto the dirty wooden floor, and you ate them?"

"After painting them and evaluating their sweet fragrance, I recalled they were in your mouth and deduced they were edible, so I washed them in a stream and tasted them." He sighs again. "That was a wonderful experience."

He looks at me on an angle. "Wait. Do you have any more?"

I look up at him and laugh. "Not with me, but maybe I can get some for you. Although have you tried mixed berries?"

He questions me and I explain my find. I'm admittedly impressed with myself for finding a replacement in the seventeenth century.

"I will invite you to try some when they're in season again," he says.

I shake my head at him. Beautiful, wonderful Marc. I grin and he smiles back in acceptance, and something else. It scares me a little, so I turn my face to the floor.

At last, a friend who has seen me at my worst and still likes me. Though the way he was just exploring my face with his brilliant green eyes spoke of more than friendship. He called me his first love, after all.

Hope flutters in my heart, but Peron's disapproving face comes to mind. I shift in discomfort and clear my throat.

"I had better head back," I say.

Marc groans, kisses me on the cheek and releases me. "For that urgent thing you had to attend to?" His voice is teasing.

"Running away is always urgent," I tease back.

We both laugh and he grabs my hand, keeping me beside him. "I'll not let you run away from me, Lily." His gaze is intense, a small smile hovering on his lips.

I stare back and excitement hums in my veins stubbornly. My hesitation melts and I shock myself by saying, "I hope you don't."

His eyes study mine for a moment, as if daring to ask, then drop to my lips. My breath becomes shallow and I can hear my heart pound heavily in my throat. I feel its vibrations all the way to my fingertips.

He moves closer, places his other hand on my back and pulls me against him. Heart hammering wildly now, I look up and watch as his chiseled face lowers to mine.

Our lips meet, his warm and soft, and I nervously breathe him in. He captures my lips again and again, melting my heart. I sigh with pleasure. With a soft growl, he tilts his head and deepens the kiss. For several long, heart-pounding moments, his lips move against mine, spilling joy through me like a warm golden glow.

It's beautiful and wild and gentle all at the same time. I'm cocooned in his arms, cherished and secure.

An unwelcome thought slithers in, shattering my bliss.

I'm leaving in three days.

The thought stabs pain through my heart, making me jerk back. We break apart, panting and staring at each other. I step back and Marc lets me, his eyebrows furrowed.

"What is it?"

"I ... I'm leaving in three days and I don't know when—if—I will return."

"What? Where are you going?"

"Home."

"Then I'll follow you. I can meet your family, show them my intentions are honorable. I'll move if you can't come back here."

"What? No. No, you can't."

Marc's frown deepens. "Yes, Lily, I can."

"No. You don't understand."

"Mari isn't too far for me. I'd follow you to Astanalle if you wanted to live there."

I stop and stare at this wonderful man. Who I think must love me. Who's willing to give up so much to be with me. But he can't come back with me. He wouldn't if he knew.

Tears come unbidden then. "You wouldn't be able to follow me where I'm going, even if you wanted to."

"I'd go to the ends of the earth to be with you if I had to, Lily. You are the only woman I have ever truly loved." He steps closer. "I love you."

My heart jumps on hearing those words and I stare back at him. He does love me. I can see it, and joy springs back up, dancing a merry jig in response.

I want so much to confess my feelings to Marc, but my future is so uncertain, and I'm still not sure how I feel about the Flea.

I can't do this to him. I can't lead him on. I care about him too much.

I look down. "I'm sorry." I sound miserable. I am miserable.

Marc envelops me in a warm embrace.

"How can I lose you after I've just found you? There must be a way to see you again."

Realization taps me on my shoulder and whispers in my ear.

I'm Lily Destin, the last Protector.

Once I pass the tests, I'll have authority. Access to what I need. Who says I can't come back?

I can. I will.

And I'll change the rules on who we can tell about Vestige.

Hope sends streams of light into my heart, filling my lungs with air. I hug Marc back.

"There is a way. I forgot."

"What?" Marc pulls back to search my eyes.

"I ... I think I can find a way back. It might take a few weeks, months even, but I'm pretty sure I can come back. No. I will. I will come back."

"You're certain?"

"*Oui.*"

Marc, looking relieved and delighted, grabs me in a hug again. "*C'est bien.*[1] Because I wouldn't have let you leave here if you'd said otherwise."

I laugh softly and he nuzzles the side of my face. I turn my face toward his and we stare at each other for a moment, happy and hopeful.

"May I kiss you again, Mademoiselle?"

"*Oui*, you may, Monsieur."

And, with a smile, he does.

To be continued...

---

1. C'est bien means "That's good"

Afterword

Thanks so much for reading *The Vestige Agent!*

If you enjoyed this read, I'll be grateful if you leave an honest reader review wherever you purchased this book, or on

https://www.goodreads.com/

Good reviews are an author's best friend!

Acknowledgements

First and foremost, Yeshua, thank you for everything you've given me (John 10:10), including the ability and courage to give writing a go. You helped me through it all.

My heartfelt thanks to my younger sister Laura, who was my beta reader from early on. Thank you for acting as my sounding board, listening as I read and giving feedback and ideas for extra laughs.

Thanks to my family, friends, work colleagues and others, who have encouraged me on my writing journey, including my Sydney Omega Writers chapter group and beta readers Jo-Anne Berthelsen, Jaye Cox, and Joanna Savage.

Thank you to my editor, Iola Goulton, for the manuscript assessment and later for editing the outcome of several rewrites. Thanks also to proofreaders Pamela Aropio, Steph Penny, and my sister Laura, you girls are awesome.

I'm grateful for the feedback I received from competition judges in The Emily, and the First Impressions contest. And to those in my Facebook Writers groups for feedback on my back cover blurb.

To the designers at Miblart, thank you so much for interpreting what I wanted and creating a book cover I absolutely love.

Lastly, thank you to YOU, Reader, for picking up this novel and giving it a chance. I hope you enjoyed the journey.

About the Author

H. E. Cooper is an award-winning author celebrated by the League of Romance Writers. Her debut novel, The Vestige Agent, earned 2nd place in the prestigious Emily Award in 2024.

From a young age, H. E. Cooper's imagination overflowed with tales of romance, adventure, and the supernatural. Inspired by night dreams, she compiled countless story ideas. One day she decided to try writing one. And so, a storyteller was born.

H. E. Cooper thrives in the corporate world of project management, service improvement and knowledge management. Residing in Sydney Australia, she is an avid reader who consumes stories like air, filling her home with a growing collection of books.

Much like Lily, this novel's protagonist, H. E. Cooper is determined to fulfill her destiny ... and rescue some animals along the way.

She writes in the hopes of sweeping you away on an entertaining journey that inspires hope and truth.

You can find out more on her website, https://hecooperauthor.com/

Extras

Organizations in The Vestige Agent:

Vestige Society (Vestige):

A hidden society who operate as Time-Dimension Keepers. They seek to correct history and right wrongs that throw worlds out of balance. They have connections to governments globally.

Governed by the Board of Directors in the absence of a reigning Protector, they serve as the guiding force until one emerges. When a Protector is in power, the Board stands in support of their rule. Vestige regards the Protector as the Creator's chosen guardian of worlds for the duration of their reign.

Vestige has headquarters in underground bunkers all over the world in the two main dimensions, Earth and ARK1—including in present day Pariseine, in the République de L'Aurente, which is similar to Paris, France.

Relic Hunter Society:

Perceived as a faction driven by insatiable greed and a hunger for power. They're seen as scavengers, willing to steal relics to line their pockets.

They don't appear to have time travel technology ... but there is at least one mole at Vestige who is helping the RH cause.

An enemy of Vestige, they hadn't broken the unspoken truce from WW2 on Earth until recently. Since then, Relic Hunters have been kidnapping Vestige agents in present day Earth, from all over the globe.

Sentinels:

Antagonists, known for their warped religious fervor. Part of a religious sect, they want to keep Vestige from gaining any more power. They believe Vestige is operating under the influence of darkness, and they employ despicable methods in their cause to foil Vestige's plans.

They don't have time travel technology, but there's always the danger of double agents at Vestige.

Protectors—a brief timeline:

1. Alexandria (Alex) Vestige reigned as Protector from 1101 to 1156 AD.

2. Nicolette (Nic) reigned from 1258 to 1338 AD.

3. Éléonore reigned from 1341 to 1402 AD.

4. Françoise reigned from 1409 to 1470 AD.

5. Henriette (Henri) Bergenoir reigned from 1491 to 1538 AD.

6. Thérèse (Terry) reigned from 1553 to 1584 AD.

7. Lily Destin will reign from around 1630 AD on ARK1 and from present day on Earth.

Did you know...

The supernatural events described in this book are grounded in truth. Across centuries, documented accounts—from ancient texts to modern testimonies—reveal moments where the impossible became real. The Bible itself—which is consistently affirmed by scholarly research and archaeological evidence—records astonishing acts: healing the incurable, raising the dead, walking through walls, divine teleportation, and receiving dreams and visions from Yahweh.

These wonders are not confined to the past. They continue to unfold across the globe today. I believe that through Jesus Christ, the miraculous is not only possible—it's his intention to weave it into the fabric of our everyday lives. Are you excited? I am!